Praise for Rene Lyons' *Tempting Darkness*

"(Tempting Darkness is) a page turner that embroils the reader even deeper into the dark world of the Knights Templar Vampires. These men are strong, masculine warriors, they truly demand a woman's attention."

~ *Stephanie McGrath, ParaNormal Roamnce*

"I was rooting for (Lucian and Jessica) and I have to say that Rene Lyons can pull every emotion out of her readers!"

~ *Gracie, Joyfully Reviewed*

"Rene Lyons writes a chilling love story in TEMPTING DARKNESS. The urgency of the situation drives Lucian, Jessica, and the reader."

~ *Robin Lee, Joyfully Reviewed*

Tempting Darkness

Rene Lyons

A Samhain publishing, Ltd. publication.

Samhain Publishing, Ltd.
512 Forest Lake Drive
Warner Robins, GA 31093
www.samhainpublishing.com

Tempting Darkness
Copyright © 2007 by Rene Lyons
Print ISBN: 1-59998-657-4
Digital ISBN: 1-59998-321-4

Editing by Laurie Rauch
Cover by Scott Carpenter

First Samhain Publishing, Ltd. electronic publication: April 2007
First Samhain Publishing, Ltd. print publication: October 2007

Dedication

Laurie, I couldn't have made it through this book without your belief in the Templars and me. I'm so lucky to have you as an editor and a friend.

Andy, thank you for lending yourself for the cover. Without you I could have never given Lucian "life."

The ladies of DHA, your support kept me writing on days when I didn't think I had it in me. Thanks for letting me in as part of your group and for sharing this whole thing with me.

Mandie, well, we made it through another one. Ready to kick me to the curb yet?

(the other) Rene, thank you for helping to breathe life into the fight scenes. With all of my heart, I thank you, milady.

Rosalind, thank you for teaching me the alphabet and for letting me name your toes. You always have been, and always will be, my DeeDee. I'm so proud you're my sister. This one is for you.

Prologue

Penwick Castle

Wiltshire, England

The Year of Our Lord 1307

Home.

In those first moments after he woke on the shore of Messina, Lucian of Penwick thought of nothing but going home.

Burned nearly to the bone, Lucian focused on nothing but this one obsession. That passion gave him the strength to trek across France and England. He realized now, after it was too late, he never should have left. Penwick was where he belonged and it's where he needed to be.

Crawling through the darkness in his frantic journey to return to Penwick Castle, he'd felt the changes taking place in him. Not alive, less than human, he'd become something dark and dirty. God had turned him into a creature only the night could love. Lucian ran his tongue over his new fangs and, if he'd been able, he would have gagged. *Vampire.* The word screamed in his head and an agonizing hunger caused his insides to twist painfully. The thirst that accompanied it turned his mouth as dry as sand. This was his punishment for abandoning his faith and continuing to kill in the name of God.

He'd become a monster, burning with the need to feed on the innocent, to take life into himself in order to exist.

Dragging his burned and battered body over the last grassy rise, Lucian caught his first glimpse of Penwick Castle. Tears of blood came to his eyes—no longer brown but silver and burning with the fire of immortality. Growling as the hunger for blood gnawed at him, Lucian clawed at the scar left behind by Michael's sword. It ached where the archangel had pierced him. The golden sword had done more than sever his heart—it had ripped the soul from him and damned him in one clean stab.

Unholy.

God, infinitely merciful to His children, had given him a chance to right his wrongs and undo his sins.

Thou shalt not kill an innocent.

Protect the Guardian.

Guard the holiest of relics.

These were His commands. By abiding his oath to God, Lucian would earn forgiveness and be allowed to enter Heaven. He'd know the Lord's grace once again.

How had he lost his faith?

Of the five of them, Lucian was the only one who'd joined the Order of the Templar Knights to serve God. The others had done it for glory alone. They'd all heard the rumors of the Templars' wealth despite their vow of poverty. The poorest of knights, they were also the richest of armies. Their power extended as high as the Pope, who feared them as much as the King of France had. Those rumors had propelled Constantine and Raphael to follow Tristan and Sebastian in joining the order of warrior-monks. It was Lucian's devotion to God and his loyalty to his brothers-in-arms that had him standing with the others when they took the vows. He gladly gave his body and soul to the Knights Templar.

In the beginning, Lucian had felt closer to God than any time thereafter. With every swing of his sword, with every village they'd razed and with every innocent they'd killed, the more he began to doubt his God. He'd looked out at the carnage the Order had left in their wake and wondered if this was God's will be done or man's thirst for power.

And then the day came when he'd killed one too many men. His faith had poured out of him as he'd watched his enemy bleed to death. Lucian had left his faith behind on the battlefield that day and had never looked back.

The seal of the Knights Templar, branded into the skin on the top of his right hand, served as a constant reminder of the oath he'd made to God. The five of them, the guilty among the innocent, taken from death by an archangel, were now merely Templars. Damned Knights Templar who had dared to kill in the name of the Lord long after they left their faith on the field of battle.

With a terrible roar of agony, Lucian detected the faint scent of blood. His vampire's body reacted violently to this first hunger. Saliva dripped from his fangs. His gaze narrowed on the massive castle rising in the distance.

Life thrived behind the high walls enclosing the keep.

He was home—where his heart lay and where his greatest sin would come to pass.

Chapter One

Penwick Castle

The Year of Our Lord 2005

Lucian of Penwick jumped to his feet when the door of the cell swung open. Vincent cast a lustful look at the woman sleeping on a pallet across the cell. Lucian growled and crouched into a battle-ready stance, fully prepared to strike should the renegade make a move toward her.

The renegade didn't come too far into the cell. Instead, he snapped his teeth together and growled back. He set a metal goblet on the floor and backed away.

"Stephan sends his regards," Vincent sneered.

Lucian wanted to rip the smirk from Vincent's face. Of all Stephan's henchman, Vincent was the one who irritated Lucian the most. The night would come when chains would no longer bind Lucian and when it did he was going to relish sending Vincent to Hell.

"Tell my brother I said to go fuck himself."

Again Vincent looked at Jessica and again Lucian growled. She sighed in her sleep and shifted on the pallet but didn't wake.

Vincent sneered and indicated Jessica with a nod of his head. "Now why would he do that? He can always just use her."

Though chained, Lucian was still able to reach Vincent. He grabbed the renegade's hand and bent it back until the bone snapped. Vincent howled and dropped to his knees. Lucian kept bending the hand until the arm bent back as well. Only after the arm bone broke did he release Vincent's hand. He wanted to do more than merely break an arm. He'd snap the prick's neck if not for fear Stephan would make Jessica suffer for his actions.

Cradling his useless arm, Vincent staggered to his feet and dove toward Lucian, who easily deflected the attack. The chains did little to hinder Lucian. He grabbed Vincent and threw him to the floor, then pounced, pressing his arm to Vincent's throat to hold him down. Though Vincent was larger, Lucian was stronger. Even in his weakened state, Lucian was more powerful than a renegade. Vincent fought to throw him off but Lucian bore his weight down and increased the pressure of his arm across the bastard's neck.

"You tell Stephan I said I'm going to bring his game to an end real soon." Lucian hissed. "Now get the hell out of here before you wake her up."

Lucian leapt off of Vincent, who then scurried from the cell like a scared rat. Not even the slam of the door or the scrape of the chains against the stone woke Jessica. Given how much blood was taken from her last night, it was no wonder she'd been sleeping the last twelve hours.

Hating to sate his bloodlust with Jessica awake, Lucian was glad she still slept. He stared at the goblet Vincent brought him, his mouth watering as the hunger tore through him. Although the thought of dead blood repulsed him, Lucian knew he had no choice but to drink it. It would take the edge off the hunger, not feed into it as his captor believed.

His body was superior to other vampires. He was stronger in both mind and body. If a renegade took in dead blood it would intensify their hunger. For a Templar, it helped ease the pain—but only for so long. It couldn't sustain him forever. Eventually his body would fight for survival, whether his mind wanted to or not.

He picked up the goblet and drank down the thick blood in one gulp. Lucian dragged his arm across his face, only smearing the blood rather than wiping it away. Coagulated and cold, the blood tumbled down his throat like shards of broken glass. Barely able to sustain him, it did more harm than good, making his body yearn for blood that was warm and rich with life.

Like a trapped animal, Lucian crouched against the icy stone wall. His gaze cut through the blanket of darkness as he listened to the soft and steady thrum of a human heart. The music of it sounded as loud as thunder in his mind. He set down the goblet and put his hands over his ears in a futile attempt to block it out. It continued to hammer inside of his head, heightening his need for fresh blood. *Her* blood.

The sound of her heartbeat brought Lucian back to the nights he'd laid awake on the eve of battle, the cold desert wind blowing over him as anticipation caused his heart to beat a frantic rhythm. All that she was made him remember life.

His body rebelled at the pittance of dead blood slowly making its way through him. If his imprisonment continued on much longer and his body was denied fresh blood... Lucian didn't dare finish the thought—not when temptation slept only a few feet away.

Jessica Vargo.

Not even this hell had robbed Jessica of her extraordinary beauty. Nor had her spirit been broken, a great feat considering the creatures who held them prisoner had devoted their nights to breaking them both.

It had been a stroke of genius on Stephan's part to lock her away in here with him. As each night passed, Jessica's presence was robbing Lucian of reason. Her scent, the rich aroma of woman and life, was slowly driving him mad. Her nearness had him fighting a continuous battle against the raging needs of his deprived body.

The hunger slowly gained strength as each night passed and he was given only enough blood by his captor to tease him—to make him need more.

With a swipe of his hand and a clatter of chains, Lucian slapped away the metal goblet on the floor. It skidded across the stone floor and hit the back wall loudly, causing the bit of pig's blood left in it to spill out.

As he raked his gaze over the small cell, Lucian remembered when he and his two brothers had played here as children—something their parents had been none too pleased to learn about. How different the dungeon had seemed then. He'd had the freedom to retreat back to the great hall when the oppressive darkness and gloom had seeped into his very bones.

He allowed his gaze to settle on his companion. Curled into a tight ball on a pallet on the floor, Jessica was lost in sleep. So weary was she after surviving another round of torture, she hadn't even stirred at the sudden clatter of the goblet and chains. Lucian envied Jessica's sleep, because it allowed her some small reprieve from the hell of this place. He wished he could be so lucky. True, there were days the death-like sleep sent him into oblivion, but it wasn't often enough.

Confronted with the sins of his past and torn apart by guilt, Lucian had relinquished his sword and allowed himself to be taken captive by his brother. And now he was home, the place he'd never thought to see again. A place he'd made sure he stayed away from for centuries.

Lucian was barely able to recall fond memories of his youth, though he'd had plenty growing up here. What he remembered were the horrors he'd committed. They overrode the happiness of his childhood and the recollections of his family.

Pain sliced through him as he remembered the night he'd returned home. They called where he'd been the Holy Land, but to Lucian it had been Purgatory.

He'd come back home seeking a place of belonging. He'd soon learned this was the last place he should have come. He still saw the faces of his family as they'd greeted his return. Their voices still rang in his ears. He saw his father's look of relief—and shock—to have his son home.

The joy had lasted but moments.

It all changed to horror when they realized what Lucian had become.

Not quite dead and far from alive.

Much as it did now, the first hunger came upon him like a lightning strike. The bloodlust was unlike anything he'd ever experienced. The pain was unbearable as his body cried out for what it needed to survive.

Lucian heard activity in the hall above and knew he wasn't the only one awake in the castle. Although, after a full day of sleep, most had already left the castle to hunt the night in search of nourishment. He pitied the prey, knowing the predators were creatures who knew no mercy. They killed without remorse, using humans as nothing more than food—or worse—playthings they tortured before taking from them what they needed to go on another night.

As he tested the chains securing him to the wall, Lucian's frustration knew no bounds. This meaningless ritual was one he performed many times each night in the hope he might eventually snap the metal and break free. Yet all it accomplished, as it always did, was making a racket as the heavy metal links scraped against the icy stone floor. Blood seeped from the already-torn flesh of his wrists. His blood was cold as it trickled down his arms.

Lucian tried not to smell past the rank odors sitting on the stale air to the sweet scent of woman and blood beyond it. He tried not to feel Jessica's presence all around him, an unseen torment teasing his mind and his body as he fought down needs he'd been able to ignore until recently.

Her mind's despair and body's pain seeped into his being, festering in him like a disease. Mingling with his bloodlust, her suffering pushed Lucian to the limits of his sanity. It took the might of ages to hold onto his reason as night after night rolled over him, taking him down a path he had walked once before. Already given a second chance to right his life's wrongs, he knew he'd not be given a third. Lucian imagined Lucifer's cool smile of satisfaction as the devil waited for his due. The soul of a Templar was the ultimate prize in his war against God.

Feeling time drag over him, Lucian pushed himself off the floor. His body ached for things he had no business wanting. He craved things that had nothing to do with him being a vampire and everything to do with him being a man.

Taking his gaze off Jessica, he forced himself to look everywhere but at the far corner where she lay. He understood why she put as much distance between them as possible. Instead, his gaze traveled over the walls. He watched the slow trickle of a leak run in a rivulet from a point near the ceiling and down the gray stones. It disappeared deep into a crack in the floor. He watched the tiny river often, if for no other reason than to give his eyes something to watch other than Jessica.

He looked at the locked iron door, which was the only way in or out of this hell. His chains afforded him enough movement to reach any corner of the cell, more of a humiliation than anything else. If the hunger grew beyond his control she'd have nowhere to escape him.

Goddamn you Stephan...

His brother was more devious than even the French jailors at Chinon had been. And those bastards had turned torture into a damn art form.

Chinon.

He couldn't even whisper the name in his mind and not have his gut twist at the memory of what he and his fellow Knights Templar had suffered. Though their imprisonment was lifetimes ago, being held here brought him right back to that time. If he listened hard enough to the silence, he almost heard faint echoes of the past. Tortured screams and the evil laughter of jailors who worked their craft of pain to perfection still haunted him.

Shaking his head as if to dispel the sounds from his ears and the stench of blood, sweat and horror from his nose, he realized those odors weren't from his memories. They came from Jessica Vargo, his companion in this dank hell.

The sounds of the past were gone, replaced by Jessica's even breathing and rhythmic heartbeat. When she shifted on the small pallet, Lucian slammed his eyes closed and tried not to listen to the rush of blood coursing through her body. He tried to focus on something other than her and found his mind reaching naturally out to Constantine. He quickly blocked his thoughts from Dragon, though before did, Lucian detected a slight frisson of electricity passing through him. He knew Constantine tried to connect their thoughts, so Lucian shook his head and tried to focus on anything but the Templars. The last thing he needed was for them to leave Seacrest Castle now, with the Obyri closing in on them. Tristan needed them there the most now and Lucian wouldn't risk all of their souls for anything—not even for Jessica's freedom. There was just too much as stake if the Obyri got their hands on the relic.

Yet Lucian couldn't stop himself from wondering why the sensation felt so strong. Constantine would have to be close in order for Lucian to sense him with such intensity. Lucian knew nothing short of an act of God would bring Constantine Draegon back to this area of England.

It was too close to where the Draegon and Greaves Castles once stood. The very ground was saturated with the evil of the lives who had once dwelled here. As long as it remained tainted, no Templar was willing to tread upon this ground knowing the pain he'd suffered here.

After the sensation passed, Lucian turned his head. His gaze searched until it found Jessica waking from her restless sleep. She'd been sleeping on her side, facing away from him, but now rolled onto her back and winced at the pain the motion caused her battered body. Slowly blinking her eyes open, Jessica came awake. Lucian watched as she stared into nothing, no emotion animating her expression.

By her shallow breathing he knew the pain was too great for her to breathe easy—which might very well be a good thing since the stench was unbearable down here. Desolation spread through her, reaching out to him. He took the burden of it willingly, knowing he was the reason she was a prisoner here.

He'd dragged his dead body back to Penwick instead of staying away as he should have, and had set the actions into motion that would bring them to this very moment.

A single tear slipped from her eye, sliding down the side of her face and disappearing into her matted mess of blonde hair. It pained him to see, knowing with each passing night she moved further away from sanity. He sensed her mind was breaking because of the brutalization of her body during the three months they'd been here.

First she'd been forced to accept what most humans couldn't—that vampires were real. Then came the realization that she was being used as a pawn in Stephan's sick game of revenge. He had to assume it would only be a matter of time before she slipped over the edge and lost her sanity completely.

Everything he was—everything he believed in—rebelled at what was being done to Jessica. She was an innocent soul and Lucian had spent many nights down here fighting to protect her as best he could. His damn chains gave Stephan and his men an advantage that brought Lucian back to the helplessness he'd known at Chinon.

Fading from life, Jessica drifted in and out of her stupor almost nightly now. He knew it would only be a matter of time before she slipped in and never returned. This must have been how Sebastian felt when Selena Ashford had been lost to insanity. He now understood Sebastian's guilt for a human's pain, and why he had taken such drastic measures to ensure he would never be the cause of it again.

Thank God for Allie.

Before Stephan had kidnapped him, Lucian had already seen the positive effect the fiery ghost hunter had on Sebastian. If anyone were able to break through Sebastian's guilt it would be Allison Parker. The woman was a force of nature. Spirited, smart, and tough as nails, he'd always believed she and Sebastian would be a good fit. He hoped Sebastian wasn't too stubborn to see it as well.

"Through Allison Parker, you can find the Daystar."

What Stephan had said on the night Lucian had allowed his brother to take him captive came back to him. Wondering if Stephan's henchmen had gotten to Allie, or if the Templars had been able to stop them, was driving him mad.

Feeling Jessica's pain, Lucian watched as she sat up slowly. She raised her hand to her forehead, lingering for a moment before pushing her hair away from her face. She looked lost and alone.

Wrapping her arms around her stomach, she pointedly avoided looking in his direction. He couldn't blame her. Not after all she'd been through. He knew the very nature of what he was repulsed her. Hating her disdain, but left with no other choice but to accept it, Lucian didn't try to offer her comfort during their captivity together. Instead, he watched helplessly as she slipped deeper into the darkness that was now her world.

Here they were, two lost creatures locked away in the darkness together. Bound by their confinement, yet infinitely alone.

As much as Stephan liked to have Lucian believe Jessica was being used solely as a means to break him, he knew his brother enjoyed torturing her. Stephan accused *him* of being a monster, even as he took delight in hurting an innocent. The irony, while lost on Stephan, didn't go unnoticed by Lucian.

Stephan's plan was not just to break him, but to also keep him from redemption. He wanted to strip Lucian of what was left of his humanity. His brother wanted to make certain there would be nothing left of him to piece together—nothing to show for seven hundred years of fighting for the right to walk in Heaven.

Stephan wanted to bring back the monster Lucian had been when he'd returned to Penwick. He wanted Lucian to be brought back to the moment of madness when the bloodlust overrode his sanity and he'd done the unspeakable. *God, forgive me.* Lucian knew he'd receive no forgiveness from God—and even if he did, he'd never forgive himself for what he'd done. Not as long as his family continued to haunt him every moment of his damned existence.

Jessica let out a small sigh. The sad sound was like a hand tightening around Lucian's severed heart. He heard her stomach growl and related as his body tried rejecting what he'd taken in earlier. The only difference was, where she craved food, his body needed fresh, living blood.

Unable to remain still any longer, Lucian stood. His chains rattled and scraped louder than gunfire throughout the otherwise silent cell. Jessica's head snapped to the side and she glared in distrust in his general direction. If looks could kill, Lucian knew he'd be dead.

Though Jessica couldn't see him, he was able to see her clearly. His sight bore through the dark, taking in every nuance of her as she sat staring into nothing. Though her lifeforce was strong, it was fading each night. He felt it all around him, teasing him with what he knew could never be his again.

Life.

She was painfully thin from lack of food, her filthy clothes—the same green medical uniform she'd been taken in—hung from her frail body. Her hair, dirty and matted, fell to the middle of her back. From the handful of times they'd spoken over the past months, he knew her to be twenty-four. Two years younger than he had been when he'd died. Though she looked younger than her years, the months she'd spent here were etched on her beautiful face.

Though they were being held captive together, he never forced her to engage in conversation. He allowed her to be as silent as she wished and to keep to herself without the added worry of having to speak with him. Lucian allowed her the space she needed, keeping to his side of the cell, trying his damnedest to fight his body's raging needs.

Stephan had taken her while they were still in Damascus, the rural area of Pennsylvania where Tristan Beaumont, the leader of the Templar Vampires, had been living for centuries and where the rest of them had gone to join him some months ago. From what Lucian had learned, Jessica was a dental assistant and had been coming out of work when Stephan had kidnapped her.

During the long trek from America to Salisbury, Stephan had kept them chained together. The long days had been spent locked away in a crate with Jessica, which Stephan, no doubt, believed had been a crafty move. He had hoped keeping the two of them in such close confines would send Lucian over the edge. Thus far, it hadn't, and his continued restraint drove his brother to more desperate measures.

What Stephan failed to realize was, in the hierarchy of the nocturnal world, the Templars were at the top of the food chain. Stronger mentally and physically than other vampires—namely renegade vampires—they were able to resist the temptations others of their kind couldn't. Or at least they could for a certain amount of time. They weren't immune to the temptations of life. They were simply strong enough to resist them for long periods of time. Although, three months of drinking nothing but dead pig's blood, and the memories of being held in Chinon, were pushing Lucian past the point of reason. He knew it was only a matter of time before his resolve broke.

Good God, he was starving. His stomach contracted painfully again as the meager blood settled inside of him. Bloodlust was adding to an already dangerous situation. To quell the hunger, Lucian removed his gaze from the temptation of Jessica. After many long minutes, he settled his gaze on her again. Much to his relief, she had looked away from him.

She moved her head to ease a crick out of her neck. He saw the bite marks ringing her neck and anger surged through him. Stephan hadn't bothered to heal them after he'd fed from her. Not that Lucian expected his brother to.

The growl that erupted from him came of its own accord as his gaze cut through the dark, watching her, feeling her pain and sorrow. Jessica gasped, obviously scared, and searched him out. He sensed her panic rise when she couldn't locate him.

It took all of Lucian's effort to push aside his rage and keep his tone level. "Don't worry, Jessica, I'm not going to hurt you."

She jumped, but seemed to accept his promise. Lucian was relieved. Here, alone with him in this cell, was the only place he knew she felt relatively safe. He'd be damned twice over if he robbed her of that sense of security.

Her disquiet of spirit heightened Lucian's agitation. Oppressive blackness lent the feeling of being trapped inside a tomb. Though he'd taken his last breath seven hundred years ago—he'd been executed by fire in 1310 by the order of King Philip of France—darkness, bone-numbing cold, and deafening silence were as close to being buried as one could get and still be on this side of the grave. By the look of her, and the shiver that wracked her body, he knew Jessica felt it too. The despondency of the dungeon seeped into their very beings.

Lucian still felt the flames licking at his flesh, slowly burning him to death. The cheers of the bloodthirsty crowd, which had drowned out the screams of the forty-nine other members of the Templar Order burning along with him, still rang in his ears. It was a horrific end to lives spent, for the most part, in the servitude of God. For five of them who'd died that day, the battles they'd fought and the blood they'd spilt hadn't been enough to save their souls. They'd faced Michael and were damned for their sins.

Jessica stood, jolting Lucian out of his memories. He rose to his feet, keeping his back pressed against the wall. Her scent came at him and he bit back a groan. As she stretched her petite body, her stomach growled again in protest of its empty state. Her hand went to her concave belly as her gaze drifted through the dark. He had a feeling it definitely wasn't him she was looking for. A small smile played upon her lips as he followed her stare, seeing nothing but cracked gray stone.

She ran her hair through her thick fall of dark blonde hair. Dirt and dried blood turned it into a tangled mess, made it an effort for her to work her fingers through it. "I'd give anything for a cheeseburger. And fries smothered in mozzarella and gravy." She looked in his general direction but missed his exact location by at least a foot. "You wouldn't know anything about food though, would you?"

Lucian flinched at the accusation in Jessica's voice. "I wasn't always dead, Jessica."

He knew food. Lucian remembered it fondly. He might never have eaten a cheeseburger and fries, but his mouth watered for those things she spoke longingly of nonetheless.

Her eyes narrowed, searching. Her frustration was palpable. "Where are you?"

"Here." He moved his left arm, rattling his chains.

This time when he moved she wasn't startled by the sudden clatter of metal. She followed the sound to where he stood. He didn't miss the shiver that passed over her. "He's going to kill me, isn't he?"

Her question came at him like a physical blow. The hopelessness lacing her words brought Lucian right back to his time at Chinon, when despair was all he'd known. Even after seven centuries as a Templar, the memories of his time in captivity were difficult for him to deal with. He hated that she knew such depth of despair. Moreover, Lucian hated knowing he was to blame for her suffering.

Lucian may have refrained from bringing harm to his brother, but that didn't mean he lacked the ability. All it would take was one small error on Stephan's part and Lucian would be able to free himself, and Jessica, from Penwick Castle.

At first he'd refused to see Stephan as a mindless monster. Instead, he'd seen his brother as the boy who'd once idolized him. He wanted to believe the man that boy should have grown into was in him somewhere. After seeing the horrors Stephan was capable of, Lucian knew that boy had died within these walls centuries ago. In his place was a renegade vampire who he'd have no choice but to bring down.

"No. I won't let him kill you. I swear it."

She walked to the wall and leaned against it heavily. "I'm supposed to trust you? You're a vampire too. Like *him.*"

No—he wasn't like Stephan. He didn't take pleasure in hurting people. He didn't torture his victims. He wasn't a sadistic bastard hell-bent on revenge. He was actually much worse. Wasn't he? God had personally damned him and the other Templars. One had to have the blackest of souls to receive such a punishment. And yet, here he was, fighting for redemption night after night. Sometimes, the struggle was almost too much of a burden to bear.

"Have I done anything to hurt you?"

Lucian expected her to hurl accusations at him. He expected her to vent her fears and hate on him. She didn't. She shook her head instead. "No, you haven't, but Stephan says you will. And if you don't kill me, we both know *he* will."

Giving her every chance to move away, Lucian slowly approached Jessica. As he assumed she would, she stood her ground. Although, in truth, what other option did she have? There was nowhere for her to run. But it was the *way* she stood there proudly that awed Lucian.

He took her chin in hand and forced her head up so that he was able to see into her eyes. Lucian loved her eyes, brown and gold and full of life. She sucked in a sharp breath at his touch. Her fear instantly flowed through him like a bitter wind. "I swear it on God, Jessica, I *will* get you out of here."

He heard footsteps approaching and turned to face the door. As he always did, he placed himself between Jessica and the threat of Stephan. Lucian heard Jessica's heartbeat quicken and her breathing turn to terrified gasps. Her fear reached out to him, becoming an almost living entity in the cell with them. She whispered a quick prayer to God for strength.

Lucian moved in a riot of clattering chains as he settled into a battle stance. He wrapped a small length of chain around each fist in a makeshift weapon. He had no qualms about doing whatever needed to be done in order to protect Jessica. Hell, he'd been beaten near to death too many times to count for doing exactly that. What bothered him was that Stephan was forcing him to make a choice—his brother's life or Jessica's.

The door opened and a flood of torchlight broke through the dark. Lucian was forced to look away. After spending countless hours locked away down here, the firelight was like needles in his eyes. Looking back toward the door, he saw a smirk on Stephan's face. His brother's hands were clasped behind his back in the arrogant stance of a man who believed in his own power.

"And how are you both this evening? I trust your day was pleasant?"

"I wouldn't be too cocky if I were you, Stephan. Remember what I did to you last night?"

Stephan had gotten careless last night. His arrogance had allowed Lucian to gain a slight upper hand and he was able to get in a shot good enough to send his brother into the wall. He'd been beaten for it, but at least it had gotten Stephan's attention away from Jessica. That was all Lucian had wanted.

"Always the noble one, aren't you Luc?" He looked over his shoulder at the vampire standing sentry behind him. The Scotsman thought he looked intimidating with his chest thrust out and his arms crossed over it. "My brother certainly lives up to his moniker of Knight, does he not, James? Let's see if we can't make this night the one where he breaks, shall we?"

Lucian bared his fangs in response to Stephan's threat. The raw hatred blazing in the depths of his brother's eyes sliced through him. Gone were all traces of the innocent young boy Stephan had been. His once-eager brown eyes now gleamed silver with immortality. His easy smile was replaced with a permanent sneer. Razor-sharp fangs peeked out from behind pale lips. Although the blush of youth was still upon him, Stephan's eyes reflected the ages he'd seen as he'd traveled from the moment of his human death until now.

"I won't let you hurt her."

"You have no choice." Stephan strode over to him. The moment Lucian moved to attack, James was on him. Although chained, Lucian's strength put him on an even keel with the renegade. He was gaining the upper hand but Jessica's scream stopped him cold. He took a nasty shot to the face that sent him staggering back.

His feet tangled in the chains and he went down. After James landed a solid kick to Lucian's ribs, Stephan called the prick off. Snarling, James kicked him in the face before grabbing a struggling Jessica away from Stephan.

"I'm going to hurt you tonight, Lucian." Stephan smiled coldly as he moved out of Lucian's reach. "And I'm going to hurt her too. So badly, in fact, I might have to force you to kill her to end her suffering," he taunted from the doorway.

Jessica whimpered and James laughed.

"Leave her be, Stephan. She has nothing to do with what's between us."

"What's the matter, Luc? Lost the stomach for bloodshed?"

Stephan strolled up to him as Lucian struggled to his feet. Something about his brother's smug expression woke a fury in him that couldn't be controlled. He glanced at Jessica and his rage soared to epic heights. He looked back at his brother, at the silent dare reflected in Stephan's expression, and growled. Without warning, he struck, his fist landing true. The punch to Stephan's face stunned him long enough for Lucian to take him down.

Stephan landed on his back. Lucian came down on top of him, pressing the length of chain against his brother's throat. Using the chain to hold Stephan's head still, Lucian rained blows down upon him. Though he fought, Stephan lacked the strength to knock Lucian off.

James, however, had more than enough.

From the corner of his eye, Lucian saw Jessica land on the floor. A second later James was on him. James grabbed his arm and Lucian's roar echoed throughout the cell. He turned sharply to counter James's attack. The two of them battled

27

across the cell until Stephan stepped in and yanked Jessica from the floor.

Her scream cut through the grunts and growls as he and James fought. Lucian's fight drained out of him the instant he saw the hand Stephan had clamped around her throat. Jessica was fighting for air, and Lucian knew if he kept on fighting, Stephan would kill her.

Though it galled him to have to do so, Lucian shoved the Scot away and faced Stephan. "Let her go."

"Your arrogance is astounding. I think being a Templar has gone to your head." He threw Jessica at James and swept his arm wide. "Look around you, brother. You aren't the one in charge. I am. I make the rules of this game."

"This isn't a game."

Stephan paced the cell with the confidence of a man who knew no matter how far he pushed, his brother wouldn't push back. "Yes it is. You started this game when you returned to Penwick."

His parents' faces flashed in his mind. The sight of blood—so much blood—came back to Lucian as well. His guilt closed in on him, crushing him under its weight. "It wasn't a game I played. I wanted to come home."

Stephan cocked a brow. "Should I tell her, Luc? Should I tell her what you did? Think she will see you as any more of a monster than she already does?"

Lucian glanced at Jessica and saw she no longer struggled. She was limp—lifeless, almost—in James's hold. "Don't." He pushed the word out between teeth clenched hard enough that his fangs cut into his bottom lip. The taste of his blood was foul on his tongue.

Stephan smiled with pure malevolence. "No, I don't think I will." He walked back to the open door. Stephan trailed a finger down Jessica's cheek, making Lucian want to rip his arm off. She didn't protest. She didn't do anything other than hang in James's arms. "I'll save that tragic tale for another night."

Stephan slipped a dagger from the sheath at his hip. Jessica started to cry. Each hiccupped sob, every tear that fell from her eyes, was a knife in Lucian's heart. "No, no, my dear, don't cry. This blade isn't for you. At least not yet."

Without warning, Stephan swiped the blade across Lucian's stomach, tearing through his shirt and flesh. Hissing, Lucian stood tall as his blood seeped from the gash. He knew this night was going to be one he remembered for years to come.

But at least for now, Stephan's focus was on him and not Jessica. For that, Lucian was eternally grateful.

Of course, Lucian had to keep reminding himself of that as his brother continued to lash out at him with the dagger. At one point during the hour-long ordeal, James set Jessica aside and tried to restrain him, just for the hell of it. Stephan's lapdog obviously didn't like being left out of the fun. Unfortunately for the hulking vampire, Lucian wasn't up for playing nice with him.

It only took one bite from Lucian to have James howling in pain and going back to Jessica. With pure evil satisfaction, Lucian spat out the bitten flesh at Stephan's feet. The foul taste of the renegade vampire was a worse torture than what his brother was doing to him with the blade.

With pride and fortitude borne of who and what he'd been in life, Lucian met his brother's fury with a mask of cold indifference.

He was a bloody mess by the time Stephan finished with him. Much to Lucian's shame, he'd done nothing to stop his brother, and now he'd lost enough blood to weaken himself. He collapsed to the ground with Stephan's and James's laughter cutting him deeper than the blade had.

His brother was true to his word. He'd hurt Lucian. Bad.

Eventually Stephan was going to stop playing his sick games and strike deadly. Lucian hoped by that time, he'd have managed to get Jessica worlds away from Penwick. God knew Stephan would not stop trying until he succeeded. The night would come when Lucian was going to have to wipe the stain of Stephan from this world.

Or Stephan would send him to Hell.

Lucian shook his head sadly. "I'm sorry for what's become of you, brother."

Stephan laughed and paced the length of the cell. "Why be sorry? I have immortality, Lucian." He fisted one hand, as if he were grasping treasure. "I can give eternal life to those I choose, or I can take life away."

In that moment, Lucian no longer saw Stephan as his brother, but as the renegade he'd been turned into. "If I could, I'd go back to that night at The Gate and send you to Hell, where your soul belongs."

Stephan roared with fury and stalked back to him. He grabbed a fistful of hair and hauled Lucian off of the floor. The sound of flesh hitting flesh cracked out like thunder as his brother slapped him across the face. The warrior in Lucian needed to attack—to fight back. The need overrode all else and Lucian lunged for Stephan despite his chains.

The large emerald family ring, which Stephan wore on his middle finger—to mock him, no doubt—opened the flesh on his left cheek. Blood trickled down his face even as the gash closed.

"I've already seen Hell. I saw it the night you returned to Penwick and brought your evil with you."

Lucian jerked forward again in a mad effort to reach his brother but Stephan stepped back and out of his reach. The chains cut deep into his flesh as he snarled, growled, and swiped at the air like a rabid animal. His rage reduced him to a mindless creature whose need to spill blood blinded him to everything else.

Only after Stephan had reached the doorway did he turn back and face Lucian. The order Stephan issued to James chilled Lucian clear down to the marrow in his bones.

"Bring her."

Chapter Two

Once the fog of unconsciousness receded, Lucian came awake and tried to peer around the cell. He cringed at the pain opening his eyes caused. Though his body had healed externally, he still ached and was weak from the loss of blood. He pushed himself up and gritted his teeth at the loud clatter of the chains. The too-tight manacles bit deep into his flesh, leaving bloody trenches as they squeezed his wrists. Cold blood trickled down his hands as he gained his balance.

Searching for Jessica, he finally managed to cast a quick glance around the cell. Seeing her gone and assuming hours had passed since she was hauled out of the dungeon, Lucian went numb as he imagined what torments Stephan was putting her through.

His frustration was palpable and was the only thing keeping him company as helplessness ate away at him. He could have prevented this by ending Stephan months ago. Instead, he'd allowed his emotions to guide his actions. Confronted with the fact that not only had Stephan survived through the centuries, but that he'd done so as a renegade hell-bent on revenge, Lucian had given himself over to his brother.

That night in the parking lot of The Gate, Lucian gave up his sword and allowed himself to be beaten and dragged away without a fight. Since then, he'd forced himself to endure

Stephan's taunts and his men's torments, never forgetting this was not just any renegade. Solely due to Lucian's lack of action, Jessica had become part of this sick game his brother played.

If Stephan hurt her... He'd what? As much as he knew Stephan belonged in Hell, he couldn't bear to be the one who sent him there. He already suffered profound guilt for what he'd done. He'd returned to Penwick seven centuries ago, heedless that evil had followed him there. He feared that killing his brother would be a burden too heavy to bear.

Quieting his mind, Lucian reached out to listen past the silence, but heard nothing. Not a damn thing. Given what Stephan was capable of, he wondered what was worse, being able to hear what was happening or the deafening silence surrounding him.

The cell was so small that pacing it was only a short trip wall to wall. On one pass, Lucian knelt and ran a hand over Jessica's threadbare pallet. Her energy lingered on the fabric. The silence, cold, and sense of vulnerability—it all transported him back to Chinon and that was one place he never wanted to suffer through again.

But then everything about the dungeon reminded him of that place.

He remembered those days all too well. He'd been locked away, trying not to listen to the awful screams of his brothers as they suffered their French jailor's tortures. Those sadistic bastards had even managed to break Constantine, something Lucian had believed would be impossible considering the suffering Dragon had endured in his life. Beaten and raped by Ulric Chambers for years, he'd trekked alone to Messina to escape his life. Breaking him had been an obsession with the jailors because he'd been the hardest one to shatter.

But they had broken him—just as they'd broken all of them. One by one the Knights had all come to the point where their pride fled and their will shattered. They'd all become empty shells of the proud warriors they'd once been, and faced the flames that had taken their lives.

If Lucian had known the consequences returning home would have wrought seven hundred years later, he would have gone straight to Seacrest Castle. But he had wanted to go home. His actions had resulted in the deaths of his family, the turning of his brother into a renegade, and Jessica's suffering tonight.

Thinking back to the time he'd spent in Damascus, Lucian knew his returning to Penwick had done even more harm and brought about more death than he could have ever imagined. Closing his eyes as his hand traveled over Jessica's pallet, he remembered the bodies of Sarah Addison, Jordan Brewster, and Amanda Driver. He'd found them, one after the other, bled to death in abandoned houses scattered around Pennsylvania. Lucian had learned why Stephan had targeted those women only after he'd allowed his brother to take him captive.

The three women were all born on Halloween under a Bloodmoon. From what Stephan told him, such an event marked the birth of a Hallowed—the human host of the power of the Daystar. Stephan used his knowledge of the Daystar as a bargaining tool to amass his followers throughout the years. Fortunately, few chose to be players in his plot for revenge.

A scent, one that caused his stomach to knot, wafted past the dank odors of the dungeon. Lucian growled at the sweet smell of Jessica's blood drifting down to him from the great hall. He fell on both knees when the silence of the dungeon was broken by her screams.

ଐ୯ଷ

At twenty-four, Jessica should have had her entire life in front of her. The reality was she didn't. She had weeks—more likely days—left of her lifespan. All the things she'd never done flashed in her mind.

Though she was a fighter and wasn't ready to have her life taken from her before she had the chance to live it, she didn't know how much more of this she could take. Fighting back tears, Jessica tried not to give in to her terror as she awaited the next torture Stephan of Penwick forced her to suffer. She'd tried to stay strong—Lord knows she'd done an admirable job all this time—but the pain and humiliation were beginning to crack her resolve.

The concept of the walking dead seemed absurd, nothing more than something out of a horror movie. It certainly wasn't reality. At least that's what Jessica had always believed until she'd come face to face with a vampire.

Oh God, why hadn't she waited in the office for Arlene to walk out with her? Because it had already been after eight o'clock at night and she had been tired and eager to get home. Every moment Jessica had lingered in the dentist's office was an eternity as far as she'd been concerned.

She'd left as soon as she'd finished cleaning the exam rooms and made sure the autoclave machine finished running its cycle. She hadn't even bothered to put away the sterilized dental tools, instead leaving them in the autoclave—something she'd never done before.

Jessica had almost reached her car when Stephan had stepped from the shadows. She remembered him slamming her against her car, the feel of his cold body against hers as he whispered the most awful things in her ear.

And the fangs—oh God, his fangs...

At first glance she'd thought them fake. Then she'd thought they were human incisors filed to points. After all, hadn't some kid come in and begged Dr. Leon to do the same for him? Her boss had refused. A family man and old school, he didn't want his name attached to such a procedure.

Only after Stephan had used his fangs on her had she realized they were the real deal. *He* was the real thing. A genuine vampire. She'd believed he was going to kill her. She almost wished he had. Instead, she was caught up in this nightmarish world where the lines of life and death were blurred.

"Are you still with us, Jessica?"

Unfortunately she was.

Standing in the center of the hall of the ancient castle, Jessica returned from her mind-trip. She pinned Stephan with a hard glare, wishing she possessed the strength to kill him.

Her captor reclined like a king upon a gilded red-velvet wing-backed chair. The chair was set before a fire blazing in a large hearth. Tattered and faded tapestries hung on the stone walls. They were now as dull and lifeless as the medieval keep they decorated. Death haunted every corner and shadow.

Stephan's body, tall and lean, was encased in black trousers and a slate gray long-sleeved shirt. He wore polished black shoes and a platinum Rolex adorned his left wrist, completing his casually wealthy appearance. His shoulder-length brown hair was pulled back in a neat queue. His clipped, upper-crust English accent lent him an air of civility, adding to the deceit of what he really was.

This was not what she'd imagined a vampire would look like, at least not until she saw his silver eyes. The fire of evil burned there, as did the promise of more pain and, ultimately, her death.

"Are you with us, Jessica?" Stephan repeated, the edge in his tone forcing a response from her.

"Unfortunately," Jessica murmured as she met his gaze defiantly.

Though Jessica knew he held her life in his hands, she couldn't help the proud tilt of her chin or the ice in her voice. Nor could she hide her loathing from him. It poured from every part of her being as she rivaled his cold stare.

She flinched when Stephan clapped his hands together and leaned forward with a sharp laugh. "You see, James? You see why I picked her?" The imposing vampire he spoke to, who was never more than a few steps away from his master, reminded her of a New York bouncer guarding the entrance of an elite Manhattan club. "Her spirit is a thing of true beauty. Too bad I'll have to eventually break her of it, if Lucian doesn't kill her first."

James, dressed all in black, hands clasped in front of him, his beefy arms barely able to touch his sides, gave a curt nod of agreement. "Eventually the hunger will overtake him." The Scot's thick brogue sent chills of dread over her as he appraised her from head to feet. "I doubt there'll be much left of her after he's done with her."

Jessica slid her eyes shut and dragged in a hard breath. Her blood ran cold at the thought of Lucian of Penwick tearing her body to pieces as he fed on her. Though he'd yet to show her anything but gallantry, she never forgot what he was. He might seem civil, but he was far from an ordinary man.

Every moment locked away with him was a torturous wait for the hunger to drive him to kill her. She wished he'd get it over with already, just have done with it nice and quick, because the wait was driving her crazy.

"Come here to me."

Stephan's command knocked the image of Lucian killing her from her mind. The idea of going over to him made Jessica physically ill. Her skin crawled at the mere thought of his hands on her. And the things he did to her with his fangs—oh dear God, she nearly vomited right then and there.

"I said come here."

Stephan didn't need to yell. The quiet way he barked out the command was enough to get her feet moving. Once she was in range of him, Stephan grabbed a fistful of her hair. Twisting, he pulled it until he forced her to her knees. She bit back a cry when some hair was torn free from her scalp. Jessica leaned into the pain lest he tear the entire chunk clean from her head.

"I thought I made it terribly clear by now that I'll not tolerate having to issue you a command twice." His voice was a low hiss of fury in her ear. "This will be your last warning, Jessica. Next time you'll suffer for your insolence."

As far as Jessica was concerned there'd be no need for another warning. That one had the desired effect. "What do you want from me?"

"Your death." His words were a slap to her face. "I need Lucian to kill you. I won't kill him until he does and I grow weary of waiting."

Oh sweet God...

He rubbed his cheek against hers, causing her stomach to roll and bile to rise in her throat. Although she was fairly certain he wasn't going to rape her—after all, he hadn't yet and she'd been his prisoner for months now—the contact of his flesh on hers made her doubt he was going to hold himself back much longer.

After all she'd suffered, rape was the one violation she'd been spared. Jessica didn't think she'd be able to endure this gross invasion of her body. At his soft intake of breath, Jessica knew he'd sniffed her hair. She was allowed only the occasional bath and she hoped her stink choked him. He released her hair and she resisted the urge to jump away. God only knew what he would do to her if she tried to get away from him.

Stephan's hand snaked around her throat, his fingers caressing her. His touch wasn't as cold as she'd suspected a vampire's would be. He felt alive—except he wasn't, which was proved by his lack of heartbeat or breath. Every time he smashed her against him she was struck by the stillness of his chest, a reminder that he was as dead as a corpse rotting in the ground.

"To speed things along, I've decided to stop feeding Lucian. That leaves you as his sole food source." Stephan cocked a brow and inhaled the air around her. "I wonder how long my brother will hold to his nobility as the bloodlust drives him mad with hunger."

The vision of her death materialized in her mind and she voiced the question she'd been too terrified to ask until now. "Why me?"

He nuzzled her neck, his lips running over the spot where her furious pulse pounded. "You were available."

In a swift motion, he pulled her across his lap. Once he'd settled her on top of him, Stephan's arms came around her to hold her in place. She swallowed down her disgust when he splayed his hands on her back. His touch let her know it would be foolish to fight him.

His fangs grazed her neck and she went stiff with dread. "Why don't I sweeten the bait? What say you, James?"

His words vibrated against her throat. Jessica struggled not to cry as cold terror pushed her past the edge of reason.

Jessica didn't have to look at him to know James was grinning like the Cheshire Cat. "I say that's a fine idea, my lord."

Fear made her mouth run dry and sent her heart slamming painfully against her ribcage. Stephan lifted her from his lap and handed her over to James, who took her and threw her to the floor. Jessica did her best to fight him off but the huge vampire stopped her struggles easily and held her down for Stephan. He pulled out a razor from his pocket. Though she knew it would do no good, she screamed until her throat was raw. With a sinister grin, he proceeded to sweeten the bait in his own sick way.

After Stephan was done with her, James carelessly carried her battered and bleeding body back down to the dungeon. Trapped in the dark once more, Jessica did the one thing she knew would do her no good in this place.

She cried.

Chapter Three

Eventually Jessica's screams stopped and the silence returned. Lucian might have thought they'd killed her, but her lifeforce was still strong within the castle. He sat on the floor, his back pressed against the damp wall. A knee was drawn up, his right arm resting on it, as he stared at the brand on his hand. The dual knights on a single mount were a symbol of the Order's vow of poverty. The Latin inscription encircling it read *Sigillum Militum Cristi de Templo*. Translated, it meant *Seal of the Soldiers of Christ from the Temple*. Once, Lucian had taken pride in the seal. Now, he knew only shame when he looked upon it. Shame in himself for what he'd become and for the blood he'd shed in God's name long after he'd lost his faith.

Lucian heard only one set of footsteps heading down to the dungeon—too heavy to belong to Jessica. He stood and sniffed the air, baring his fangs as the strong metallic scent of blood assailed his senses. He stumbled back as a wave of thirst made the back of his throat feel as if it were coated with needles. The lock was released and the door kicked open. Lucian's gaze cut through the dark. Jessica dangled limply in James's arms. Her eyes were closed and her head was thrown back. Her complexion was as pale as death. From what he could see, her arms were covered in small cuts and her uniform was bloody.

What had they done to her?

Acting on instinct, Lucian leapt for James. The burly renegade took a single step back out of his reach. The chains rattled loudly as Lucian snarled and growled. He swiped at the air and snapped his teeth like a crazed beast. James merely smiled coldly at Lucian's animalistic behavior.

"Get back or I'll make her wish she were dead."

By the look of her, Lucian reasoned Jessica probably already did.

As much as Lucian wanted to tear James to shreds, the threat forced him to back down. Though he was fairly confident the bastard wouldn't be stupid enough to kill Jessica knowing he'd have to face Stephan's wrath, that wasn't something Lucian knew for certain. As long as there was a shadow of doubt, he wasn't about to take a chance with Jessica's life.

Lucian moved back until he collided with the wall. James dumped Jessica's unconscious body on her pallet as if she was nothing more than a bag of trash. The cocky vampire turned back to him, letting his gaze trail slowly over Lucian as if assessing him and finding him lacking.

Lucian narrowed his eyes, frustration riding him. It would be nothing for him to tear James apart and send him straight to Lucifer. Hell, he'd brought down bigger men. As a Templar Knight, he'd been part of an elite brotherhood of warrior-monks. They were without equal on the battlefield, instilling terror in the hearts of the enemies of God. The Templars ruled the night, with only the Order of the Rose a close second in strength, power, and wealth.

"Before this is over we're going to have a go, you and I."

James snorted. "I look forward to it, Templar." Meandering out of the cell, he turned back to Lucian once he was beyond the doorway. He motioned to Jessica with a curt nod. "Enjoy Stephan's present."

The arrogant bastard slammed the cell door closed and locked it, before strolling back up to the great hall.

Once he knew James was out of the dungeon, Lucian rushed over to Jessica. Kneeling, he hesitated to touch her. He pushed aside the fall of her thick blonde hair and sucked in a hard breath at how ashen she looked. If it weren't for her soft, shallow breathing he'd think her dead.

And they called *him* the monster.

There were cuts covering her arms. God only knew what the rest of her looked like. Thin lines of blood stained her shirt and pants from the wounds hidden by her clothes. None of them, much to his relief, were deep or life threatening. The cuts were only deep enough to make her bleed in order to drive him mad with hunger. Thank God.

Though he fought against it, the bloodlust rushed through Lucian like a raging storm. He stumbled back as far from Jessica as he was able, given their small confines. The sound of the chains roused her. A scream seemed to catch, and die, in her throat. She bolted upright, cringing in obvious pain. Shivering, she searched through the darkness for him. Lucian made no sound to betray where he was.

She took a deep breath and squeezed her eyes closed. He was relieved to be given a reprieve from the impact of her wide-eyed brown gaze. But as she drew her legs up and rested her cheek against her knees, he realized she was crying. He swore his dead heart kicked to life for a split second, only to die all over again at the sounds of her quiet weeping.

This was the first time he'd heard her cry. No matter what Stephan threw at her, she'd faced him with a dignity Lucian admired. The sight of her tears now was too much for Lucian to endure. In a fit of rage, he slammed his fist against the wall. The unrelenting stone tore away the flesh and shattered the bones of his knuckles. He now understood why Constantine liked to slam his fist into things. It certainly helped release some of the anger and frustration.

She'd obviously heard the smack of his fist against the stone, heard the bones break. Jessica lifted her head to regard the dark questioningly. With a savage growl, he leveled her with a hard glare, fighting the smell of her blood. Fighting the hunger threatening to take over the man he was trying desperately to hold on to.

"Are you all right?" The sadness in her voice pained him and had him wanting to punch the wall again.

No. "Yes."

"You punched the wall, didn't you?"

"No."

She looked so damn tiny and delicate. Dear God above, her blood smelled so sweet, he couldn't block the scent from his senses.

"Yes you did." She pulled at the hem of her raggedy shirt. It took some effort but she managed to tear off a small, uneven strip. "Here."

He stared at her outstretched hand, at the scrap of dirty green cloth dangling loosely between her skeletal fingers. "I'm fine."

The piece of material would be useful to bind the broken flesh until it had a chance to heal completely. Too bad Lucian didn't trust himself to get closer to her than he already was. Even one more step would be too close to her, and not because she was bleeding from the myriad shallow cuts. Everything about her was a temptation. He was finding her harder to resist as each night passed.

When he made no motion to take the cloth, Jessica dropped her arm and used it to dab at her own wounds. How selfless of her to think of him first. Her generosity was astounding, especially considering her disdain for what he was. Lucian watched her carefully examine her arms, legs, and stomach. As she dabbed away the blood, he saw her struggle to hold in her pain.

"He's not going to allow you any more blood." Though her tone was flat, Lucian sensed disgust ripple through her.

His entire being rebelled at that information. With the hunger already relentless, it would only be a matter of time before he was in the full throes of the bloodlust and unable to fight it off. His body's basic instincts for survival would overtake him and he'd become nothing more than a crazed beast.

"You *heard* Stephan say this?"

She nodded grimly and put aside the cloth. She was barely bleeding, but he knew those cuts must hurt like hell. "He told me right before he started to cut me." Her gaze seemed to find him, though he knew she couldn't really see him through the dark. Nevertheless, her gaze sliced him with its intensity. "He's done waiting for you to kill me."

Lucian closed his eyes and raked his undamaged hand through his shoulder-length brown hair. Though his body was far past needing it, it was instinct to drag in a hard breath. Pain pounded through his chest until the air was completely gone from his body.

Opening his eyes, Lucian saw Jessica was again resting her head against her knees. He felt her pain as keenly as if it was his own and he wanted to go to her and offer her whatever small comfort he could. He didn't of course, doubting she'd accept it. Instead, he sat on his pallet, his body suddenly too heavy for legs weak with hunger to support. A spasm contracted his stomach, forcing him to bite back a groan. He prayed for strength and wisdom to escape this hell without having to end his brother.

"No matter what happens I'll never harm you. I'll force Stephan to kill me it if comes to that."

"How noble of you, vampire." She lifted her head, giving it a curt shake before curling into a fetal position on her pallet. "I'm sure death is a real sacrifice for something already dead."

Some*thing*. Not some*one*.

The way she'd spat that had him swallowing a mouthful of shame. He didn't need her scorn to remind him of what he was. The constant hunger, the brand on his hand, the relentless cold—they were all reminders of what he'd become.

And as for some*thing* dead not fearing more death, she had no idea what awaited him beyond this existence. No idea at all.

ℰℴℭℬ

"How long do you think it will take before my brother breaks?"

Stephan reclined on an elegant wing-backed chair. With his fingers steepled beneath his chin, he stared into the dancing orange flames of the fire burning in the hearth. The thrill of torturing Jessica still sang through him. Her blood sat on his tongue, tasting of life. He was almost sorry that it would be Lucian who would kill her. Stephan would have liked to be the one to drink her in as she took her last breath.

He thrived on making such an intimate kill. He liked to take his time, torment his victim for a while. It made the kill that much sweeter.

He hadn't been this way as a living man. He'd been good and kind, a son his parents had been proud of. The Obyri who'd turned him had brought out the beast in him, making him appreciate the power he had over life and death. Although Stephan enjoyed what he was, Lucian still needed to pay for what he'd brought about by returning to Penwick. Lucian shouldn't be allowed to go on without suffering in Hell for his sins.

Of all the vampires he'd recruited over the centuries, James was his most loyal servant. Stephan had found him in the gutter back at the turn of the twentieth century. He'd earned a small bit of renown as a boxer before he'd found robbery was a more profitable profession. James had been dying of a bullet wound the night Stephan had found him and turned him. From the moment his eyes had opened and he beheld the man who'd given him immortality, James's steadfast loyalty was something Stephan never failed to appreciate.

James, who had a bored look about him as he leaned against the mantle, idly examining a knife he'd taken from his kill a few nights ago, grunted. "I think not long at all, my lord. You should have seen his reaction when I brought the wench back to the cell."

"Good." Stephan nodded thoughtfully. "I'd have liked to have a go at her before Lucian drains the life from her. Her beauty and spirit never cease to please me." He waved a hand through the air in careless dismissal. "Ah well, what's done is done."

He'd been entertaining the idea of taking her body since the moment he clapped eyes on the girl. He'd happened upon her strictly by chance. Never one to shun a boon from fate, he'd stalked her until the perfect moment came to take her. He wasn't sure of the reason he'd held himself back thus far.

Normally he acted on his impulses, as the countless bodies he'd left in his wake proved.

If Lucian didn't kill the girl soon, Stephan would finally give in to his desire for her. He'd use Jessica's body and toss her back in the cell with his stink all over her. That ought to drive his brother insane with fury. And Stephan would use Lucian's rage to push him into forgetting his false sense of humanity.

Humanity.

There was no such thing hidden within Lucian, no matter what his brother liked to believe. Stephan had been there when Lucian returned from the Holy Land.

Burned and bloody, Lucian had dragged his ruined body back to Penwick. One look at him and it was clear no one could have survived the damage done to him and lived to tell about it.

That much had certainly been true.

Within moments they'd all realized Lucian was no longer alive, yet not dead. He had been both and neither at the same time. He'd brought his evil home and they'd all suffered for it.

The hunger growing, Stephan clapped a hand on James's shoulder. "Go fetch the delectable morsel we have locked away in the tower and bring her to my chamber. And afterward, make certain you dispose of her body better than you did the last one."

James nodded. "Of course, my lord." He hesitated, a rarity, because he usually rushed to do his master's bidding. "The hunger has me, my lord. May I have a go at her?"

"Of course, James. I'll leave a taste of her for you."

With a grateful nod, James hurried up the stairs to get the lively blonde he'd captured over a week ago. Stephan took a moment to relish the fact that, at long last, his revenge was finally coming to fruition. Lucian's prized nobility was beginning to fracture. Once Stephan managed to break him, Lucian would kill Jessica, a pure soul. Hell would open and take him.

Stephan would not allow Lucian to continue on the road of redemption. It wasn't fair for his brother to be forgiven his sins and allowed to enter Heaven.

Lucian belonged in Hell and Stephan was going to make damn sure that was where he spent eternity. This time around there would be no merciful archangel to give him a chance to prove his love of God. Lucifer would greet him and show him a whole new level of pain.

Chapter Four

Every part of her body hurt. The salty sweat and filth of her body made her cuts burn. Her throat was raw from screaming. Her spirit ached from enduring yet another round of torture.

Jessica knew she should be grateful for the pain. It meant she was still alive. Although, at this point, she wondered if that was good or bad. Lord only knew what awaited her next. After what Stephan had put her through tonight, she didn't want to think of what else the sick bastard would do to her.

Listening to the silence, Jessica sensed Lucian hidden in the dark—watching her, no doubt. So far, he'd exercised a measure of control by not killing her as Stephan hoped he would. She didn't think it meant he still *wouldn't* kill her. She wasn't about to fool herself into having that much hope.

The complete blackness of the cell was a hell of a thing. It suffocated her and made her dizzy. She'd often find herself groping around in the dark, disoriented and vulnerable. With her sanity slipping, her mind saw things not truly there. Her mother and father, her brother, even her ex-boyfriend Charlie made an appearance. They stepped through the blackness, easing her fears and loneliness. She almost felt their arms around her, trying to protect her from the evil surrounding her.

The constant damp and cold were also wearing on her. She had a constant ache in her lower back from sleeping on the floor. Her joints hurt. So did her jaw from the force of clenching her teeth to keep them from chattering.

Feeling empty after being cut and fed from, Jessica would have given anything for an aspirin and a package of Band-Aids. A hot shower and a good meal would be heaven-sent. The fuzzy feeling on her teeth, the filth on her body, the hair growth under her arms and legs were nauseating to her, given her fastidiousness when it came to personal hygiene.

Raking a hand through the matted mess of her hair, Jessica shivered with disgust. Her hair gave a whole new meaning to the term *dirty blonde*. She wondered how much of it she'd be forced to cut if, by some miracle, she survived this hell. Probably all of it, she thought regrettably, given the severity of some of the knots she felt.

Losing her hair was the least of her problems. Right now, her first priority was survival. She'd worry about how bald and scarred she was going to be after she made it out of Penwick alive.

"Jessica?"

Like some disembodied entity, Lucian's voice sounded directly beside her. It startled Jessica clean out of her torn skin. Gasping, she looked toward him, as if she'd see him standing beside her. "What?"

"How are you feeling?"

He was closer than she'd thought. She didn't like him being so near, an unseen threat hidden by the dark. "Why do you care?"

She heard the chains scrape against the floor and knew he moved away from her. "I don't."

She swore she heard disappointment in his voice. Why would he care if she snapped at him nastily? Why did he make it seem as if he cared about her at all? For God's sake, Lucian

51

of Penwick was a vampire, and he had no right to sound crestfallen. It confused her. It made her think of him as less of a monster than Stephan was.

Tired of silence, loneliness, and fear as her only companions, Jessica found herself wanting to talk to him. She wanted to hear something other than the ringing in her ears caused by the oppressive quiet.

"I'm fine. He only scratched the skin."

She wasn't being entirely truthful.

After James had ripped off her scrubs, leaving her clad in nothing but her bra and panties, he'd held her down for Stephan. The torture had gone on for an eternity as Stephan inflicted shallow cuts on her arms, chest, and legs.

A long silence stretched between them. Lucian's tone was tight and controlled when he spoke. "Will you allow me to look at them?"

She raised a brow, wondering if that was a good idea. Given what he was, she didn't want him near her. "No, I don't trust you."

"Nor should you." It seemed Lucian was going to match her honesty with a healthy dose of his own. "But right now I just want to make certain you weren't cut too deep. I swear it on God I won't hurt you."

She ran her fingers over the sliced skin of her left arm. All the cuts stung like hell. A few of them were worse than she'd first suspected. Stephan obviously allowed his delight at hurting her to get away from him a time or two. Still, she didn't think she wanted Lucian near her.

"I told you, your brother didn't cut me deep. Not like he cut you."

No, not like he'd cut Lucian at all. Jesus Christ, at one point Jessica thought Stephan was going to sever Lucian's left arm clean off. She'd been horrified that one brother would do that to another, though given what'd she'd seen thus far, Stephan was sadistic enough to do just about anything. His ruthlessness made each moment here a nightmare that seemed to last forever.

Jessica heard Lucian's chains scrape the floor as he came back to her. She leapt off the pallet, slamming into the wall as Lucian continued his advance. He gripped her shoulders with freezing hands. She rasped out a startled breath and wrapped her hands around his wrists. The manacles bit into her palms as she tried to pry his hands from her.

Though he held her gently, his grip was firm enough to tell her he'd win this battle of wills. "You're lying, Jessica."

"Let go of me."

"I feel your pain."

She tried to shove him away, but not only was it like trying to move a mountain, the effort pulled the skin on her arm. One of the deeper cuts opened, causing her to whimper, despite how hard she tried to hold it back.

"If you kill me, I swear to God I'll come back and haunt you."

"No you won't. You'll go to God." He applied just enough pressure to force her down without hurting her. "Now sit down before you fall."

Lucian joined her on her pallet. Being this close to Lucian was like sitting next to a glacier. There were times she'd heard his chains rattling softly and knew the movement was caused by his shivering. True, she was always cold as well—the dungeon was damp and icy—but she occasionally found warmth buried under the pallet. Lucian didn't. She knew his cold came from within, not without.

Stephan took delight in informing her that Lucian had no soul, hence the sub-zero body temperature. The misery she'd felt on those freezing December mornings back home when all she'd wanted to do was hide under the covers and savor the warmth of her bed made her want to offer him her heat. The insane desire to wrap her arms around him was a ridiculous notion. He was a vampire and she was human. The two simply didn't mix.

Oh yeah—she was definitely losing her damn mind.

He took her hand and extended her arm. Jessica hissed as the skin pulled around the cuts. Using extreme care, Lucian ran his fingers over her torn flesh. As much as Jessica wanted to swat him away, she refrained. She needed this—his touch. She needed to connect with him after all this time of being together, yet very much alone.

His fingers lingered over the more serious of wounds before he dropped her arm. He repeated the action with her other arm before gently letting it go. "I'm so sorry, Jessica."

"For what? You didn't take the razorblade to me."

His rumbling growl reverberated through her. "I could have prevented all of this if I'd just killed Stephan back in Damascus."

Something about Lucian made Jessica believe that his conscience would never allow him to bear the burden of killing his brother. He may be a vampire—like Stephan was—but it was clear to her that Lucian lacked the ruthless streak his brother possessed. Or maybe he did have it and he was just playing a good game with her. Earning her trust. Playing with her to make the kill that much sweeter. After all, isn't that what Stephan had claimed at least a dozen times already?

Oh God, Jessica didn't know what to believe anymore. The line between reality and fiction had blurred. It stood to reason that the line that separated honesty and lies was just as distorted.

Morbid curiosity won out over reason. Lucian went to move away from her, Jessica reached out to find him. Her hand brushed through his hair, which felt like silken strands through her fingers. He went so still at her touch that she nearly pulled away.

He sighed softly as her hand explored him. She ran her fingers through his hair before moving to his mouth. She drew in a deep breath and pushed past his lips with a single index finger. The breath left her when she encountered his fangs.

Though she tried not to think about it, she wondered how many people he'd killed. She wondered if he would kill her like in the movies. Would he take her in his arms, bite her neck, and almost lovingly drain the life from her? Or would it be a savage kill, a vicious bite and then leave her to bleed out on the floor? Suddenly, the how ceased to be a worry and the wonder of who Lucian of Penwick was became her paramount concern. They'd spent three months together and yet they were complete strangers. If she was going to die by this creature, she wanted to know who her killer was.

Putting her other hand into play, her pain was shoved aside as she learned the lines of his face. To her surprise, he sat still and allowed her to explore him with her hands.

She ran her fingers over his face, past his chiseled cheekbones and down his Roman nose. Her fingertips lingered on his full lips, amazed at how soft they felt. She rounded his chin, almost smiling at the arrogant tilt of it.

Though she knew what he looked like, it was strange to see him with her hands. He had a good face, a handsome face, one she would have done a double take to get a better look at if she had encountered him anywhere other than this hellhole.

Jessica rested her hand on his broad chest. His lack of heartbeat and the absolute stillness unnerved her. Curiously, she brought her hand back to his face. Trailing her fingers over his mouth, she tucked her index finger past his lips to feel his fangs. She swallowed hard and pulled her hand away.

"Is it true you were a Knight Templar?"

"I was."

She didn't know much about them, only what she'd read in school, which wasn't all that much. "So you were a monk?"

"Yes."

She frowned in confusion. How did someone go from fighting for God to damnation? "How did you become a..."

"Vampire?"

He supplied the word she couldn't utter aloud. "Yes. How did it happen?"

"You want the short or long version?"

They certainly had time for the long version. Too bad Jessica wasn't up for hearing it just yet. Her fear of him prevented her from wanting to know too many details. "The short version, I think."

She felt him shrug. "I lost my faith and God damned me for it."

"When did you—die?" It sounded crazy to ask such a thing of someone, some*thing*, who still seemed very much alive.

This time he took a moment to answer. "1310."

From the clipped way he answered, it was obvious this was a topic he didn't want to talk about. She had just one more question. "The oath you made to God, the one Stephan always mentions, it prevents you from killing humans?"

"As long as my existence isn't threatened I can't take a human life."

Good to know. Though it didn't ease her fear of him—who knew what he might perceive as a threat to his existence—it was a useful nugget of information to have in her pocket.

Lucian doubted Jessica realized her hand was still pressed to his chest. If she did, he had no doubt she'd snatch it away. He saw her mind working as she tried to see him through the dark. Saw her confusion as she fought with herself over what she should do. Move away or allow him to comfort her.

Her whispered request surprised him. "Can I trust you, Lucian? Even if just for now?"

If not for his advanced hearing, he might not have heard her whispered request. He felt the turmoil in her, knowing it killed her to have to ask anything from a monster.

Take her.

The monster in him wanted to taste her blood, wanted to devour her, drink her in and have her life flow through him. He needed her energy and her warmth, especially after so many long months of suffering the bloodlust.

Drain her.

No. Not her, not after all she'd already been through because of him. He couldn't deny her whispered plea to make the hurt go away. Closing his eyes for a moment, Lucian begged God for strength to hold back his needs and help her.

"Yes, you can trust me."

Taking her small, trembling hand in his, Lucian took her in his arms. He wrapped himself around her, absorbing her body heat as she took in his cold. She felt—he could barely describe it—*right.* Yes. She felt *right* in his arms. As if God Himself meant for her to be here.

"Did your knuckles heal?"

He flexed his right hand, the still-torn flesh taking its time to mend. At least the bones were no longer shattered, which lessened the pain somewhat. "Yes." Why he lied, he didn't know.

Her vulnerability was a fist around his heart. The scent of her blood was agony, tempting him almost beyond his endurance. It would be nothing to lay her back on the pallet, rip the clothes from her and use her body to sate his lust and her blood to ease his hunger. His pain would stop, the constant need would quiet, and he'd feel whole again.

And then he'd be no better than the monster Stephan wanted him to be.

This time when he stood and dragged himself to the other side of the cell, she didn't stop him. He tried not to want to feel her soft hand snake out and grab hold of his arm to keep him close. He couldn't be near her, not after almost seven hundred years of death as his constant companion. Yet being here in this tomb-like dungeon with Jessica was the closest he'd come to life since his death.

With hunger making him weak, he allowed the weight of his chains to drag him down. Sitting on the pallet, he actually welcomed the rank stench of it, glad it helped to block out the scent of Jessica's blood.

Goddamn Stephan, if this was the first strike in his new game, Lucian didn't want to know what his brother's next move was going to be.

Chapter Five

"I see you didn't like my gift."

Lucian cracked open an eye as Stephan sauntered into the cell. "And here I went through all the trouble of making sure you would. I see I'll have to do better next time."

The whimper coming from across the cell had Lucian, who was lying on his back, turning his head to look at Jessica. Crouched on the pallet, staring wide-eyed at Stephan, she looked like a caged animal. There was a wild gleam in her eyes that bespoke of her terror.

Lucian stood and gave Stephan a bored stare. He wasn't going to play into his brother's hands and give him the rise he obviously sought. "It takes a real man to hold down a woman and slice her."

Stephan cocked a brow and sneered. "Ah yes, I forgot you expect us to believe you hold human life in such high regard. How very noble of you, Luc." He motioned to Jessica with a nod. "Next time I'll make certain the damage runs deep enough to break your fine sensibilities."

Lowering his head, Lucian glared at Stephan through a veil of filthy hair. "Touch her again and I'll make sure your head and body lose their connection."

With a wave of his hand, Stephan carelessly dismissed Lucian's threat. "You'll do no such thing and we all know it."

Baring his fangs, Lucian growled viciously. Unfazed, his brother stalked boldly toward him. The backhanded smack caught Lucian off guard. His bottom lip split. His pride rebelling, Lucian lunged for Stephan, who jumped back with a vampire's speed and agility.

Stephan nodded to James, who stepped into the cell and hauled a fighting Jessica up by her hair. Lucian went mad with rage at the sight of her grabbing at the roots of her hair to keep James from tearing it clean from her scalp.

Summoning reserves of strength he'd hadn't known he possessed, Lucian pulled savagely against the chains. His growling echoed throughout the cell as he damaged himself trying to break free. Only Jessica's whimpered plea for him to stop calmed him.

Stephan stepped in, slapping Jessica across the face. Blood spat from her mouth and her head was thrown to the side. All the while, Stephan kept his gaze locked on Lucian. "Misbehave again and I promise you, it'll be *her* head and body that lose their connection."

Lucian moved back. "Let her go."

James's hand snaked around Jessica's throat, instantly stopping her struggles. Stephan walked over to her, closed his eyes, and inhaled the air around her. "Can you smell it, Luc? Can you smell the sweetness of her blood?" All the fury rotting his brother's soul was in his eyes when he opened them. "I know you crave the taste of her. Do you want me to show you what she tastes like?"

"Don't do it, Stephan."

Stephan grabbed Jessica. She screamed as she was yanked away from James. Captured in Stephan's hold, she tried to fight his grip on her but he was obviously much stronger. After the fight went out of her, she hung in his arms, completely at his mercy.

Stephan lowered his head and sank his fangs deep into the side of her throat. Lucian's roar mingled with Jessica's scream.

Heedless of his chains, Lucian charged Stephan. The chains, however, were unyielding, snapping him back when they'd reached their limit.

James's laughter rang out as Jessica clawed at Stephan's back, trying desperately to break his hold on her. Her every gasp and whimper was an assault on Lucian's mind and his heart. Stephan kept on drinking, her struggles nothing to him. Even when her legs gave out and she crumpled in his arms, he held her fast, taking from her until she was drained nearly dry.

Hearing her heart decelerate to a sickeningly slow rhythm, Lucian thought she was going to die and he was going to be powerless to prevent it. It killed him to know he was as helpless now as he'd been back in Damascus.

He hadn't been able to save those three women Stephan had murdered there. After seeing their battered and drained bodies, he'd sworn he'd do everything within his power to prevent one more woman from falling victim to such a fate. Yet here he was, chained and unable to end Jessica's suffering.

Jessica turned her head and locked her gaze on him. Lucian felt as if she was looking not *at* him, but *into* him. For a moment he swore she saw past what he was to what lay hidden beneath the surface. In her eyes he saw her pain, fear, and what small hope she refused to surrender.

"Enough."

That one word from Lucian had Stephan lifting his head from Jessica's neck. He released her and cast Lucian a smug, bloody smile. Jessica crumpled to the floor like a rag doll. Her attempt to crawl away was stopped by James, who planted a booted foot on her back. Grunting, she lay facedown on the floor with James standing sentry over her. His silent threat worked wonders at keeping Lucian docile.

Stephan sauntered back toward Lucian and spat a mouthful of Jessica's blood in his face. Lucian staggered back in a tangle of chains. He hit the floor, hard, unable to see past the sting of blood in his eyes. Dragging an arm across his face, he smeared the blood, causing some of it to make its way past his lips. Like liquid fire on his tongue, Jessica's blood tasted sweeter than life itself as he struggled not to swallow. The vampire he was overrode the man he fought to be and forced him to swallow.

Jesus Christ, please give me the strength and the will to fight this.

And fight he did.

He pushed off the floor and met his brother's self-righteous look with one of rage. If Stephan had been within his reach, Lucian knew he'd have ripped his brother to pieces.

"Wipe the smug look from your face, Stephan," he warned. "I killed you once. You're just forcing me to do it twice."

Hatred twisted the smooth, youthful planes of Stephan's face. "I'll never give you the chance."

"You won't have to. It's already done. I just haven't turned you to ash yet."

"We'll see, Lucian." Stephan remarked casually as he turned and stalked from the cell.

James followed, but not before he gave Lucian a cocky grin. Once alone and engulfed in darkness, Lucian wiped his face with his shirt and lumbered over to Jessica, who was still lying on the floor. For a moment he believed she wept, but as he neared, he realized what he'd mistaken as sobs were nothing more than short and rasping breaths.

She didn't put up a fight when he lifted her. She was limp and lifeless, the chill of her flesh was cold enough to almost match his own. Cradling her, Lucian carried her to his pallet. Careful so as not to jostle her, he sat and settled her on his lap. Gathering Jessica close, he tucked her into him, nestling her under his chin. Her heart beat a slow and steady rhythm against his body.

Lucian rested his chin on the top of her head as he gently rocked her. "Don't worry, Jessica, I swear I'll find a way to get you away from here."

He felt her sag against him. This was the first time she'd allowed him to comfort her. It made him feel almost human again. Jessica dragged in a hard breath. Her pain sliced through him as if it were his own.

"I hope so," she whispered. "Because he's killing me."

₧₨

Sometime during the long day, Jessica woke shivering uncontrollably from cold and weakness—both byproducts of the blood loss. Lying against Lucian's icy body certainly didn't help matters. Not that she minded. In fact, she felt almost safe with his arms wrapped around her. The illusion of safety made her press even closer into him.

The absolute dark, the cold, the emptiness she felt after having a monster drink the blood from her left her feeling half dead and it unnerved her right down to her soul. Her body aching, Jessica shivered until her bones hurt. She tried in vain to hold back her groan of misery, but it sneaked from her.

Her body aching, Jessica shifted in Lucian's embrace. He came awake instantly, leaning on his elbow. Absently, he ran his hand over her hair, smoothing the tangled mess away from her face.

"What's the matter?" Lucian's murmur was slurred and sleepy.

A vampire nearly drained me dry, she answered in the privacy of her mind. "Nothing. I'm just cold."

Lucian rose and shuffled across the cell. Funny, but she was colder with him gone than with him wrapped around her. Unable to see where he'd gone or what he was doing—not that he could have gone far or done much—she gave up trying to see him through the dark.

Jessica heard the loud clatter of his chains as he crossed the cell and wondered how he endured the relentlessness of them. She couldn't imagine being bound, always having chains weighing her down. She'd have gone crazy for sure already if they added another layer of captivity to her imprisonment.

Yet Lucian never complained. Not once had he ranted or raved about the chains or about being locked in this damn cell. He handled this situation with a dignity that rivaled her turbulent emotions. The only time she'd seen him lose his cool was when Stephan and his men pushed. That's when Lucian lost it and pushed back as much as he could even though he was chained to a wall.

Lucian returned to her a moment later and, as much as Jessica hated to admit it, she was glad he came back. He dropped down heavily next to her and pulled something over her. It was her pallet. The thing smelled and made her itch, and yet she was grateful for the meager warmth it provided. Lucian's thoughtfulness astounded her.

Once he was satisfied she was all tucked in, Lucian gathered her back into his arms. "Go back to sleep. You'll be safe for the rest of the day."

Safe? Jessica wouldn't feel safe until she was away from this place and back home with her family—or dead. Jessica had the feeling dead was the more realistic possibility.

Snuggling as close to Lucian as possible, Jessica tried to ignore the ringing in her ears from the silence and the strain on her mind from the complete darkness. She closed her eyes and reminded herself Lucian was a vampire who was most likely going to be the one to kill her. Yet, even as she forced herself to remember that fact, she found herself snuggling even closer up to him.

Madness, that's what she thought a moment later. Yes, it had to be madness that made the unexplainable desire begin to build within her. How else could she explain her body's crazy reaction to being this close to Lucian?

Heat came to settle at the junction of her legs, bringing with it an uncomfortable pressure. Her body undulated, needing to have Lucian fill the aching emptiness. Fisting her hands, Jessica fought down her body's cravings.

It was a losing battle.

Maybe if Lucian's arms weren't so muscular or his chest so massive, she'd be able to continue to see him as a monster. Or maybe if he weren't so nice to her she'd be able to hate him. But he was nice and he was gorgeous and she was finding it harder to resist him as each day passed.

Even if she did somehow get out of this, she wondered if she'd ever be able to get back to normal again. After the things she'd seen, the things done to her, she feared finding normal was about as impossible as touching the stars. She couldn't even imagine going through the motions of everyday life after this ordeal. Her eyes were open now to the things no human was supposed to see. The lines of fiction and reality had blurred and there was no going back to being blind to what took place in the dark. She'd be constantly looking to the shadows, wondering what dangers were about to leap out at her, dragging her back into Hell where all she would know was dark and cold and pain.

And yet, as she drifted into sleep, all her fear left her and all that mattered was the feel of Lucian at her back.

Chapter Six

"There's something vastly satisfying about bringing a dog to heel, wouldn't you agree?"

His shirt stripped from him, a thick chain securing him to a metal spike set into the stone floor, Lucian's back had been whipped raw. Stephan was forcing Jessica to watch as James tore away big chunks of Lucian's flesh with a thick leather bullwhip.

He faced her and she marveled at his indifferent expression. God knows she wouldn't be able to handle the pain if she were on the receiving end of the whipping. But not Lucian. No, he remained as still as a statue and as silent as a grave while the whip came down across his back again and again.

Lucian's gaze never wavered from Stephan, who watched his brother being beaten with vicious delight. His hair hung around his face in knotted ropes. His lips were compressed into a thin line. Every muscle of his body was held taut. The only indication of his agony was the slight slumping of his shoulders.

The sound of the whip hitting flesh was sickening. The sight of blood splattering from the gashes the leather opened brought bile up in her throat. Blood pooled at Lucian's bare feet. And yet, he met the pain with dignity and honor.

Over the last few nights Jessica had seen a change in Lucian. He'd begun to fight back, and though he'd been doing so since they'd been brought here, something was different about the *way* he fought back. There was urgency to his fight that told her he knew how close Stephan was to putting an end to this.

Jessica found it astounding how Lucian risked himself time and again to protect her. He rarely fought for himself, as if he were conserving what strength he had solely for her. She knew if it came down to her life for his, he'd freely give up his existence to save her.

And yet, Jessica couldn't bring herself to fully trust him. Not after all she'd seen of a vampire's nature. Although, seeing Lucian wince for the first time since the beating began, she couldn't keep silent after all he'd sacrificed for her.

"Please stop this."

Stephan turned to her and Jessica shrank from the ruthlessness in his stare. "How human of you to feel compassion for my brother. Think he feels the same compassion for you? I assure you, Jessica, he doesn't. Eventually he's going to kill you and feel nothing but satisfaction as he drains you dry."

Jessica ignored the shiver of dread that moved through her at the conviction in Stephan's tone. "Whatever he's done, you've made him suffer enough."

With a feral snarl Stephan was on her. He took her down to the floor. Jessica's back hit the stone, the wind knocked out of her as he settled on top of her. His hand was around her throat, cutting off her air, crushing her windpipe. Vaguely, she heard the clatter of chains and Lucian let out a growl.

"What the fuck do you know about his suffering?" he snarled. "Only after he kills you and he's rotting in Hell will he have suffered enough for what he's done to me."

Hauling her from the floor, Stephan held her by her throat as Jessica kicked and clawed at him. The hard backhand he delivered would have sent her right back to the floor if he hadn't been holding her.

Jessica almost cried with relief at the unmistakable sound of metal breaking and the length of chain hitting the floor. James was already in the middle of bringing the whip down. Lucian turned as much as he could with one of his arms still bound and caught the end of it. With a flick of his wrist he yanked the whip away and flipped it, catching it by the handle. Before James was able to jump back and out of striking distance, Lucian cracked it across his face. James staggered back, his hands flying to his face as blood spurted from the gash.

Stephan moved away, dragging her by the throat. James lowered his hands and faced off against Lucian. James tried to knock the whip out of Lucian's grip but it was obvious that wasn't going to happen. Much to Jessica's horror, however, James managed to get close enough to Lucian to land a few well-placed blows.

Lucian grabbed James by the wrist and snapped the bone. The bone broke through the skin, forcing a bellow from the renegade. Never letting go of the whip, he stepped behind James, forcing the taller and wider vampire down on his knees. He wrapped the broken chain around his neck tight enough to force a sick sound from James as his skin split from the force of the metal pressing into him.

Lucian tightened the chain. Blood trickled out of the corner of James's mouth. "This ends now, Stephan. Let her go."

Like the coward he was, Stephan put himself behind Jessica, using her as a human shield. "But I like her where she is."

Lucian lowered his head, glaring at Stephan through the fall of filthy hair. "It's over. I won't tell you to release her again."

"Over? I don't think so. This isn't over until I say it is." Stephan squeezed his hand, cutting off her air. Jessica coughed and gasped as she fought for breath.

Jessica, believing Lucian was going to kill his brother—but not before Stephan took her with him—closed her eyes and tried to stem the flow of tears gathering in her eyes. Against her will, they slipped down her face as Stephan ran his hands over her face and neck, before coming to rest on her stomach. His touch was tender, caring almost, as he held her against him and made her want to gag.

"I warned you."

Without another word, Lucian twisted James's neck, snapping it in one quick motion. Lucian released him and James slid to the floor. The vampire wasn't dead but he was broken to the point that his body twitched and jerked around sickly on the floor.

With a violent shove, Stephan threw Jessica aside. She went sprawling to the floor. He strode to Lucian, who wrapped the chain around his fist and stood battle-ready. Stephan went to strike him but Lucian caught his fist and nailed him in the face. The chain split his lips and right cheek.

Jessica darted away from the two vampires, her back slamming into the wall. She eyed the double doors but knew any attempt at escape would only get her killed. She turned back to the fight. Lucian had Stephan by the throat. He dragged his brother close, fangs bared and eyes blazing.

"You fool. It didn't have to end like this. You could have had your revenge on me. All you had to do was let Jessica go."

Stephan rasped out a laugh. "You won't kill me and we both know it."

Lucian growled and Jessica shivered. Though she had yet to see such savagery from him, she knew the ferocity was inside him. It lay dormant, waiting for the right time to reveal itself. She prayed to God Lucian would end the bastard and set them both free permanently.

"Unchain me, Stephan."

Stephan had the nerve to tsk sarcastically. "I'm afraid I can't do that."

Lucian gave him such a hard shake Jessica thought his head was going to snap. "I said unchain me."

"This is pointless, Luc. You won't kill me and I'll never let you leave here alive."

"Jessica." Lucian barked at her. "James has a dagger in his boot. Get it." Jessica gaped and shook her head as fear caused her heart to slam painfully. "Get the goddamn dagger, woman."

His shout shook her out of her stupor and had her moving. With a cry, Jessica pushed away from the wall and raced to James, who was still flopping around on the floor. Her stomach turned at the sight of his head nearly twisted completely around. She snatched the dagger out of his boot. His hand clamped down on her wrist and she screamed. She jerked her hand away and sliced at him as he continued to try to grab at her. When he went to grab her left arm, she thrust the knife and cut off his hand.

His roar bounced off the walls. Jumping over James, Jessica ran behind Lucian and slapped the dagger into his waiting hand. In one fluid movement, Lucian turned Stephan around and slammed his brother's back against his chest. His free arm snaked around him and he pressed the dagger to his throat.

"Jessica, take the keys out of Stephan's pocket and unchain my arm."

This time, Jessica didn't hesitate. Not with the promise of freedom within reach. She hurried out from behind him, though she hesitated when confronted with Stephan's wrathful gaze. Tentatively reaching into his pocket, she grabbed the keys and pulled them out, ignoring his hiss of fury.

"You better pray he kills me, because if he doesn't, when I find you I'll make you pray for death."

"Shut the fuck up," Lucian warned.

Remembering all he'd put her and Lucian through in the last few months, she cracked her hand across his cheek, wishing she possessed the strength to do more. Growling, he lunged for her. Lucian stopped him by cutting his throat. Gasping, Stephan's hands flew to his opened throat as he collapsed to the floor.

Although her hands were slick with sweat and shaking, Jessica unlocked the manacle around Lucian's wrist. He grabbed her by the arm and forced her into a mad dash for the hall. By this time, the remaining vampires who had been milling about in other parts of the castle while their master amused himself with his playthings finally arrived after hearing the commotion. It took them all a single moment to take in the situation.

They charged as Lucian broke through the doors and literally threw Jessica out of the keep before running out behind her. She fell and rolled away as all five vampires attacked Lucian at once. She pushed herself up from the dirt and watched in horror and awe as he fought them off with the skill of a man raised from birth for battle. Not to mention the inhuman strength of a vampire.

The renegades had swords, one of which caught Lucian's attention first. With a vicious snarl, he lunged at the one brandishing a sword with a red cross in its pommel. Lucian disarmed him, easily knocking the weapon out of the smaller vampire's grasp. Grabbing him in a headlock, Lucian changed his hold and, with a hard turn of his hands, snapped the vampire's neck.

The vampire collapsed to the floor just as Lucian grabbed for the sword. For a moment, he seemed to relish the feel of it in his hands before he brought the weapon down in a brutal hack. He took the vampire's head off in one clean cut.

Turning, Lucian crossed swords with another vampire. Scared, Jessica moved as far from the melee as she was able. Never had she seen such brutal combat and such swift movements. Kicking the vampire away, Lucian used the split second of time to cut a deep gash in his opponent's stomach with James's dagger. A rush of blood spilled out as the vampire doubled over.

As Lucian continued to battle one vampire, another used his distraction to come after her. Defenseless, Jessica's only recourse was to run, though she didn't get far. Faster and stronger, he took her down and pinned her to the ground. She managed to claw his face, watching in horrified fascination as the marks healed even as the blood continued to drip down his face. His fist connected with her mouth, opening her bottom lip. Pressing the blade of his sword to her throat, he smiled with evil delight as a string of saliva fell from his right fang.

With nothing left for her to do, Jessica screamed for Lucian.

The moment Lucian's gaze locked on them, it was obvious the vampire had made a lethal mistake in going after her.

Letting out a battle cry that rocked the night, Lucian fought his way free of the remaining vampires. He took them out one by one in a furious blur of blood and ash before charging the vampire on top of Jessica. Knocking him off her, he easily deflected the vampire's sword as the agile bastard jumped back far enough to avoid Lucian slicing him across the middle.

Lucian sized up the situation. The moment he moved to attack, Lucian saw Jessica's face contort into a horrified expression. A gasp caught in the back of her throat as she looked down at the blade protruding from her right side.

Time froze as the vampire's laughter rang out across the courtyard. It mixed with Jessica's ragged intake of breath as Lucian watched the spread of blood form on her ragged scrubs. She looked back at him, tears slipping down her ashen cheeks. Lucian locked his gaze on the vampire, and would have struck him down had the bastard not been holding the hilt of the sword buried in Jessica's side.

The vampire pulled the sword free. Jessica's scream shattered the night. If Lucian's heart hadn't already been destroyed, her scream would have broken it to pieces. Wanting only to get at her attacker, he shoved Jessica to the side. Once she was out of the way, he advanced on the vampire. The medieval warrior he still was combined with the vampire he had become. Those two entities, which usually warred within him, merged into one power.

With a savagery he'd never known, he cut the vampire down the chest, relishing the bastard's agonized howl. He slashed again, severing the left arm, which evaporated into dust before it even hit the ground. Sneering, Lucian advanced on the wounded renegade, wanting to play with him even though he knew he had to get Jessica the hell away from Penwick. One clean swipe across the vampire's throat ended him in a cloud of dust.

The bloodlust still riding him, Lucian swept Jessica up into his arms and raced across the courtyard. Sensing the coming dawn, he ran to where he and Stephan used to sneak out of the castle's grounds. Once he reached the thick outer wall, he followed it to a small metal grate. Holding Jessica tight, he kicked the ancient bars free of the stone. With no time to be careful, he pushed her roughly through the small opening.

Once she was through, Lucian tried to follow. Almost too large to fit, his shoulder broke as he forced his body through. Once out of the hole, he landed on the damp grass with a grunt. His arm was useless.

Jessica looked up at him and he saw how pale she was and how badly she trembled. He felt her pain as if it were his own. He went to lift her but she slapped away his hands. "I can walk."

From the look of her and the severity of her wound, he doubted she would even be able to stand much longer. Lucian wanted to argue that point with her but he heard his brother's furious yell come from the direction of the keep. It was followed by a commotion in the courtyard and he knew they had to get moving.

Now.

Grabbing Jessica's hand, Lucian dragged her along behind him. Although he knew she had to be in horrendous pain, there was no time to worry about being gentle. He forced her to move as fast as her body would allow through the clearing into the dense forest. Stumbling over her own feet, she was clumsy as her legs lost their strength. She was losing too much blood to get far on her own. And given the all-too familiar prickling at the nape of his neck, he knew dawn was inching too close for him to keep the same pace.

The sun whispered to him, promising Lucian a slow and agonizing death if he didn't find shelter soon. Thank God he remembered the place his brother Robert used to take his betrothed, Mary, to be alone. It would offer them shelter during the day—if they made it there before the sun broke through the night and sent him to Hell.

Breaking through the line of trees, Jessica's pace slowed even more. Lucian went to reach for her despite his broken shoulder. "No, you can't carry me."

"You can barely walk, Jessica."

"I'm fine. Come on. Let's get moving."

Lucian saw pain etched all over her face. Her complexion was deathly pale and she had a hand pressed to her side. Blood coated her hand and soaked her clothes. "Stubborn wench," he muttered before he grabbed for her.

With limited use of his left arm, he gripped her firmly with his right. She wrapped her arms around his neck, her ragged breaths hitting his neck after she settled against him.

He glanced at the sky, which was turning from the blue-black of night to a brighter hue as the moon dipped low to make way for the coming dawn. Letting out a string of curses, his shoulder hurting like hell, he sprinted through the trees toward a cave hidden deep within the forest.

As everything around her blended together in muted browns, greens, and blacks, the only solid in Jessica's world was Lucian. His scent, his strength, they were the things she held onto as she felt herself slipping into unconsciousness. Jesus Christ, of all the ways she'd imagined dying, being stabbed by a sword had never been one of them.

She didn't want to go out like this—here—so far from her family. She had an entire life to live and she'd be damned if she wasn't going to live it. So, imagining her family, Jessica struggled to remain awake even as oblivion pulled at her.

"Hold on, Jessica, we're almost there."

Whether Lucian said that or it was her murky mind playing tricks on her, Jessica wasn't sure. All she knew was that whispered plea helped her hang on to life.

Finally, and surprisingly, the pain stopped. Her body went pleasantly numb as Lucian ran with her deeper into the forest. They passed a small hunting lodge, which she was sure he'd chosen as their hideaway from the sun. But he kept on running until he came to a cave hidden by trees and rocks and ducked into it. As soon as they were inside, Jessica realized they weren't the only ones looking to use this place for refuge.

Though growling was something Jessica had heard often these last months, she hadn't heard a sound quite like what she was hearing now. She'd learned a vampire's growl was like no other—least of all that of a pissed-off wolf.

Slowly setting her down, Lucian never turned his back on the wolf that was crouching low and ready to strike. Yellow eyes and bared fangs didn't scare Jessica half as much as Stephan's snarl had, although it did run a close second. The animal sniffed at the air, obviously catching the scent of her blood. It flicked its tongue over its fangs and pawed anxiously—or was it hungrily—at the dirt floor of the cave.

"Here, you bloody bastard. Look at me."

The wolf directed its attention back to Lucian, who was in a battle stance of his own. The wolf growled. He snarled right back at the animal in some kind of feral standoff.

The wolf took a step toward him, putting its head low, its fangs dripping with saliva. Scratching its paws in the dirt, it was clear the animal wanted to protect its home, yet didn't know what to make of the stink of death emanating from Lucian.

"Come on then, make your move."

As if understanding, the huge silver wolf leapt at Lucian, who easily knocked it to the side. The wolf hit the ground with a yap. It scurried to gain its footing but Lucian never gave it the chance. He jumped on top of the animal, wrapping it in a hold strong enough to make the beast yelp. The pathetic whimper filled the cave and made Jessica cringe. The sound turned into an almost human scream when Lucian sank his fangs deep into the back of its neck.

Jessica threw her hands over her ears to block out the pathetic sound of the dying animal. Horrified, she slammed her eyes shut as Lucian drained the poor beast of its blood.

After he'd finished with the animal, Lucian didn't spare her a glance as he hauled the carcass out of the cave. He returned a few moments later. "We have to get as far back as possible."

Jessica didn't think she could move. She tried to stand but her body simply wouldn't comply. When Lucian helped her, the pain came back swift and strong. She shook her head to stop him from lifting her. "No. It hurts too much."

"I know, Jessie, but we have to or else I'll fry."

Her head slumped to the side and she saw sunlight begin to inch past the entrance of the cave. The deadly light crept further in and would eventually reach them since they were only a few feet from the opening.

Dragging in a breath, Jessica reached out her hand to Lucian. "Okay, but let's do this quick."

Lucian lifted her with infinite care. "Let me do all the work. Just relax, Jessie. Just relax into me."

She did as he asked. Jessica relaxed against him as Lucian carried her to the back of the cave. The dark had her panicking, reminding her of the cell. After he set her down on the floor, she shivered at the cold and damp wall against her back. It felt like the dungeon. Cold. Damp. Dark. Still.

Dear God she didn't want to die in here. She wanted to go with the sun on her face and the warmth of her family around her. She shouldn't have to die in a cave with a vampire as her only companion.

Exhaustion winning out over her determination, her eyes fluttered shut. Jessica heard Lucian demand she fight but ignored him. Holding on to life was becoming harder to do by the second. Death slowly wrapped around her and pulled her down a long, dark road. In the distance, a brilliant white light, which promised love and peace, beckoned her.

The sound of her heartbeat, slow and uneven, overrode Lucian's voice coaxing her to fight for her life. A thick coating of liquid coated her mouth and throat, causing Jessica to gag. She continued to gag as she heard Lucian commanding her to drink, pleading with her to come back. Though where he thought she'd gone, Jessica didn't know.

Jessica realized the cold metallic liquid that slipped down her throat was blood and her entire being rebelled. Death wasn't nearly as frightening as becoming a vampire. She wanted to push him away but her body needed what he offered. She didn't want this and yet couldn't stop herself from drinking him in. As much as she didn't want to die, she didn't want to be pulled further into this nightmarish world of vampires.

She wanted to go home.

As if beyond her control, Jessica's body wanted life and it was going to take it no matter where it came from—even if it came from death itself.

The more she drank the more her body's warmth returned and the pain began to fade. Jessica felt whole again, strong, even as sleep beckoned to her. After Lucian stopped feeding her his blood, he shifted her so that she was lying on the ground. Jessica vaguely thought she felt him running his fingers through her hair as he whispered reassurances to her.

She drifted off to sleep wondering what she was going to wake as. She wanted to believe Lucian wouldn't turn her, but whether that was true or not remained to be seen. Jessica gave into the oblivion, drifting into the peaceful darkness as the early autumn sun lit the world outside their dark sanctuary.

Chapter Seven

The smell of damp rock and the steady echo of dripping water woke Jessica. There was enough faint daylight lighting the cave so that when she opened her eyes she was able to spot Lucian sitting opposite her. He looked relaxed with his back against the wall of the cave. If it weren't for the profound look in his eyes and the rigid set of his jaw, he would look like a man in relaxed repose. She wondered how many times he'd sat just like that, watching her through the dark of the cell without her knowing.

The events of last night were still hazy in Jessica's mind. She sat up, her body aching. She felt as if she'd gone through a battle and come out the other end wrung out emotionally and physically.

"What happened?"

"You nearly died." His tone was flat, his deep, resonating voice echoed softly throughout the cave.

Died? Her hazy mind spun at that bit of news. She licked her lips and winced. Her mouth tasted awful, like old metal and salt. It was the taste of old blood. The past night came back to her in a sudden rush and she gaped in horror at the vampire who'd forced her to take in his blood in order for her to live.

Jumping up with agility her body protested, Jessica lifted her shirt, searching for the stab wound that should be in her side. Poking at the large, dark scar that marred the otherwise smooth flesh, she knew if it hadn't been for Lucian she'd indeed be dead. He'd saved her life—again. But at what cost to her?

Pressing a palm to her chest, Jessica let out a breath of relief at her steady heartbeat. Thankfully she was still very much of the living.

When Lucian stood—his gaze never moving from her— Jessica saw his clothes were torn and covered with blood. She assumed the wolf's blood had taken the edge off his bloodlust because the feral gleam she'd seen burning in his eyes was gone. Now he seemed almost...civilized. All traces of the savagery he'd displayed last night were gone.

"Thank you."

His eyes narrowed and he looked away from her. He shrugged with a carelessness she had a good feeling was false. "I did nothing."

No? He'd risked his life to get her away from Stephan. He'd offered up his blood to save her life—and Jessica knew beyond a shadow of a doubt she had been perilously close to the edge of death.

Jessica moved toward him. Lucian moved away. He kept on stepping back as she advanced until his back pressed against the rock wall. When her hand touched his face he hissed as if he'd been burned.

"If it weren't for you I'd be dead...or worse. You risked yourself to free me from Stephan and for that, I'm so grateful."

He stepped to the side and Jessica dropped her arm. Lucian's upper lip curled back to reveal lethal fangs she still hadn't grown accustomed to seeing. "Keep your goddamn gratitude. It's because of me you're here. The least I could have done was gotten you away from my brother."

Jessica regarded Lucian for a good, long moment, almost absorbing his emotional anguish. After spending months locked away with him, she was seeing him as if for the first time. She dragged her gaze from his head to his feet, seeing the way his rich brown hair tumbled around his face. Each feature of his exquisite face was a sculpted work of art. From his cutting cheekbones and Roman nose, to the proud tilt of his jaw and the deep set of his silver eyes, it all made for one gorgeous face. His fangs scared the hell out of her, but as long he kept them safely tucked behind those full, sensual lips, she'd try not to be so afraid of him and what he was.

"No. The least you could have done was free yourself and leave me behind."

Leaving her behind had never been an option. In fact, getting her away from Penwick was what had kept him from surrendering to his guilt as the nights passed. Returning her to her family had become a burning passion within him—one that couldn't be ignored. An innocent soul so full of life, Jessica's existence needed to be protected and preserved. What a shame it would be if this world had to do without her spirit.

Lucian watched her as she began to pace the width of the cave. Her hair was a mess of caked, dried blood, but still Jessica's beauty shone through. She raked a hand through her matted hair and winced. He could relate. He ached for a shower, but didn't think all the soap in the world could cleanse the filth from him.

She looked over at him. Her eyes searched him. "I'm starving."

So was he, only with him, that was a very dangerous thing. The wolf's blood had only quieted the hunger, taken the edge off. The bloodlust continued to roar through him and it took every ounce of his control to fight it back. Giving Jessica blood had made it even harder to fight, yet as a Templar, he'd find the strength. They always did when it came to the hunger.

"Don't worry, we'll be on the move again as soon as the sun goes down. Once we reach Malmesbury we'll secure a place for the day and get you something to eat."

Jessica walked all the way to the entrance of the cave. He was about to warn her not to leave since it was possible Stephan had human henchmen searching for them, but she stopped and wrapped her arms around herself. She just stood there staring out the mouth of the cave. Lucian had the sickening suspicion she was crying.

Goddamn it, he couldn't go to her. She was too close to the entrance—too close to the sun. He couldn't even continue looking at her, the light was making his eyes hurt. She turned and looked back at him, tilting her head to the side questioningly.

"Would you really burn from the sun, like in the movies?"

"No. Not like in the movies." Lucian had already experienced what it was to have his flesh melting off his bones. He knew the sounds of his own screams as flames licked at him, slowly burning him to death. The sun would do exactly that to him and he wasn't up for that party twice. "In the movies you can't smell the flesh burning. And though I'd try not to give voice to them, I'm sure my screams would be forthcoming."

"I'm sorry."

He shrugged with a nonchalance he didn't feel, especially being this close to the greatest temptation he'd ever known— Jessica. His body hardened uncomfortably, straining against the worn fabric of his jeans, which were stiff and foul from three months without washing. Thank God he wasn't able to get body odor. If he did, he didn't even want to contemplate his own stink. Jessica, at least, was allowed the occasional bath. Stephan wasn't as generous with him.

Lucian leaned back against the ragged wall and was able to look at Jessica now that she had moved back into the heart of the cave. He resisted the urge to adjust himself as raw lust ripped through him. He'd been able to ignore his sexual needs for centuries, but he couldn't fight his desire for Jessica. She turned his entire existence upside down with nothing more than a glance.

"Don't be. I did this to myself."

She looked surprised. "Stephan said God did it to you."

Lucian rubbed his hands over his face and passed them through his hair as every life he took in the name of God came back to haunt him. "Like I said, I did this to myself."

"What was being a Knight Templar like?" Obviously Jessica wasn't too keen on the dropped hint in his tone that he had no desire to speak about this. Ever.

"Brutal."

She nodded absently. "It must have been hard back then, without all of the modern conveniences that we take for granted." She walked back to him. Close enough that Lucian could reach out and touch her. He didn't, but that didn't stop him from wanting to. "And then to have gone on a Crusade... I can't even imagine it."

The sun and sand had nearly driven him mad. He'd watched helplessly as men dropped dead from heat, hunger, and thirst around him. All the while, he had wondered when it would be his turn to fall. Or worse, if he'd have to watch Tristan, Sebastian, Raphael, or Constantine succumb to the elements.

Somehow, they'd gotten through their years fighting in the deserts of the Holy Land. They'd served their time in Hell, only to find themselves arrested and thrown in Chinon.

"It was Hell on earth."

"War has a tendency to be that way. Not that I would know firsthand. But if it weren't horrific everyone would sign up for it. Although I guess it must have been a lot worse in your time. You couldn't press a button and blow up an entire country. You fought hand to hand."

"Sword to sword, actually. You only went at it hand to hand if you dropped your weapon."

His half-hearted attempt at humor was lost on her. Jessica sat and drew her knees up. Hugging her legs, she licked her dry lips. Lucian watched the tip of her tongue peek out from between her pink lips. He bit back a groan as his body grew even harder. He had to draw up one leg when he sat to hide the state of his arousal and shift around until he found a way to accommodate his heavy erection.

As she sat across from him, staring at him intently, Lucian saw an array of emotions play out across Jessica's face. Regret, relief, and confusion all took their turns as she watched him with a steady gaze.

"I want to be repulsed by you. God knows I do. Yet no matter how hard I try, I can't bring myself to hate you." He started to reply but Jessica held up her hand. His words died in his throat as tears gathered in her eyes and rolled down her cheeks. "And it has nothing to do with you saving my life. All that time down in the dungeon and you never once did all the things Stephan said you would."

Suddenly, Lucian felt every one of his years crawl over him. He felt old, tired. He should be dead, his body rotted away by now, lost in some bit of earth in France. Instead, he went on living night after night, his body going on long after his mind wanted to surrender.

"I may be a vampire, but I'm also still a man." He ached to go to her and wipe the tears from her face. "I'd never hurt you, Jessie. I hope you know that by now."

"I know." Her tone lacked conviction. "Stephan isn't a man any more, is he?"

Regret tore through him at the memory of how his brother had been as a boy. Stephan had had laughing eyes and an eager smile. He had been the gentle one of the three brothers, the one destined for the Church.

"No. When he was turned, he left his humanity where he died."

"How did it happen? How did Stephan die and become so different than you?"

"My brother and I aren't as different as you think. The only thing separating us is that I'm forced to control the nature of the vampire. Stephan isn't."

He blatantly avoided answering the question of how Stephan was killed. He was infinitely grateful she didn't press him about it.

Jessica looked toward the mouth of the cave and shivered as if a cold wind blew over her. "He's going to find us, isn't he?"

Lucian wanted to tell her no. He wanted to give her hope, but Stephan had crossed the world over to find him once. He'd no doubt do so again—only this time, he'd be searching for Jessica as well. "Eventually. I need to get you to Seacrest Castle. He can't get to you there."

Her brows furrowed together in a deep frown. "How do you plan on making it all the way back to America with no money? Besides, you can't even go outside during the day."

"Not the Seacrest you know in Damascus. The original, in Northumberland."

Understanding dawned on her. "I hadn't realized there were two."

Lucian shifted, glad his body had calmed and he wasn't raging with desire. Talking with Jessica calmed him—made him feel as normal as a creature like him could feel. He ran a hand through his knotted hair to get it out of his face. "Before going to America, Tristan had a replica of his ancestral home built. It made the transition easier for him."

"Tristan? As in Tristan Beaumont? He's a vampire too?" Lucian cringed, not meaning to reveal too much about the Templars, but at the same time not wanting to keep her in the dark either. Lord knows she'd been in the dark too long already. "No wonder no one ever sees him."

"Edward will make certain you get back home."

"I take it this Edward is at Seacrest?" Again, Lucian nodded. "And you won't be coming back with me, will you?"

"No, I won't."

He had to stay here and face his brother without the worry of Jessica getting caught in the middle of the battle. She was still in danger, but at least with her back in America he'd know she was safe and he'd be able to take care of business without the worry of her holding him back. He had to stay and end this.

Unfortunately, Jessica looked as if he was abandoning her.

"How far away is Seacrest?"

"We're in southern England, Northumberland is near Scotland."

"Basically, we're as far as we can possibly be."

Her flippant humor had him smiling. "Once the sun goes down I'll find a phone and call Edward. He'll get money to me and I'll get us transportation to Seacrest." He ached to touch her, even if only her hand, to comfort her and ease the fear he sensed in her. "Don't worry, Jessica, I won't let Stephan get to you."

His conviction left no doubt in Jessica's mind Lucian would do everything humanly possible—and beyond—to keep her safe. It helped calm her, even as she found it insane that she was putting her life in the hands of a vampire. Looking at the situation realistically she knew she had no choice since he was the only thing standing between her and a raving lunatic vampire hell-bent on using her as a means to gain revenge.

"Is Edward a descendant of Tristan's?" He confirmed her assumption. "Are you related to him too?"

"No," he said with a shake of his head. "Not by blood anyway, only by spirit. After we were turned, it just felt natural for us to make our way to Seacrest. Truth was we had nowhere else to go."

"Did you ever try going home? Is that why Stephan is so mad at you?"

Without a word, Lucian rose and came toward her. Jessica wanted to scoot away. Instead she stayed where she was, even after he sat next to her and wrapped his arms around her. Much to Jessica's surprise, she found herself leaning into him.

"I'd rather not talk about it."

She wouldn't push him on the matter. His past obviously hurt to talk about. After everything they'd both suffered, she didn't want to add to his torment by pressing him on the matter of his family—even though her being involved in this was a direct result of his past.

Instead, Jessica relaxed in his arms. She tried to put her mind at rest and enjoy the feel of his body against hers. She'd never known a man as muscular as him. Lean and corded with thick muscles, he wasn't like one of those no-neck body-builder types. His body was one that had been honed from years of swinging a sword. It was a body most men would kill to have— and most women would kill to have all for their very own.

Lucian began to stroke her hair. The motion was soothing and soon Jessica was fighting to stay awake. "Why don't you rest now, since we'll probably be traveling through the night?"

That sounded like a wonderful idea. She'd be safe while she slept. Lucian, she knew, would make sure if it. He'd keep the monsters away.

ঙেওও

Furious that Lucian and the wench had escaped, Stephan paced the hall. He held his hand to his throat, which was raw after being cut. Looking at James didn't help his anger to abate. If anything, it only threw fuel on an already raging fire.

James sat on the leather sofa in the room Stephan used to enjoy the creature comforts of the modern world. A plasma television was mounted over a stand that held an assortment of electronics. Here, he had a computer, which he'd spent hours on as he tracked down both the Daystar and his brother. He also came here to escape the reality of what he was.

Not even James had breached his sanctuary until now.

The Scot cradled his right arm to his chest. The hand was gone, which made him next to useless now as far as Stephan was concerned. Shame really, since he'd been such a loyal dog.

James's body, much as his was, was healing much too slowly. Their injuries had been too close to lethal for Stephan's comfort. So much so, that even feeding off the wenches they held in reserve here at Penwick hadn't been enough to heal their damaged bodies.

There was no doubt in Stephan's mind Lucian would have killed them all to free the girl. What had held him back, he didn't know. Stephan didn't dare believe it was love. After what he'd put Lucian through, if his brother still held that sentiment for him, he was a bloody fool. The devil knew Stephan held no love for Lucian. No, he had only contempt for the bastard, who'd returned to Penwick and brought an evil with him that had led to the death of them all.

Pushing away from the hearth, Stephan turned his attention to the iron cross hanging over the entrance of the hall. His father had put it there as a testament to his family's devotion to God. The castle was rife with such items of Christianity. He should have removed them long before now, yet he'd kept them despite the pain it caused him to look upon them.

"Damn You," he snarled at the cross, his eyes blazing with silver fire as hatred washed through him like a violent tidal wave. "Where were you to protect us when a demon invaded our home?"

"My lord?" James's voice was hoarse, his throat far from fully healed. Lucian had nearly taken his head clean off.

Stephan let out a rumbling growl as he whipped around and pinned James with a hard glare. "I don't care what you have to do, but I want them found. Am I making myself clear?"

James tried to nod but couldn't. "Aye, my lord."

"If you come back without them, I can promise you I'll cut you to pieces." He waved his hand through the air dismissively. "Now go. I don't want to see you again unless my brother and that bitch are with you."

Like a good lapdog, James scurried from the hall as fast as his weakened body would allow. Glaring at the ancient iron cross, Stephan felt his eyes begin to burn. How had he ever believed in a God who created demons? How had he once put faith in a God who had done nothing while a monster destroyed His children?

At the sight of his brother trudging through the courtyard, Stephan's relief had known no bounds. His body burnt nearly to bone, it was evident something was terribly wrong with Lucian. No man could have survived such injuries. Stephan had known immediately his brother was unholy. Yet their parents had seen past the damage of their returning son's body. Their joy to have their son home had blinded them to what Lucian had become.

Not a sennight earlier they'd received word Lucian was dead. They'd been told Philip of France had executed him along with the other Templar Knights. Their mother had gone into mourning after losing a second son, their father had not spoken to anyone for days. In the span of a moment, their father had withered into an old man.

The moment they saw Lucian standing in the courtyard, Lord David and Lady Catherine came back to life. Although all their joy turned to horror when they realized Lucian had returned as a creature caught between life and death.

Before he left again, Lucian had taken blood from them all. He'd cut a path of destruction through Penwick that had left them vulnerable to the creatures who'd come to finish what he'd started.

With those heartrending memories tearing through his mind, Stephan roared with the emotions that raced through him. He leapt and ripped the cross from the stone. The flesh of his palm burning, melting from the bone, he flung the offensive thing into the hearth. He watched as the flames licked at it, scorching it black before it glowed red-hot. His fury burned as hot as the iron.

Lucian would not get away from him. He'd send his bastard of a brother to Hell where he belonged. It was the least he could do to avenge his family.

Fighting back the bloody tears that stung his eyes, Stephan swore he heard his mother's whispered weeping echo throughout the chamber.

Chapter Eight

Having been away from Wiltshire for so long, Lucian had forgotten how far Malmesbury was from Penwick. It took a good part of the night to trek there with Jessica glued to his side all the while. Her fear scented the damp, cold air. He assured her he'd sense if other vampires were near, although given the way her nails dug into his forearm, he was fairly positive it did little to soothe her terror.

Lucian welcomed the warmth of the tiny inn in Malmesbury even as the cold of the innkeeper's glare chilled him to the bone. Her arrogance evaporated the moment she saw his sword. She also came dangerously close to ringing the police. It took a lot of persuasion and some intimidation to keep the woman from picking up the phone.

"I want no trouble," the innkeeper declared as she glared down her nose at them, despite the fear wafting from her.

"Nor will we give you any." He stepped closer to her desk. She took a step back, though she raised her chin a notch in a silent dare. As much as he admired the innkeeper's spirit, Lucian knew she was taking a foolish chance with her life. If he were anyone else, she'd be dead by now. "Do you have a phone I can use?"

"I'd rather you just leave."

Unfortunately for her, that wasn't an option. "I'm sure you would, but you see, that's simply not possible. Now, I need to use your phone."

The woman was obviously debating with herself over what the best course of action would be. Finally, she stabbed a finger at a table across the room. "You can use that one."

"I thank you," he said to her with a nod.

"Just make your call and leave."

She was not a woman easily intimidated, Lucian realized. She shifted her attention to Jessica, her gaze raking over her. In a vain attempt to make herself more presentable, Jessica patted down her matted hair and tried to wipe the dirt from her face.

Jessica was only a step behind him as Lucian walked to the phone. After he'd dialed Edward's number, he put his hand out for her to take. He felt the way her hand trembled and he ached to take her fear away.

"It's me," he said curtly into the phone at Edward's cheerful greeting.

"Luc? Is that you, my boy? Where have you been? Are you all right?"

Edward's barrage of questions reinforced the fact that he was as close to a father as most of the Templars ever had—in life and in death. "I need help, Edward. I'm in Wiltshire and I'm not alone."

Even across the distance Lucian felt Edward's concern reach him—or was it Constantine he sensed? The sensation was a pinch on his mind and a stirring in the place where his soul once resided.

"The others are with you?"

"No."

"Jesus Christ, Luc, why aren't they with you?"

"It's a long story, Edward. One best left for another time."

"Of course, son. Just tell me what you need."

"Money. Enough to get me to Seacrest."

He imagined Edward nodding vigorously, his stock of brown curls bouncing wildly. "Of course. Where can I wire it to you?"

Lucian looked at the innkeeper, who was hanging on his every word. "Is there a Western Union near here?"

She pursed her lips together for a moment and Lucian thought he'd have to pry the information from her at swordpoint. "Goodman's Travel. It's right up the road."

"Wire it to a Goodman's Travel," he said to Edward.

"Let me write that down." After a short pause, he continued. "Who's with you, Luc?"

Lucian passed a long look over Jessica, whose wide-eyed gaze was fixed on the door. "No one you need know about this moment."

"Very well, then. I'll ring Tristan and tell him you're all right."

"No." Lucian rushed out. "I don't want them to come here."

"Lucian, be reasonable. They need to know…"

"I said no." His tone brooked no argument. "I won't risk the others."

Lucian was fairly positive Edward was going to fight him. Instead, he was surprised when Edward let out a rasping cough and said nothing more about alerting the others of his welfare. "Be careful, son."

"I will." He ended the call and walked back to the innkeeper. "We'll need a room for the night." Jessica shot him a questioning look. He gave her hand a small squeeze.

"I told you, I don't want you here."

"Nor do I wish to be here." Lucian cocked a brow at her hesitation.

He rested his hand on the pommel of his sword in silent warning—not that he'd ever use the weapon against a woman, but the innkeeper didn't need to know that. All he knew was that Jessica was hungry and dirty and she deserved a comfortable bed to rest in for a few hours.

His hand curled over the pommel, the circle that enclosed the Red Cross Pattee feeling so right against his palm. After his brother had taken his sword from him, Lucian thought the weapon—sacred to all Templars—was lost to him. It had been a boon when Stephan thought to use Lucian's own blade against him.

The innkeeper flared her nostrils in indignation. Her haughty demeanor annoyed him. "Fine. I'll allow you to stay here one night. I want you gone by dawn."

"Fear not, good woman, we will be." She seemed less than convinced. Then to Jessica he said, "Go take a shower. I'll be back shortly."

She clung to him as if to letting go meant life or death. "I'll come with you."

He shook his head. "Stay here, Jessie, and get some rest. Remember what I told you about the thing I can sense?" She nodded, looking as if she were on the verge of tears. "I meant it, and right now I can't feel anything."

She looked slightly relieved. Over Jessica's head he saw the innkeeper giving them an imperious, yet curious, look. "Hurry back, okay?"

Jessica stared at him with tears glistening in her brown eyes. This was not the same woman who'd faced Stephan, silently defying him with her regal bearing. This was a woman

97

who'd looked death in the face, escaped, and never wanted to have to face such a threat again.

"I will, I swear it." He strode toward the innkeeper, inadvertently dragging Jessica with him. "I'd appreciate it if food is made available to her." Sizing her up, he added, "And clothes, if you will."

The woman looked flabbergasted, which was better than the haughty expression she'd worn since they arrived. "You want me to give her my clothes?"

Lucian raised a brow in a way that put her arrogance to shame. "You'll be compensated well for the inconvenience."

Jessica tugged at Lucian's arm. "I don't need her clothes."

He indicated her disgusting scrubs with a curt nod of his head. "You want to put those back on after a shower?"

She slipped her hand from his and shook her head. Stealing a look at the innkeeper, Jessica gave her a small smile. "I understand if you don't feel comfortable…"

A gleam of greed lit her eyes. "How much are you offering?"

"Enough to keep you from asking questions. Or telling anyone we were ever here."

The innkeeper pondered that for a moment before raking Jessica with a self-satisfied sneer. "Well, in that case," she turned and removed a key from the wall. "Room two-twelve is available."

He figured as much.

Jessica took the offered key and thanked the lady. She turned back to him and Lucian realized how vulnerable she was with him not by her side. "I'll be back before you're out of the shower."

She nodded, putting on the same brave face he'd witnessed a hundred times over the past months. "Swear it on God."

His lips curled with the hint of a smile. "I swear it on God." That satisfied her. "Here." He went to hand her his sword.

She looked at him as if he'd lost his mind. "What in the world do you want me to do with that?"

"Keep it close to you while I'm gone."

She eyed the sword warily. "Are you kidding? I won't even be able to lift it."

"You're taking it anyway. And if anyone besides me tries to get in your room, run them through."

The innkeeper gasped and stepped back, a hand flying to her throat. "I said I don't wan..."

"I know what you said," he snapped.

Gripping the weapon in both hands, the weight of it drew her arms down. "See? I told you."

Frustrated, Lucian took back the sword. He hated leaving Jessica unprotected, yet he had to go and the weapon would be useless in her hands. Moreover, God forbid the worst happened and he sensed renegades who got to her before he could, the sword would end up doing her more harm than good. He'd be leaving his enemies his own blade to use against her.

He pulled Jessica in close and rested his cheek against hers. "Though a vampire may enter the inn, he won't be able to get into your room unless you invite him in," he whispered so that only she would hear that.

He felt her nod. "Don't you worry, you're the only one I'll be letting in my room."

He pushed her away and directed her to the stairs. As he watched her head up to the second floor, he saw the way she dragged her tired body. It was obvious Jessica was worn out, pushed nearly to the limits of endurance. He hoped a shower and some food would give her back some energy and strength.

Lord knew she'd need it if they were to move fast enough to stay ahead of Stephan.

Only after he heard the door to their room open and shut did he turn to leave. The innkeeper cleared her throat in a bid to get his attention. As much as Lucian wanted to just walk out and ignore her, he wasn't rude, so he gave her the attention she sought.

"Whatever trouble you two are in, I don't want you to bring it here. I've got my own worries."

"I told you, no trouble will breach your inn." Lucian wasn't at all positive about that, but again, that was a piece of information she need not know about.

"Why don't I believe you?"

He spared a glance down at himself and saw himself through her eyes. Of course she was leery of them staying there. In he and Jessica had come, bloody, dirty, with him carrying a sword. It was a miracle she hadn't found a way to call the police. Actually, she still might…

"I need to trust that you won't call the police while I'm gone."

She crossed her arms over her chest and raised her chin a notch. "Are you threatening me?"

Lucian slapped his hands on the desk. The innkeeper sucked in a breath and retreated back until she hit the wall. "No, I'm asking you for your word that you won't. If you call the police you'll be putting us all in danger, and the trouble that you want to avoid will find its way here."

She weighed that for a moment. "Fine. But I want the money you promised me."

Lucian stepped away from the desk and nodded. "You hold to your word, and I'll hold to mine."

Wanting to get back as quickly as possible, Lucian left the inn and followed the street to Goodman's Travel. As he strode down the darkened street he'd walked as a boy, he couldn't help but thank God for Edward. None of the Templars would have gotten this far without Tristan's family. They'd saved them from the sun, from enemies, even from themselves for the past seven centuries.

Something told Lucian the Beaumonts would continue to be their protectors for as long as the Templars haunted the night.

ℬ⚬ℭ

Sitting on the floor of the shower, a hot stream of water cascading over her, Jessica wrapped her arms around her drawn-up legs. Her chin rested on her knees as she expended her turbulent emotions in a flood of tears. She struggled to erase the images of Stephan, James, and the other vampires from her mind, but she couldn't banish them as she wept for all she was worth. Jessica was just thankful Lucian wasn't here to witness her breakdown. She'd made sure she stayed strong over the past months, but now it all poured out of her in a rush of tears she couldn't hold back.

Her tears mingled with the falling water as she watched the bubbles made by the soap she'd dropped disappear down the drain. She'd washed herself at least a dozen times, and yet still felt dirty. Her skin actually hurt from the number of times she'd washed her hair, her nails digging into her scalp to scrub it clean. Jessica wondered if she'd ever feel clean again. Somehow, she doubted it.

Thinking about the food the innkeeper had promised to bring her, Jessica's mouth watered and her stomach contracted in anticipation. Strange, something as simple as a meal and a change of clothes were now the greatest of treasures. It showed how drastically her life had changed.

Since this was the first time she'd been alone, Jessica thought she'd relish not having Lucian near. Instead, she felt more than just alone—she felt abandoned and vulnerable. And she didn't like it.

Lucian had been the one constant in her life over the last three months. He was a companion more reliable than the pain that had come to be so much a part of her. She may not have been able to see him in the dark but she'd known he was with her. As much as Jessica hated to admit it, more often than not, Lucian's presence had comforted her.

Her reaction to him confused her. There was no getting around what he was, yet there were times his being a vampire seemed almost insignificant. He'd been kind and considerate toward her. He'd sacrificed himself time and again in an effort to spare her from Stephan's cruelty. His actions were what mattered to her, not what he was. She prayed she wouldn't be proven wrong by trusting him.

After Jessica's tears finally stopped, she stood and took stock of herself. Looking at her body, which bore evidence of Stephan's punishments, she saw just how sloppy he'd gotten in his growing frustration. Lucian's blood had healed the cuts Stephan had inflicted upon her. What was left was a scattering of scars over her arms, legs, and torso. They, along with the scars that ringed her neck, would be constant reminders of her time in Hell—if she and Lucian managed to get to Seacrest Castle before Stephan got to them, that is.

Retrieving the soap, Jessica washed one last time. The lavender-scented soap stung her nose, but right then she didn't care about the smell, which had never been one of her favorites.

With the hot water turning warm, she reluctantly gave up the shower. Wrapping a towel around herself, she hugged the fluffy terrycloth to her as she stepped from the tub. Her hair dripping, she went over to the sink and untangled the mess of wet blonde strands with the brush she'd found in the bathroom cabinet.

Wiping a hand across the steamed up mirror, Jessica felt new tears sting her eyes. She didn't even recognize her reflection. Sickly thin, her cheeks were sunken and her eyes were shadowed to the point that they looked like the hollowed sockets of a skull. Jessica's stomach turned, knowing she looked less than human after her ordeal. How was she going to face her family looking like this?

Once Jessica had brushed the last knot from her hair, she dressed in borrowed clothes and returned to the cozy Victorian-decorated bedroom.

Looking around the room, which was small by any standards yet felt like a palace compared to where she'd been, she was awed by the creature comforts. The bed, covered in a thick quilt and topped with two fluffy pillows, looked extremely inviting. She longed to lie down and fall asleep on something comfortable instead of a rotting pallet on the floor.

Jessica was about to pounce on the beckoning bed but a sharp rap at the door stopped her. Fear took hold of her as she crossed the room. Pressing her ear against the wood, she tried to hear any sounds coming from the hallway. Hearing nothing, she gripped the lock on the door. Beads of sweat formed on her brow and upper lip, her hands went slick with it as her heartbeat raced. Her mouth ran dry as images of Stephan and his men bursting into her room assailed her mind.

"Who is it?"

"I have food for you."

Jessica had been expecting the innkeeper to return with food. Nevertheless, she was reluctant to open the door. Her stomach growled and a stab of hunger sliced through her, which propelled her to inch open the door. In case vampires were using the innkeeper to get Jessica to open the door, Jessica didn't invite the innkeeper in until she was sure she was alone.

The tray of sandwiches and fruit made Jessica's mouth water after months of scraps of barely edible food she'd been given in the dungeon. She watched in avid fascination as the innkeeper set the overloaded tray down on the small, round table between two windows.

After she'd set down the tray, the innkeeper went to leave, until Jessica's torn-up arms caught her attention. By the look on her face, she clearly hadn't noticed them when they'd first arrived. But then, Lucian's sword had held her attention, not the scraggily woman standing next to the intimidating man brandishing the weapon.

"My God, girl, what did that man do to you?"

The innkeeper reached for her, but Jessica threw her up her hand and stepped back. "Nothing. He didn't do this. We were in an accident. A car accident."

By the look on her face, the innkeeper didn't believe a word of her explanation. "Look, it's none of my business, but, if I were you, I'd get away from a man who could do that to a woman."

How ironic... "That's exactly what I'm trying to do."

The woman pursed her lips together, regarded Jessica for a long moment, and then gave her a curt nod. "I still want you both gone by morning."

A glance at the window showed it was still night—it also revealed just why they weren't going to be here once the sun rose. "Trust me, we will be."

"Good," the innkeeper declared before she marched toward the door. She stopped in the threshold and turned back to Jessica. "And I want the money promised me."

Before Jessica had the chance to assure her she'd get paid, the innkeeper left and slammed the door shut behind her.

Alone again, Jessica perched on one of the uncomfortable wooden chairs around the table and dove into the veritable feast provided for her. As she devoured the two sandwiches and all of the fruit, and threw back three glasses of water, all Jessica thought about was being back home. And yet, as much as she wanted to go home, she was terrified of facing her family. What if they saw what she'd endured? How could she explain what she'd been through? How would they treat her if they knew what had happened to her?

Jessica pushed away the now-empty tray and bit back the catch in her throat as tears stung her eyes. *They can never know.* They could never know where she'd been and the things done to her. She wouldn't taint them with the filth of what happened in the bowels of Penwick Castle.

Besides, how was she to tell them about vampires? They'd lock her away in an asylum, believing she'd lost her mind from her ordeal. Lord knows she felt as if she were crazy herself. She found it ironic that the one person everyone in town believed was a nut was actually the sane one, and everyone else was blind to what went on once the sun set.

If she ever made it back home, she and Allie Parker would have plenty to discuss.

&OCR

The world around Penwick Castle had changed drastically since he'd last been here, yet somehow managed to remain the same. Believing he'd never see this part of England again, Lucian took in Malmesbury. How odd that he'd once run down this very street and caused mischief with Richard and Stephan. Now, instead of dirt beneath his feet, there was concrete. The town retained an old world feel even as it passed into the modern age. It brought Lucian back to his youth and filled him with fond memories.

For once, the shame of his past was set aside as he hurried through Malmesbury. He almost felt normal again. For one blessed moment he didn't feel damned.

He remembered his childhood fondly. His parents had been doting, showering their son with love in a time when cold discipline was the norm. But after Richard went off to war and died, the world he'd known had begun to break apart. Until, finally, he'd left for Crusade after Guy Sinclair had come calling for able bodies to join his army.

Tristan, Sebastian and Raphael were already among the ranks, and the four formed an instant bond. Constantine found his way into Sinclair's army in Medina the night before they'd left England for the Holy Land. He'd been half-wild and, though one of the youngest of their number, he was more savage than men twice his age and size.

How he'd become part of their four-man group, Lucian couldn't recall. Only after they'd died and shared memories did they understand Constantine's pain and why he was the man he was.

The anger festering within him came from years of abuse, not only by his parents, but also by the lord they'd sold him to as a squire. Even Lucian's family had heard of Ulric Chambers and his sadistic ways. They'd never associated with the lord of Graves Castle—or with the Draegons for that matter. That was the reason why he'd never met Constantine before the night he'd joined Sinclair's army.

The day they'd left England, Lucian thought to return home in a few years, marry his betrothed, and raise fine sons.

Of course, it was not to be. The call to God deafened him until he was no longer able to resist. The day Tristan had announced he was joining the Order of the Knights Templar, Lucian had eagerly followed him. The others had as well, though Sebastian, Raphael, and Constantine did so for the glory. Tristan had as well, if the truth were known. Lucian, raised in a devout family, had been the only one to take up the cross and join the Knights Templar solely out of his devotion to the Lord.

He'd lost his faith soon after, leaving it behind on the battlefield even as he continued to fight and kill in the name of God.

Lucian's memories dissolved when he arrived at Goodman's Travel. The aroma of food turned his stomach the moment he stepped inside the shop. Brochures of places he'd never see were piled high on two desks. He heard rustling sounds coming from the back room.

"Hello?" Lucian heard the crinkle of foil and the shuffle of feet coming from an open doorway. Emerging from the shadowed back room was a rail-thin man wiping his mouth. "May I help..." His sentence trailed off when he got a look at Lucian—or rather the sword he held. "Bloody hell, man. Are you here to rob the place at swordpoint? How perfectly medieval."

Filthy, with blood on his clothes and skin as pale as a corpse's, he couldn't blame the man for his assumption.

"No, I'm not going to rob you." Lucian retorted with exasperation. He knew he should have left the sword with Jessica. "I'm here to collect a money transfer."

The man continued to eye the sword as he walked to a chaotic-looking desk. "If you tell me your name, I can tell you if your transfer came through."

Though Lucian was reluctant to give his name, he did so nonetheless. The man nodded as he pulled a thick envelope from the locked top drawer of the desk.

"Normally I need picture identification to release the money, but... Is that thing real, mate?"

Lucian narrowed his eyes in a glare at the man who wisely didn't ask twice. He sighed long and loud. If he weren't civilized, he'd have already taken the envelope from the man, with force if necessary. Since he *was* civilized, he refrained, regardless of the effort it took to maintain his composure and patience. "Yes."

The man let out a nervous laugh, his gaze fixated on the sword. "You always go around carrying that?"

Lucian ignored the question. "Just give me the money."

The man handed the envelope to Lucian, who opened it and pulled out a wad of bills. After handing the money to the man, he slipped into his pocket.

"What's this for?"

"Your silence," Lucian explained.

"I'm probably going to lose my job for this."

Lucian watched the man tuck the money into the pocket of his jeans. "That should be enough to compensate you for the loss."

The man grinned and shrugged. "Old man Goodman is a pain in the arse anyway."

"I need a car as well."

The man eyed the sword again, swallowing a lump lodged in his throat. "I'll make arrangements for you."

Lucian gave him a curt nod, glad Edward's money could purchase them a sound plan of escape. "You'll tell no one about me." Lucian warned, putting enough menace in his tone to turn the man white. "Do you understand?"

He nodded furiously. "No worries, mate. I won't."

After the man made the arrangements for a rental car, Lucian quickly left the shop, wanting to get back to Jessica. He hated having to leave her, but he wanted her clean and fed and comfortable. She deserved time alone, a hot bath, and a fine meal after the months she'd spent as Stephan's captive.

He had to get her to Seacrest as quickly as possible. Too much time had already been wasted. They couldn't afford to waste any more. They'd rest for a while at the inn and head out before dawn, giving themselves enough time to get to another hideaway where they could spend the day. He'd eyed a boarded-up, abandoned building that would do nicely as a haven.

Because they were only able to travel by night, it would take a few days to get to the castle after they procured a car. Once Jessica was safely on her way back to America, Lucian would hunt down Stephan and end him once and for all.

Chapter Nine

Jessica's scent reached Lucian as he strode down the hallway to their room. It beckoned to him and awakened desires that were best left dormant.

He didn't want to read into why his hand shook as he fit the key into the lock. After inching open the door, he found Jessica sitting at a small table. Her long legs were stretched out and her bare feet were propped up on a chair and crossed at the ankles. Her head turned to the door and she jumped up so fast she nearly tripped over her own feet. She grabbed a butter knife from a tray resting on the table, brandishing it as he would his sword. Realizing it was Lucian, she dropped the knife and released a sigh of relief.

Lucian grunted when Jessica ran to him. She slammed into him and wrapped her arms around his waist. He couldn't explain the painful tightening in the region where his heart used to beat as he settled his arms around her. All he knew was that she felt damn good in his arms.

Her heartbeat thundered wildly against his chest and the rush of her blood was a roar in his ears. It caused his insides to convulse as bloodlust nagged at him. He had to feed. Soon.

As much as Lucian would have loved to take advantage of having Jessica in his arms, the best thing to do would be to push her away, which was exactly what he forced himself to do.

The chill in the room and the damp of the outside air rushed back to him after the warmth of Jessica's body was gone.

Propping his sword against the wall near the bed, Lucian felt Jessica's gaze on him as he glanced at the tray on the table. Nothing but scraps and an empty pitcher were left. He looked back at Jessica, taking note of how the innkeeper's clothes draped over her frail body.

"She fed you well?"

"Better than I expected." Jessica crossed to the bed, sat, and folded her hands on her lap. Lucian noticed the way she wrung her hands. "He hasn't found us, has he?"

"No, Jessie. I didn't sense Stephan or his men. We'll be safe here for the rest of the night."

At least Lucian hoped so. By the look of her, Jessica needed rest—in a bed—before they had to move on to where they'd have to hide out for the day.

She looked down at her hands, wringing them some more, before directing her gaze back at him. All of Jessica's fear was laid bare for him. The guilt at knowing she was part of Stephan's plan to break him was like a sword slicing through his heart.

"You took so long that I thought Stephan had found us."

He'd taken longer than he'd thought, but he hadn't worried about Jessica noticing how long he'd been gone. He'd expected her to have fallen asleep long before now. Even now, Lucian watched as she fought to stay awake.

"I had to procure a car. Luckily the travel agent was good enough to lend a hand in the matter." He took the money from his pocket and placed it on the table. She eyed the stack in surprise. Lucian smiled and saw the way Jessica's gaze fixated on his fangs. His smile was gone instantly. "As always, Edward came through. We have more than enough to get to Seacrest."

She swallowed and nodded, again eyeing the money before looking back at him. "How long until we leave?"

"There's plenty of time for you to get some sleep." Jessica's relief was palpable. "I saw an old building not far from here where we can stay until sunset."

"Why do I sense there's a but in there somewhere?"

How astute of her. "Come the morning you need to go pick up the rental car."

He didn't think it possible, but her pallid complexion turned paler still. She jumped up as her jaw dropped. Snapping it closed, Jessica looked at him in horror. "Alone? You want me to go alone?"

He nodded, hating her fear, but unable to do anything about it. He couldn't go and do it himself and, given the finagling the kid at the travel agency had done to get them a car, there was no other time to pick up their transportation.

"I've already arranged it with the travel agent. All you need to do is pick up the car and drive it back to where we'll be staying." He offered a small smile, making certain to keep his fangs hidden. "Tell me you know how to drive stick."

From the look on her face, Lucian was sure she was going to tell him she couldn't. He was surprised by her answer. "My father had to replace the clutch after teaching me, but I learned."

Lucian imagined Jessica learning how to drive. He imagined her growing up, living her life, doing all the normal things women of her day did as they moved through life. And then he imagined her years from now, married with children, and he swore his dead heart ached from his imaginings.

He would have liked for it to be him she shared her future with. His children she carried under her heart. Lucian wanted what he'd once had—a family and light and laughter. And he wanted it with Jessica.

Giving himself a mental shake, Lucian cast such wants away. He dismissed what he felt as nothing more than seven hundred years of being deprived of human contact and an existence devoid of a woman's touch. It was the only reason why he ached for things with Jessica he had no business wanting.

"I'm sure you'll do fine," he snapped, suddenly irritated at all the things Jessica was going to do that he'd never get to see.

How he envied her future husband.

"It's the wrong side of the car thing I'm worried about."

Unable to resist, Lucian laughed. He'd had the same problem when he'd gone to America. "I'm certain you can conquer driving on the right side for a few blocks."

"I hope you're right." She gave a little laugh as she shrugged her slight shoulders. Good God, she was so painfully thin it was a wonder she still had the strength to remain upright. "If you're not, we're screwed."

After everything she'd been through, that Jessica was able to find laughter told Lucian just how strong a woman she was. Her strength would see her through, he was certain of it. Now all he had to do was live up to his end of things and get her home.

"Why don't you try to get some sleep while I go take a shower?"

Jessica padded over to the bed and picked up some folded clothes. "Here." He took the clothes and their fingers brushed. The tiny frisson of sexual desire that passed through him was like a small shock of electricity through his body. "The innkeeper brought these for you, although you are a big boy, Lucian, so I doubt they'll fit."

Back in his day, all fighting men were his size. It was only as the ages progressed and men no longer fought as they once had—and life got easier due to machinery and other modern advances—that men grew smaller. Now, most men worked their bodies only out of vanity, not necessity.

Shaking out the clothes, Lucian saw they were a pair of black jeans and a gray long-sleeved shirt. Jessica was right, they'd fit snug, but at least they were clean. He'd throw the innkeeper a bit more for them, which he was fairly certain was the reason she'd offered them up in the first place.

Lucian watched Jessica sit on the bed. The mattress seemed to swallow her as she sank into it with a satisfied sigh. She folded her arms behind her head. Her eyes slid closed and a dreamy smile curled her lips. She looked positively enchanting.

"Soft?"

"Unbelievably soft." She opened her eyes and sat up. Her gaze cut clean through him. "Wait until you give it a try. You're not going to want to get up after all that time spent on the floor."

Bullshit. Lucian wasn't going to want to get up simply because he'd be lying next to her.

The primitive creature dwelling within him that he fought constantly wanted to push her back on the bed and devour her. Or was it the man who wanted to sink deep into her body and forget the past seven hundred years as he lost himself in her?

After all these centuries, Lucian no longer knew what part of himself was the vampire and what part was the man. By now, both halves seemed to have blended together. Nevertheless, he didn't trust himself around her until he got fresh blood in him. The bloodlust warred with his sexual lust and brought him closer to the edge of beast than anything Stephan had done to him at Penwick.

"I'm going to take a shower. If you need anything just yell."

"Don't worry, I will."

Jessica's light laugh followed him into the pink Victorian bathroom. As he closed the door, shutting out the sight of her, Lucian doubted she'd even be awake by the time he got out.

ಬಂದ

Being a fastidious man, Lucian relished a daily shower. Stephan knew this, which was why the lack of bathing had been particularly cruel on his brother's part.

Even while he'd been alive and it was normal for people to go months—sometimes an entire year—without washing, Lucian washed almost daily. Sebastian wasn't the only one who'd hated the vermin infestation in their hair while they were held at Chinon. It had driven Lucian nearly mad, only he had never voiced his torment. Sebastian had, and the jailors had refused to cut his hair until the night before their execution. They were sadistic enough that they'd found it humorous to give Sebastian relief from the torture of the lice for only a short amount of time.

The memory of the infestation had Lucian giving his body a good scratch before shampooing his hair for the second time. He scrubbed until his scalp was raw—and then he washed it once more for good measure.

He dried quickly, shaking from the cold. He missed the days when his chill could be relieved by a roaring fire and he'd actually spent long hours marveling at the invention of electric heat. Unfortunately, even that wasn't enough to relieve the constant cold that plagued the Templars. The relentless chill was part and parcel of their damnation.

Draping the towel on a hook, he looked down at his nude body, marking each scar with his gaze. Some he touched as the memory of how he'd received each one came back to him. He'd led a brutal life, most of which had been spent on the battlefield.

His scars were blatant reminders of all the times he'd charged into battle without a thought of dying—and if he had thought of the possibility, he'd pushed it aside and rushed in anyway. As far as he'd been concerned, God was at his back. What more could a warrior ask for than his Lord protecting him?

Of course, once Lucian had lost faith, God no longer cast a protective hand over him. He'd been lost without his belief in God—lost and alone, with luck replacing faith. In France, his luck had run out.

It had run out for all of them.

Threatened by their power, King Philip of France orchestrated the mass arrest of the Order throughout Europe. Lucian and his fellow Templars had been in France at the time. Arrested and charged with heresy—as well as other trumped-up charges—they were taken to Chinon, where Lucian had believed they'd be executed immediately. Not so. Instead, they'd been held at Chinon for three years and ultimately burned to death.

Of course, the charges were unfounded and eventually the remaining Templars were released. Unfortunately, many Knights were put to death in Philip's master plan to dissolve the Order.

Lucian's years as a Templar Knight and then as a prisoner at Chinon had taken their toll. As Lucian dressed, his hands moving over his scars, he wondered if a woman would see the evidence of his years of harsh living and find him displeasing. No woman had ever seen him nude, and as he pulled on the too-tight pants the innkeeper had provided, he doubted a woman like Jessica would find pleasure in his damaged flesh.

Swiping his hand over the steamed-up mirror above the sink, Lucian looked at his face, thinking it was rather handsome as far as faces went. He'd never paid his looks much attention nor had he wondered if a woman would find them pleasing. He'd had no reason to wonder such things, as he'd taken an oath of chastity in life and thought to hold fast to his vow in death.

But he wondered now. He worried, actually, that Jessica would find him ugly. Thankfully his features were unmarred from battle, unlike Constantine's face, which bore a long scar. Women still found him appealing, however, which gave Lucian hope that Jessica wouldn't be put off by his appearance. And yet, his body was riddled with marks of battle. He imagined Jessica recoiling should she ever chance to see what war had done to him. Though why he cared, he didn't know. He'd never given the matter much thought before.

Once he'd taken his vow of celibacy in life, his devotion to God had aided him in fighting his sexual desires. Eventually he'd stopped thinking about sex altogether. Even after he'd lost his faith, sex wasn't a priority to him. Not like it was to the others. As soon as their bodies healed from their deaths, they'd gone off to slake lust that had been repressed for years.

He'd hung back as the others cut a sexual path through Northumberland, retreating into his damnation to spend the last seven centuries lost in the shadows.

But Lucian was thinking about it now—and he was afraid he'd be found lacking.

The flesh of his left thigh was puckered from a well-landed blade. The attack should have cost him his leg. Instead, Lucian had been quicker than his opponent and he'd managed to jump back before too much of the leg was cut. His chest was a maze of thick scars, the one over his heart the most prominent. All Templar Vampires possessed the mark. It was where the archangel Michael had run him through, severing his heart and taking his soul.

Donning the tight gray shirt, he covered his chest before running his hands through his wet hair. Before he opened the door, he listened for a moment to Jessica's slow and even breathing. He entered the room as quietly as possible so as not to disturb her sleep. Inhaling her sweet scent, Lucian stopped at the foot of the bed and watched her sleep for a long while, loving how peaceful she looked.

Jessica must have sensed him watching her. She opened her eyes, blinking away the fog of sleep as she bolted up. Only after she focused on the room—and then on him—did she relax. She smiled. Lucian was struck by how innocent she looked.

Her hair was a disheveled mess, her eyes hooded. She wore a dreamy smile now that she realized she wasn't still in the dungeon. He ached to take her in his arms and kiss her senseless.

"You clean up nice."

Lucian came around the bed, fighting the need to smile at her compliment. "Lie down and go back to sleep."

She patted the bed shyly. The invitation felt like a hand squeezing his heart. "Will you come lie with me, Lucian?"

His name on her tongue was music to his ears. "You don't want me next to you."

"Yes I do." She pulled up her legs and hugged her knees. Her gaze stayed locked on him. "I'm tired of being alone and feeling scared. Please lie with me."

Did Lucian feel a hand squeezing his heart? No—it was a vise, reminding him of emotions best left forgotten. What he felt now was dangerously close to what he'd felt each time he'd ridden under Penwick's gate and known he was home. A warm and wonderful homecoming—that was what he felt around Jessica. He ached to keep such a feeling in his heart, even though he knew he was bound to lose it once he returned her to her life.

How could he deny her? He climbed on the bed. It took him forever to settle next to her, and still he wasn't comfortable. The too-small clothes pulled and gathered in all the wrong places. When Jessica laughed at the spectacle he made, he gave her a glare worthy of Constantine.

"You look like a sausage."

He shrugged and leaned against the headboard. "Beggars can't be choosers."

She unwrapped her arms from her legs and lifted her head from her knees. "You can take them off and get comfortable." She looked away bashfully. "Don't worry, I won't peek while you get undressed."

Lie next to her naked?

As much as he believed his resolve would shatter if he were to be so close to her without clothes, Lucian got up and peeled off his shirt and pants. He slid on the bed and quickly covered himself lest Jessica see how his body hardened at her nearness.

"Better?"

He nodded curtly. "Much."

"Good." Jessica settled next to him. She took him by surprise by wrapping herself around his body. He hissed at the feel of her against his bare skin. She moved away with a frown. "What's wrong?"

He shook his head and gathered her back up against him. "Nothing."

Jessica laid her head in the crook of his arm, her arm draping over his chest. Her warmth flooded him and her soft breaths fanned his flesh. He heard the rush of blood through her body, as well as each steady beat of her heart. Those rhythmic beats drummed against him as she relaxed in his arms. In that moment, Lucian marveled at how right this felt— how perfectly Jessica fit in against his body.

The shudders that wracked Jessica jarred Lucian. The sound of soft sobs pierced him. "Jessica? Why are you crying?"

She shook her head and crushed herself even closer. Her arm tightened around his chest. Her sobs were muffled as her emotions poured from her. Lucian hugged her close as she wept, wishing to God he could take every moment of the last months from her mind. But he couldn't. All he could do was hold her and pray to God it was enough.

Lucian was her anchor as she wept. Without his arms around her, Jessica knew she would have shattered into a million pieces. She realized then that he'd always been there, a silent comfort in the dark. His nearness alone had gotten her through their hellish time at Penwick. Whenever her mind had slipped further toward the point of insanity, the clatter of his chains as he moved had been a beacon in the darkness.

Jessica could have never survived without him. Stephan would have broken her if it hadn't been for the strength Lucian's presence lent her when hers deserted her. Without him she'd be dead, or wishing she were. If Jessica had learned anything over the last months it was that there were worse things that could happen to a person than death.

He'd sacrificed so much to see that she'd survived. He'd fought for her, bled for her, had risked his life—as it were—to free her from Penwick. There simply weren't enough words to express her gratitude for all Lucian had done to protect her.

Once Jessica's tears were spent, she unburied herself from the crook of his arm, wiped her face, and looked at him with watery eyes. "I'm sorry for that, but I couldn't hold it back."

Lucian kissed the top of her head before smoothing his hand over her hair. "Don't apologize."

The calluses on his palm caught on her hair. She liked his hands. They weren't the soft hands of a pampered man, but the roughened hands of a warrior who'd spent lifetimes wielding a sword. "You'd think I'd realize how useless tears are."

"You don't have to be strong around me, Jessie."

Jessica propped herself on her elbow. She searched his body curiously, resting for a moment on the scar over his heart before coming back to his face. "Do you ever get tired of living?"

He folded his arms behind his head in a relaxed manner she hadn't seen while they were in the dungeon. "I'm dead, so it's a moot point."

Though his words were said matter-of-factly, somehow Jessica sensed Lucian wasn't as indifferent to his death as he made out. "Is it really?"

"No, it's not," he admitted. "In theory, immortality is a good deal. In reality, not so much. There are times when I can feel time crawling over me and I fear I'll go mad from it."

Though Jessica nodded in understanding, in actuality, she couldn't possibly know what it was like for him. She couldn't fathom going on for century after century, fighting the urges she knew he must have. That he refrained from giving in to the things Stephan did proved Lucian's strength of body and mind.

"Stephan seems to enjoy the whole living forever thing."

"My brother is a damn fool."

"No arguments from me about that."

Jessica danced her fingers over Lucian's chest. Though his flesh was cold, she liked the feel of him. She loved that his body bore the scars of battle. She hated that he'd suffered receiving them, but each mark was a testimony to the life he'd led and the harsh times he'd lived.

He was as different from the men of this era as day was from night. Jessica wondered how anyone could look at him and not see him for the medieval warrior he was. But then, she knew, people often saw what they wanted to see. Vampires weren't supposed to exist. People didn't live forever. So when someone looked at Lucian, they saw what he was supposed to be and not who and what he was.

"I'm sorry," Jessica whispered, thinking about how difficult it must be for him to face the fact that his brother was evil.

His slashing brown brows came together in a puzzled frown. "For what?"

"For your brother's hatred."

"There's no need to apologize, Jessica." Lucian's pain was reflected in his gleaming silver eyes. "I've brought that on myself."

Being as close as she was to her own brother, Jessica couldn't imagine the depth of animosity Stephan felt for Lucian. "Why does he hate you so much?"

"I can't talk about that, Jessica."

No, she didn't imagine he could. Nor would Jessica push to talk about something so obviously painful. Instead, she flattened her hand over his heart and met his gaze, ignoring that she felt no heartbeat against her palm. "Are you ever going to go back to Pennsylvania?"

"I have to." By the way he said that she knew it wasn't something he was looking forward to. "Don't worry, Jessica, I promise I won't bother you."

As much as Jessica wanted to tell him that he wasn't a bother, and in fact, the thought of never seeing him again damn near killed her, she kept silent. She wasn't going to come across as needy or demanding. That wasn't fair to Lucian. He was part of a world she couldn't bring herself to live in and he certainly couldn't exist in hers. She was of the living and he was of— something else. Caught between two planes of existence, his soul on the edge of both Heaven and Hell.

"Do you believe we'll make it to Seacrest before Stephan catches up with us?"

"Rest easy, Jessica," Lucian assured her. "I swear to you that I'll get you home to your family."

She had no doubt about that. She was simply scared and needed to hear him say it. "I know you will, Lucian."

Jessica moved so that she was lying beside him. He gathered her close and held her tight. Jessica settled into him and closed her eyes. She let the world around them disappear so that it was just the two of them. Sighing, she draped her arm across his chest, wishing she could make this one moment last forever.

Lucian sensed the moment Jessica slipped into sleep. He ached to hold onto this perfect moment for lifetimes. It felt right to hold her even as he knew he had no right to pull her into the darkness of his existence. She didn't belong trapped in the dark. She belonged under the glow of the sun, not with him, hidden in the shadows and lost to the night.

Once he returned to Damascus he knew it would be torture to keep away from her. Somehow, however, he'd manage. He had to—for her sake and for his sanity's sake. If he could, he'd avoid going back there even though it would mean being separated from the other Templars. Yet he had to return there. Damascus was where the Templars had to be. It was where their fight with the Obyri—the Templar Knights who'd made no oath to God—was going to take place. It was where the Templars were going to fight their final battle for redemption.

After he got her to Northumberland, Lucian would arrange for her to go home to America. Only then would he return to Penwick, and as much as it would kill him to have to do it, he'd be forced to end Stephan.

The images of Sarah Addison, Amanda Driver, and Jordan Brewster flashed through his mind, reminding Lucian of what Stephan was capable. His brother couldn't be left to continue his bloody rampage. Although it pained him to do the deed, Lucian would not put Stephan's death in another's hands. He was the cause of what his brother had become and he would be the one to end him.

In doing so, Lucian would set free the souls Stephan had stolen so the innocents could go to God and finally find peace.

Chapter Ten

At the persistent call of her name—spoken in the most musical baritone she'd ever heard—Jessica grumbled and rolled over onto her stomach. Given how heavy her body felt, and how fogged her brain was, it seemed as if she'd just fallen asleep. Hugging her pillow, she just wanted to lie here for a few minutes more, at least until the remnants of the awful dream she'd had faded.

An ancient castle, a dungeon, and vampires? Jesus Christ, where did her mind find such horrendous imaginings? She shivered and hugged her pillow tighter, thankful to find herself home in her own comfortable bed, far from where the monsters in her dream could get her.

"Jessica, you have to get up. We have to leave soon."

Jessica came fully awake and realized this wasn't a dream—rather it was a nightmare.

Oh God, she heaved a sigh and sat up. She flipped back her hair and was met by the sight of Lucian sitting next to her on the bed. He was back in the ill-fitting clothes, watching her with intense, glowing silver eyes. His lips were parted and she saw the tips of his fangs. Her mouth ran dry and a sick feeling settled in the pit of her stomach at the sight.

She blinked away the sleep from her eyes and tucked her hair behind her ears. Glancing out the window, she saw it was still dark out. "How long until we have to leave?"

Jessica saw a glimmer of fear light behind his eyes. His fear, she assumed, was of the sun. She'd be afraid of it too, if it could burn her to ash.

"We need to be out of here in less than an hour."

That was much too soon as far as Jessica was concerned. She didn't want to give up the warmth and comfort of the bed, yet knowing how vital it was for them to be on the move, she tossed off the covers and threw her legs over the side of the bed.

"Did you sleep at all?"

When he didn't answer, she peered at him from over her shoulder. He shook his head. His wealth of brown hair tumbled around his face. "No."

"Oh. I mustn't have been asleep long, then."

He shrugged and stood. "About two hours or so."

Two hours? It didn't seem that long at all. Two hours was nothing given how battered and weary she was in both mind and body. "What did you do all that time?"

He came around the bed. Jessica didn't shrink away when he fingered a lock of her hair. "I held you."

That shocked her right down to her toes. "Really?"

He leaned in close enough that Jessica assumed he might try to kiss her. She wondered if she'd move away if he tried. No. She didn't think she would, which confused the hell out of her.

"You felt good in my arms."

The man didn't mince words. And the words released a bevy of butterflies in her stomach. They fluttered around furiously as warmth spread through her at his simple, sweet announcement. Her reaction to his words only confused her even more.

"I want to hate you but I can't."

"I don't want you to hate me." He moved away and Jessica almost reached out to grab him back.

She watched as Lucian ducked away, as if saying that cost him greatly. But then he stopped, as if some unseen force froze him in his tracks. He muttered a curse and turned back around. Jessica sucked in a sharp breath as he came at her in three long strides. He grabbed her by the shoulders, his hold demanding. He lowered his head and at that moment she wasn't sure who leaned in toward whom. All she knew was that his mouth came down on hers and Jessica's entire world spun out of control.

Lucian's lips were soft, cold, and tasted of mint-flavored toothpaste. His kiss reminded her of a crisp winter day, if such a thing were possible. He was ice and snow and wind, yet she melted in his arms from the heat of his kiss.

With an expertise that left her breathless, Lucian played her mouth with his tongue until Jessica felt lightheaded. He teased her, making her want more of him, and then giving her what she craved. She moaned. He answered her moan with a growl that sent delicious shivers over her. His hands settled on the small of her back, applying just enough pressure to press her up against him, Jessica ran her hands up his back and buried them in his soft brown hair. She tugged gently and pulled another primal sound from him.

Although Jessica felt his fangs, she didn't pull away. Instead, she ignored them and went right on enjoying his kiss.

Lucian's body was hard and unyielding, his erection pressing against her, making her ache to know what it would feel like to have him fill her. She shivered when he ground into her. Pulling at his hair, her body went slick with desire.

Lucian pushed her away with a hiss. Jessica fell back on the bed, blinking at his sudden change. "What's the matter?"

"I can't, Jessica... I can feel myself losing control." He looked as if he were in agony. "I'm sorry. I had no right to kiss you."

Jessica stood and closed the space between them. She laid her hand against his smooth cheek. "No apologies. I kissed you too."

He stepped back and ran a hand through his hair, unable to ignore the sensation of pinpricks at the nape of his neck. The night was fading fast.

Lucian scratched the back of his neck and shook off the unpleasant warning of the coming dawn. "We have to go."

She gave him a curt nod, noticing the urgency in his tone. "I'll be ready in ten minutes."

In the bathroom, Jessica stared at her reflection in the mirror. She no longer resembled the girl she'd been months ago. She was at least ten pounds thinner, probably more. She looked skeletal, especially with the clothes she wore, which were at least a size too big. Her face was drawn and reflected all the suffering she'd endured. Truthfully, she looked awful, and as she washed her face, she wondered why Lucian had kissed her. God knew she looked as far from kissable as humanly possible.

After washing her face, she loaded her finger with toothpaste she'd found in the medicine cabinet and scrubbed her teeth as best she could. Primitive, yes, but at least it helped to make her feel somewhat cleaner. Having done her business in a bucket with Lucian only a few feet away, she nearly wept with relief at having privacy in a bathroom.

Though she knew they didn't have much time before they had to leave, Jessica couldn't resist a fast shower. Going three months with irregular baths at most, she wasn't going to pass up the chance to wash. After all, she had no idea when she'd get the chance to shower again.

Feeling slightly better after her shower, Jessica left the bathroom. Lucian was pacing the room, his gaze locked on the window. "Ready?"

Jessica nodded. "I thought you said we had some time."

"After being held in a dungeon, it seems my senses are a bit off."

That was not good on so many levels, Jessica couldn't begin to think of them all. "I didn't think that could be possible."

He tugged her out of the room. "Neither did I."

Once they were downstairs Lucian used the phone again. He called Edward to tell him they were leaving. The brief conversation with Tristan Beaumont's descendant ended with a curt assurance that all would be well and they'd hopefully reach the castle within a few days.

Jessica hoped to God that were true.

"Come on, Jessica." Again, Lucian extended his hand to her and Jessica put her trust in him. "The building is only two blocks away, but we have to hurry."

Jessica was reluctant to leave the comfort of the room, but she knew staying here would be a foolish risk. Though the innkeeper was being paid for her discretion, she didn't want them there and might sell them out. So, as much as she wanted to throw a blanket over the window and sleep the day away in a nice, comfortable bed, logic won over want.

As soon as they stepped out into the crisp early morning air, the cold slapped Jessica in the face. She swallowed a hard breath as Lucian pulled her down the street. She barely had a chance to take in the picturesque town as they raced down the street and around a corner. She did spy an ancient abbey and almost stumbled over her own feet in amazement. As a lover of history, Jessica wished she was here under different circumstances. She'd have loved the chance to explore the town and the abbey.

Jessica felt as if she were surrounded by the past and present at once, especially since she held the hand of a man who'd been around since these buildings were young. He was every bit as medieval as everything around her. She wondered if he felt out of place in this modern world, even though he'd gone through the ages, seeing the changes in the world as he passed through time. How could he not?

When they came to the building where they'd spend the day, Jessica eyed it warily. Chipping white plaster and thick, leaded-glass windows lent the place a creepy look. She wasn't looking forward to spending an entire day in there.

"I'll help you through the window."

Lucian made a step for her with his hands. Jessica backed away, shaking her head. "I'm not going in there first."

He straightened and took hold of her shoulders. "There's nothing in there to hurt you. Trust me."

She nodded, unsure of why she was so afraid. "That's easy for you to say. You're a vampire. What can hurt you?"

"The sun," he quipped. "Now hurry. I can feel dawn coming."

Jessica peeked at the sky, and sure enough, the sky had gone from inky black to dark blue as the sun began its ascent. "Fine. But you'd better be right behind me."

"I'll be directly behind you, I swear. Now hurry."

Lucian moved forward again. This time, Jessica didn't hesitate. She gripped the crumbling wall and let him heft her up. Worming her way through the narrow opening feet first, she was met by nothing but air. A frisson of fear passed through her and she almost threw herself back out the window. Only the thought of Lucian bursting into flames had her propelling herself forward.

Jessica landed with a thud. She lost her balance and stumbled backward. Scrambling to her feet, she slammed herself against the wall and began to hyperventilate. Oppressive blackness surrounded her, a musty stench choking her. She was vaguely aware of Lucian coming through the window after her.

"Easy, Jessica. Nothing in here will hurt you."

His voice cut through her panic and Jessica felt more in control. After dragging in a breath, she nodded and put her hand in his as he pulled her from the window. She couldn't see anything once they were deep in the building and away from what meager moonlight shone in. Obviously Lucian saw just fine. He led her to where there were high stacks of boxes, a perfect place for him to hide from the sun.

And the sun was coming.

Lucian felt the dawn like pinpricks all over his body. He dropped Jessica's hand after they rounded the high wall of boxes, which were the only items in the building. This place was obviously being used as a warehouse, with no hint of its original purpose to be found.

Jessica dropped to the floor and drew her knees up the moment he let go of her hand. It was what she did when she was afraid. She made herself as small as possible. Sitting beside her, Lucian put an arm around her. She smiled as she scooted closer to him and rested her head on his shoulder. He didn't understand why she trusted him now, and hadn't in the dungeon. Nor did he take too much time analyzing it. Not when he'd much rather enjoy the feel of her against him.

"What happens if someone comes here and finds us?"

He hugged her even closer. "Let's not think about that, shall we?"

He'd do whatever was necessary to ensure her safety and his continued existence. Basically, the rules governing Templars were simple. They had to guard the relic, protect Tristan at all costs, and kill only if their existence was threatened. If even one of them deviated from those rules, all of their souls would be sent to Hell. That was something every Templar fought to avoid since the night they'd woken as vampires.

The stab in his stomach and the dryness of his mouth reminded him again that he needed to feed. With the hunger upon him, it would only continue to grow until he fed, making him more dangerous to Jessica as the day wore on. They couldn't leave Malmesbury until he fed.

Jessica must have sensed his body stiffening in his effort to hold onto his control because she leaned away from him. Her gaze was searching, causing Lucian to shift under the weight of it. "Are you okay?"

She looked too serious by half, which given their situation, he couldn't blame her for. "I'm fine."

She cocked a brow at him. "No you're not." Her eyes narrowed on him, like she saw through him to the hunger gnawing at him. "You need blood, don't you?"

Lucian couldn't deny his shame at his body's need. "I said I'm fine."

"You don't have to lie to me about it. You seem to forget we've spent the last three months together."

Forget? Never would he forget one moment of their captivity.

Raking a hand through his hair, Lucian sensed the rising sun, an added agitation to his already growing unease. He didn't dare glance around the boxes to see how much of the sun spilled in through the missing windowpane and the cracks between the boards that covered the remaining windows.

Lucian shrugged with false indifference. "You don't need to be reminded of what I am."

Jessica raised her brows, regarding him in astonishment. "Do you think I need a reminder?"

"No. I'm sure you don't."

Lucian pulled back slightly when she shimmied out of his arms. She ran her hands through his hair, the gentle caress a touch upon his heart. "I don't see you as a monster, Lucian. Not anymore, anyway."

He found it ironic she'd say that because of his devious thoughts about her. "You should, Jessie. If you knew the things I want to do to you..."

"Stop it. Stop trying to make me afraid of you." Her hands came to rest on his cheeks. Her touch was warm—gentle—bringing to life tender emotions in him he was only now realizing he possessed. "Haven't I spent enough time being afraid? Can't I just enjoy this moment with you?"

Her whispered questions caused an ache in his heart. A low growl rumbled within him as he struggled with himself not to mislead her, but to be as frank and honest with her as he could. "I'm a monster."

She shook her head and trailed her hands down to his shoulders. Her thin arms settled around his neck. Her face was so close all he had to do was lean forward and he'd be able to capture her lips. He closed his eyes and swallowed a groan

133

when she hugged him. Her breath fanned his cheek and her breasts, small and firm, pressed against his chest. His body reacted instantly to her, hardening and pressing painfully against the fabric of the too-tight pants.

"You had a million opportunities to hurt me and you never did." Her heartbeat hammered against his chest as her lips touched his cheek in a whisper of a kiss. "A monster wouldn't have held back or protected me as selflessly as you have."

Lucian wished he could hold on to this moment for eternity. But as it always did, life—or rather his death—managed to intrude.

The stab of hunger forced his eyes open as everything about Jessica drove him mad with need. She made him hurt in ways he never knew possible. Back in the dungeon, her fear helped him to fight the hunger. But now, with her fear gone, the way she opened herself to him was a new kind of torture for Lucian. One he'd never known before. He'd never allowed himself to get close to any human, which made resisting Jessica a difficult battle to fight. It raised the pain of hunger to new and brutal heights. There was nothing keeping him from refraining, save his own will, which right now was tenuous at best.

Nevertheless, Lucian drew Jessica even closer, until he no longer knew where he ended and she began. He buried his face in the rich fall of her hair and inhaled her clean scent. She rested her head on his shoulder and relaxed into him. Lucian felt as if the world came to a dead stop and nothing and no one but the two of them mattered.

With desire ripping through him and the bloodlust steadily growing, Lucian wanted more than to simply hold Jessica. He ached to push her to the floor and take her and sate his body's sexual desire for her. Lucian could almost imagine Constantine's gruff approval that his resolve had finally begun to crack after lifetimes of abstinence. Hell, Raphael would probably clap him on the back and remark that it was about damn time. That nosy bastard had tried everything over the centuries to break Lucian's control. Somehow Lucian had managed to tamp down his sexual needs. He'd stood back and watched Raphael and Constantine cut a sexual path through the ages, using women to sate their every need. Tristan had as well, only he was more discreet about it. But then, he needed to keep a low profile so as not to attract the attention of the Obyri.

Lucian had watched Sebastian struggle with his self-imposed celibacy for three hundred years, never understanding why the fight was so tough—until now. Lucian finally understood Sebastian's torment.

"You've no idea how badly I want you."

The words tumbled from Lucian unbidden.

Jessica pulled away from him. In the span of a single moment she'd gone from soft and warm in his arms to hard and cold—as she'd been in the dungeon. "I won't let you feed from me."

"That's not what I meant."

Though that wasn't exactly true, Jessica didn't need to know how he struggled against *that* particular craving.

"Oh," she mumbled and looked away.

He took her chin in hand and forced her to look back at him. "I shouldn't have said that."

"I'd rather have your honesty."

Honesty? His entire existence was shrouded in secrecy. From why God had chosen the Templars to be damned as vampires and not simply sent to Hell, right down to the sins of his past. And yet, Lucian had been more open with Jessica than even Lady Felicia, to whom he'd been betrothed prior to going off on Crusade.

Felicia had evoked a small degree of affection from him, but as the years passed and Lucian grew from boy to man, he'd come to realize all he'd felt toward her was a sense of loyalty. What he'd felt for Felicia was a far cry from love, and it was drastically different than what he felt for Jessica—something Lucian still hadn't worked through to fully understand.

Lucian always knew Felicia would have made the perfect wife. Well-bred, comely, kind and obedient, she would have given him fine sons. Unfortunately, once he'd seen Jerusalem, had walked the same ground his Lord had once stood upon, Lucian had found a stronger calling than to home and hearth. He'd answered the call to God by joining the Templar Knights, and had not regretted his decision until the day came that he'd left his faith on a bloodstained battlefield.

Facing Jessica, whose eyes blazed with elegance and strength of spirit, he wondered if he'd have made the same decision in life if she'd been his betrothed rather than Felicia. Would he have made the same choices if it was Jessica who would have bore him children, and who would have been waiting for him to return each time he'd gone off to battle?

Unable to resist, Lucian took the chance and claimed Jessica's mouth. He expected her to fight his kiss. Instead, her arms came around him and she clung to him. He growled into her mouth and crushed her to him as their tongues met. She tasted of life and strength, fuel to the already raging fire of desire burning within him.

With her hands buried in his hair, her fingers brushing the nape of his neck, Lucian deepened the kiss. The scent of her desire was intoxicating and had him pushing her to the floor. He laid Jessica down, her legs opening to allow him to settle between them. He covered her, reveling in her heat. Her hands moved away from his hair to travel down his back. He jerked in surprise when her fingers accidentally grazed his side. He laughed into her mouth, realizing for the first time he was ticklish.

She turned her head and broke the kiss. "What's so funny?"

"I'm ticklish."

Her smile, shy yet playful, was enchanting. "You should have warned me."

"I didn't know I was."

Jessica gazed at him as if he'd sprouted a second head. "Are you serious?" He nodded. "How can you go this long without realizing you're ticklish?"

"No one's ever touched me where you just did."

If he'd thought she looked at him oddly a moment ago, that was nothing compared to the look she was giving him now. "Really? Never?"

"Never."

"Well, I guess a warrior wouldn't find himself in too many situations where he'd be tickled."

He smiled back at her. "No, he wouldn't."

Lucian had only a moment to wonder at Jessica's narrowed eyes and her wicked grin. She deliberately grazed his side, causing him to jerk again. She giggled. He rumbled low in his throat, the sound half growl, half moan.

"That wasn't nice."

She laughed and shook her head. "No, it wasn't."

When she did it again and he laughed, Lucian knew if the Templars could hear him, they'd think he'd lost his mind. He never laughed. He was always much too serious, his past a

137

constant burden, preventing him from indulging in humor. Yet here he was, lying on top of Jessica and laughing as she tickled him.

"You realize you're going to pay for your impertinence."

Jessica had no time to consider the consequences of her actions. She gasped when Lucian's mouth crashed down on hers. No one had ever kissed her with the enthusiasm Lucian did. His lips and tongue played havoc on her senses, so much so, she barely took notice of his fangs. She didn't mind his fangs as much as she thought she would. She liked kissing Lucian too much to focus on them.

And oh God, did she like kissing him.

His lips were cool, unyielding, and demanding. He braced himself with one hand while he moved the other over her. She liked his weight on top of her. His size and strength made her feel delicate, something she'd never known before, having grown up with an older brother who'd toughened her up by terrorizing her since they were children.

But most of all, Jessica loved how Lucian worshiped her mouth.

He kissed her as if he'd never kissed another woman before. As if he was savoring every moment of the kiss. The frantic need in which he claimed her mouth woke the same sentiment in her. She matched his passion, clawing at him, needing to be even closer to him. Jessica needed to have all of her body mold to all of his.

As Lucian kept on kissing her, the world disappeared. What might come if Stephan found them wasn't a nagging fear as long as Lucian's mouth remained on hers. No impending doom overshadowed them. Stephan, the dungeon, how she was going to face her family—all of it faded under Lucian's gentle, yet demanding, kiss.

Lucian took his mouth from hers and Jessica felt a moment of dread at the feel of his lips on her throat. He kissed the spot over her pulse as his hand slipped under her shirt. He worked his way up her stomach to her bare breast. His rough palm awakened her nipple as he dragged his tongue down the side of her neck. The sweet assault on her body had her arching into his hand.

Lost in the sensations he woke in her, Jessica fisted her hands in his hair and let out a breathy moan. He rolled her nipple gently between his fingers and Jessica nearly shattered. She felt Lucian smile against her neck as he trailed kisses down to her collarbone. Secretly, she was glad to have him away from her neck.

A wonderful pressure began to build between her legs when he ground his erection against her. In that moment Jessica knew she wouldn't stop him if he took this even further.

But he didn't. Instead, Lucian pushed himself off her. She wanted to pull him back to her but didn't. He knelt there staring at her, his eyes literally glowing. His lips were parted, the tip of his fangs showing. His nostrils flared and he growled. Jessica nearly died of shame when she realized he was inhaling her scent.

But then she smelled something odd and scooted away from him. Sitting up, she saw, much to her astonishment, that his foot was smoking.

Horrified, she saw a stream of sunlight cutting across the floor—right over his foot. "Lucian, your foot is burning." He glanced over his shoulder, cursed, and moved out of the sun. "Why didn't you say something?"

He lifted a brow as he shifted so that he was now sitting. His foot was still smoking. The stench of burnt flesh was nauseating.

"I hadn't realized it was burning."

"How could you not know?"

He smiled cockily, even as he cringed now that the pain was setting in. "I was otherwise occupied."

Jessica knew if she lived ten lifetimes, no other man would ever claim to be so caught up in kissing her he hadn't realized his person was burning. Of course, if she lived ten more lifetimes, Jessica doubted she'd ever find herself being kissed senseless by another vampire.

"You have to go get the rental."

She was not looking forward to leaving his side. She genuinely felt safe being near him. "I wish you could come with me. The thought of going out there alone terrifies me."

He took hold of her shoulders and pulled her in for a strong embrace. "All will be well, Jessica."

"What happens if Stephan's men are out there?"

"If you have even the slightest suspicion you're being watched or followed, you get yourself back here immediately."

That was something he didn't need to demand of her.

"Don't worry, I will."

He kissed her hard before pushing her away. "Hurry back to me."

As long as he provided safety, she'd get back to him as quickly as she could.

Chapter Eleven

After awkwardly climbing out of the window, the bright sunlight nearly blinded Jessica. Flattening her back against the wall of the building, she needed a moment to allow her eyes to adjust to the light and to get her bearings. She also needed a moment to fight down the panic of being alone. Out in the open, Jessica knew how vulnerable she was. At any moment, one of Stephan's human henchmen could snatch her up and drag her back to the castle. Just the thought of going back there had her gasping for air as fear snaked around her throat to choke her.

Regulating her breathing, Jessica fought for calm. She didn't have time to indulge her fear. Reminding herself that if she didn't get the car, they'd have no hope of getting to Seacrest got her moving.

Crudwell Road. Down two blocks and make a right. That's where she had to go. It was a short and simple trip, and yet as she looked up and then down the street, it seemed as if she had to trek across the world.

Knowing how important it was for her to do this, Jessica shoved aside her fear and pushed off the wall. Finding fortitude somewhere deep within her soul, she walked at a brisk pace down the street. The day, though sunny, was cool, and she wrapped her arms around herself in an effort to ward off the cold.

The town, she noticed again, retained a medieval feel. The ancient buildings, though somewhat upgraded, still looked much as they must have when they'd first been constructed. Jessica tried to imagine Lucian here as a boy, before he'd gone off to war and long before he'd been—changed—into what he now was. It had to be a hell of a thing for him to be back here, where he'd been raised, after being away for as long as he had. Seeing how things must have changed, even as he'd stayed the same, must be disconcerting to say the least. Lord knew it would be to her, Jessica mused as she hurried toward Crudwell Road.

She'd walked only two blocks when the aroma of fresh bread reached her. Though she'd eaten at the inn, it was hardly enough to fill her after months of practically being starved. Her stomach constricted in hunger and her mouth watered at the delicious smells coming from a teashop across the street.

Following the scent, Jessica ducked her head against a gust of frigid wind that made her eyes sting and tear. Hunger, coupled with the wad of cash in her pocket, compelled Jessica into the teashop. Thankful for the short reprieve from the bitter English cold, she pushed open the door and hurried inside. The chime of a bell as she entered startled her.

The interior of the teashop wasn't as quaint as the exterior, but had a cozy feel that drew Jessica right in. Decorated in white and pink, it was feminine and welcoming. In the rear was a gathering of small tables. On the walls hung paintings of what one imagined typical nineteenth-century English country life to be—women and children in bonnets and men in three-piece suits sitting around a garden sipping tea. Up in the front was a long glass display case holding assorted foods, which Jessica walked toward with a rumbling stomach.

"Good morning, ma'am. May I help you?"

She smiled stiffly at the plump woman dressed in white behind the glass counter. "Hi, um, I'd like..." *One of everything.* Scanning the glass case filled with an assortment of scones, breads, cookies and cakes, her sentence trailed off. She couldn't decide what she wanted. Hunger, Jessica found, was a terrible shopping companion.

"Don't tell me you're an American."

Jessica nodded shyly, not knowing how an American would be received here. She was well aware of the whole arrogant American reputation. Besides, the last thing she needed was to draw undue attention to herself.

"Well now, you're a far way from home." The woman smiled even wider and gestured to one of the round white metal tables. "Go on and sit down and try one of our famous scones."

Jessica sat, in need of a friendly face. The woman gathered up a scone and what looked like a wad of butter and placed it on a dish. Placing a napkin and a butter knife on it, she carried it over to the table. "Here. Don't be shy. Enjoy. It isn't every day we're visited by an American."

"Thank you," Jessica mumbled before sinking her teeth into the warm scone. The woman corrected the way she was eating by cutting the scone and slathering it with what she informed Jessica was clotted cream. It was heaven. Pure heaven.

"Would you like some tea?" Jessica nodded, though she hated tea. The scone was really dry and with her mouth full she couldn't ask for water. The woman hurried to make her a cup. She brought it back and sat across from Jessica. She waited until Jessica chewed and swallowed another bite of scone before firing off a barrage of questions. They ended with her asking what Jessica was doing in Malmesbury.

I'm running from the vampires who live in Penwick Castle. "I'm just passing through."

"Where are you headed?"

The eager gleam in the woman's bright green eyes did nothing to prompt Jessica to talk. She didn't know whom to trust, who might be working for Stephan. For all she knew, this woman could be a human drone for that sadistic bastard.

"I'm just sightseeing before I go home."

"Well, at least you can say you've had one of Lily's famous scones."

"And I can honestly say it was delicious." She offered the woman a hint of a smile, not really up to a full grin. "Thank you."

The woman, Jessica assumed she was Lily, beamed at the compliment. "Would you like anything else before you go?"

She wanted Lily to bag up everything. "Just a few more scones, please."

Lily walked back behind the counter and dropped a few scones into a bag. Jessica glanced out the window to see a couple strolling hand in hand past the teashop. They looked happy. Jessica wanted to know that happiness. And one day, maybe she would. All she had to do was survive long enough to get back home.

Wiping her mouth and hands on the napkin, she carried the dish to the counter. "Here. Thank you."

Lily tsked. "You didn't have to clean up."

Jessica shrugged. "It's no problem."

The bell above the door rang and Jessica nearly jumped clean out of her skin. She whipped around and saw a middle-aged man stride in. Eyes wide, breath rasping in fear, she watched him walk over to the counter.

"Good morning, Lily."

So Lily *was* the woman's name. "Good morning, Will. The usual today?"

Will laughed and glanced at Jessica, who sidestepped away from him. "Of course."

"Just let me finish up with..." Jessica wasn't forthcoming with her name. Lily looked at her curiously, probably sizing her up as a rude American. "I'm sorry I didn't catch your name."

"Mary," Jessica lied.

"Mary is from America. Isn't that positively exciting?"

Will turned to Jessica and grinned. "An American? Where in the States are you from?"

Jessica was so consumed with irrational fear she could barely form a coherent thought. "New York."

The lie slipped easily from her tongue.

"How do you find our little town after coming from such a busy place?"

Jessica began to sweat. She wasn't prepared for conversation. She should have gone directly to the car rental office, hunger be damned.

"It's lovely." Her mouth ran dry even as the palms of her hands went slick with sweat. "How much do I owe you?"

After Lily tallied up her order and told her the cost, Jessica stuck her shaking hand in her pocket and pulled out the wad of cash. Peeling off a bill, she slapped it on the counter, hoping it was enough to cover what she'd ordered. She hadn't the slightest clue about the English pound.

Panicking, she snatched the white paper bag and raced from the teashop. Outside, she dragged in great gulps of chilly air as she glanced up and down the block, expecting Stephan's men to leap out from every store or alley.

Swallowing her fright, Jessica set off toward Crudwell Road. The bag clutched tightly in her grasp, she ducked her head and strode briskly down the street. A few people were now emerging from their homes, all going about their business without sparing her a glance.

But it was those few who did that terrified Jessica. Of course, she was too far gone in her fear to remember how odd she must appear dressed in clothes a size too big, her hair around a face sunken from near starvation and as pale as death. She didn't know how far-reaching Stephan's influence was. Anyone could be working for him, and it was that fact that had her close to hyperventilating as three big men, all bruisers by the look of them, talked among themselves in hushed tones as they walked toward her.

They eyed her and laughed, one going so far as to throw her a lopsided grin. The idea of being dragged to Penwick and thrown back in the dungeon had Jessica panicking. She ducked into a store as the group of young men barreled past her. She hid behind a rack of clothing, keeping her gaze glued to the door. She waited with bated breath for them to rush in and grab her.

Instead they passed right by the store.

Jessica tried to calm down but a tap on her shoulder scared her. Choking on a scream, she spun around and came face to face with an old man, who looked as startled as she was.

Hand to her chest as she fought for calm, Jessica met the man's concerned stare. "Jesus Christ, you scared me half to death."

"Well now, you gave me just as much of a fright." He took a step back and smiled. "I was just going to ask if I might help you with something?"

Jessica was about to mumble some excuse for why she ran in there like the devil was chasing her when she saw the kind of store she'd run in to.

She thought about Lucian stuffed into the clothes given to him by the innkeeper. "Actually, I think you can..."

හ)ශ

What was taking her so damn long?

Lucian was a pacer. Whenever he was aggravated he paced, but with his heel burnt, that was out of the question, which meant he had to sit there until it healed with no outlet for his agitation. Never a good thing for a man used to venting his frustration.

Flinching and holding in a hiss, he finally pulled off his boot. He'd been avoiding seeing how bad the damage was. Tossing the heavy boot aside, Lucian saw his entire heel was burned down to the bone. Given the severity of the injury, it said how caught up in Jessica he had been. Totally and completely lost in her. But then, how could he not be? She had been so open to him, matching his desire until he'd been nearly mindless with need. How he managed to regain control and pull away from her, Lucian didn't know. He credited it to centuries of honing his discipline so that in any given situation he'd be in full control of himself.

And still, Lucian had felt his restraint slipping. Just as it was now, waiting for her to return.

God damn it all. Jessica was long overdue to return and here he was, trapped in this building while she was out there, unprotected, for nearly an hour. Lucian's mind worked furiously, knowing anything could have befallen her. Not the least of which could be Stephan's men getting their hands on her.

Though it hurt like hell and took great effort, Lucian found his footing and limped around on his damaged foot, partly testing his foot and partly giving in to his compulsive need to pace. The injury, he assumed, would take a long while to heal without fresh blood to help it along. Walking was going to be a bitch and, given their circumstances, wasn't a good thing at all.

Lucian had gone on in battle with far worse injuries. So, biting back the pain, he continued to pace. His nerves were at a breaking point and if he didn't keep moving he'd do something foolish—like run out into the daylight in a desperate attempt to get to Jessica. He'd get all of five feet or less before the sun roasted him. Still, given how the wait for her to return was killing him slowly, the quick end by the sun would be far more merciful than what he was experiencing right then.

Of course, there was always the possibility that Jessica had taken the money and run. If that's what she'd done, she was a bloody fool. She wouldn't get far on her own. This was Stephan's world. He knew these lands inside and out. Jessica, on the other hand, had no idea where she was or whom to trust. She'd never outrun him or hide from him here.

If Jessica wasn't back by nightfall, Lucian had every intention of taking himself right back to Penwick Castle. Whether or not she ran from him was irrelevant. He'd not abandon her to Stephan. He was a Templar for God's sake, and with that title came a nobility renegades didn't possess and humans simply couldn't understand. It was inherent from their days of living as Knights Templar, still as much a part of him now as it had been in life.

Restless with anger and worry, Lucian ran a hand through his hair and made a limping pass across his tiny space. An odd chill ran through him. *Constantine.* Lucian felt Constantine as keenly as if he were standing right next to him. This was the second time he'd felt such a sensation. It left Lucian confused. There was no way Constantine would tread this land. The things Ulric Chambers had done to him ensured Constantine would never walk the ground where he'd endured such pain and shame.

That left the question of why he would sense Constantine here. And sense him so strongly. It had to be a result of his prolonged captivity. His time in the dungeon must have taken a toll on his mind. It was a hell of a thing to cage a Templar, especially after what they'd endured in Chinon. Sweet Jesus, he wondered if he'd ever forget the cheering of the crowd as the fifty of them, all the Knights Templar, burned.

He'd expected Hell. What he'd gotten, the fate *all* the Templar Vampires had received, was so much worse. They should have gone to Hell for continuing to take life in the name of God after losing faith. Instead, God had other plans for them. Being damned as vampires was both a blessing and a curse. It gave them hope of redemption even as they were forced to fight the instincts that came with this existence.

Lucian was on his last nerve when he finally detected Jessica. Relieved, Lucian peered around the boxes before he thought better of it. He growled and threw his arm over his eyes as he ducked back behind the tall stack of boxes.

Letting out a string of curses, Lucian knew his feelings for Jessica were making him sloppy. He couldn't continue to let that happen. Though he knew he couldn't be indifferent when it came to Jessica, he had to stay sharp or else he could get her killed—or worse.

Movement at the window told him Jessica was climbing through. He muttered a curse just before he heard a loud thud.

After some scuffling, she whispered his name. Answering her with a curt, "I'm here," Lucian had to refrain from shaking the hell out of her for having taken so long.

The aroma of fresh scones reached him. A vampire's body couldn't tolerate anything save blood. The smell of the scones reminded him of all the times he'd needed to force food down his throat in order to blend in somewhere—to appear normal—and how his body rejected it.

As soon as Jessica rounded the boxes, Lucian grabbed her by the shoulders and gave in to his need to shake her. Hard. The three bags she'd been holding hit the floor. Her jaw dropped in shock and a gasp caught in her throat.

"Damn it all, Jessica, what took you so long?"

His fangs were bared as he rasped out the words. Jessica stared at him wide-eyed with fear, but right then he didn't care how scared she was of him. She'd worried the hell out of him and it felt damn good to shake her.

She glanced at the fallen bags. "I stopped to get something to eat."

Though he understood she needed to eat—hell, he was just as hungry, only not for food—her reason didn't calm his temper. "Over an hour, Jessica." His voice was nothing more than an angry rumbling erupting from deep within him. "You've been gone for over an hour. Have you any idea how..."

His tirade trailed off into a frustrated grunt, unable to give voice to the path his thoughts had taken. Instead, he pushed off her with a mumbled complaint and retrieved her fallen bags.

Jessica snatched the white bag from him, hugging it protectively in the crook of her left arm. "I'm sorry I worried you." She motioned to the bags he held. "I picked up some stuff for us that I figured we'd need."

Lucian looked down at the bag, then back to her face again. Wind-blown and ruddy from the morning chill, Jessica was an enchanting sight. His anger began to abate in the face of her beauty and the weary look in her eyes.

"What is it?"

She shrugged slightly, still clutching her bag as if she feared he'd snatch it away from her at any moment. "Just a change of clothes."

Retrieving the dropped bags, Lucian opened one and rummaged through it. He found a dark gray long-sleeved T-shirt and pants. Both looked to be about his size. She'd even bought him boxers, something he never wore, but the thought she'd put into buying him clothes touched him.

Something among the clothes caught his eye. With a cocked brow, he reached his hand in the bag and slowly pulled out a black lace bra. "I assume this isn't for me."

Jessica turned an adorable shade of red and grabbed it out of his hands. "Here." She dug in her pocket and pulled out a handful of money. "I didn't spend a lot. There's still plenty left."

Lucian took it and tried to tuck it back into the pocket of his pants. Wasn't going to work. He couldn't fit air in there, they were so tight. He slapped it on top of a box. "Where did you park the car?"

She glanced over her shoulder and gestured with her chin toward the direction of the window. "Right where you told me to. Directly in front of the window so we can watch it. Or rather, *I* can keep an eye on it." She must have noticed him still favoring his foot. "How bad is it?"

"Not bad enough to hinder me," he lied.

Jessica rummaged through the other bag and pulled out more clothing. "I picked us up jackets. They aren't the most stylish, but I got them in a thrift store."

151

Lucian sensed something. He sensed a lingering fear in her. "Did anything happen that I should know about?"

She shrugged and plucked faded blue jeans and a plain black sweater out of the bag. "I thought three men were after me so I ducked into the thrift store." She smiled ruefully. "It turned out to be a blessing in disguise."

A chill of dread worked up his spine. "*What?*" His roar echoed throughout the old building. "You were followed?"

Jessica cringed. "No. I said *thought*. That's the key word. Obviously I wasn't or else I wouldn't be here, now would I?"

Lucian grabbed the black pea coat she offered him and threw it on the box where he'd put the money. He pulled Jessica into his arms and gave her a fierce hug. Surprisingly, she melted into him. He fully expected her to pull away, not needing nor desiring his comfort.

"I'm sorry you had to go out alone."

She said nothing for a long while, just slipped her arms around his waist and held onto him as if it meant life or death.

"It wasn't that bad. I just let my imagination get the better of me." Her words were muffled into his chest.

He ran his hand over her hair, loving the silken feel of it against his roughened palm. Lucian swore he felt his heart beat when she leaned into his touch. "I'll get you back home to your family, Jessie, I swear it. I'll get you back to your life and you can put this nightmare behind you."

And forget all about me, though I'll never forget you. I'll carry the memory of you with me for the remainder of time.

Of course, Lucian admitted that only to himself.

He loved the way she shuddered and gripped him tighter. "I know you'll find a way to get me home, Lucian. But I also know I'll never be the same now that I've..."

Her words seemed to die in her throat. Lucian leaned away from her and cupped her chin. He forced her to look at him. Unshed tears glistened in her eyes. All of her pain was laid bare in the reflection of her eyes. "You've stared into the night, Jessica, and had the night stare back."

"I guess if anyone would understand how I feel, it would be you. I can never put this behind me."

She gripped his shoulders and stepped up on her tiptoes. She rested her cheek against his and he felt it was wet with tears.

Her breath tickled his ear when she whispered words to him that would haunt him until the stars burnt out.

"I'll never forget you, Lucian. Never."

ಬಂ

Jessica meant what she'd said. She'd never forget Lucian, and not only because he was part of the nightmare she'd found herself caught up in.

Standing in the circle of his embrace, Jessica knew something profound passed between them. It ran so much deeper than the kisses they'd shared and far beyond their imprisonment together. It was the unexplainable force suspended between them that left her breathless.

Lucian stared deep into her eyes, and for a moment, Jessica swore he saw clear to her soul. "Don't you want to change out of those clothes?"

Lucian didn't immediately answer. Instead, he replied with a slow nod, all the while keeping his gaze locked on her. Suddenly shy under his close scrutiny, Jessica reluctantly stepped out of his arms.

She offered him a smile as she handed his clothes to him. "Here. I promise not to peek."

His expression told her he might not mind her peeking—or doing more.

Though Jessica gave him her back, a part of her desperately wanted to go against her word and sneak a peek at Lucian. But then she recalled how he'd never violated her privacy during their time in the dungeon. She'd been forced to do everything in that cell. Everything. All she had been able to do was pray Lucian hadn't added to her shame by watching her. He assured her he hadn't, but honestly, it had been pitch black. Only he had been able to see through the dark. She had no guarantees he hadn't sneaked a peek. All she had was his word and, given what Lucian had proved to her thus far, his word was enough for her to believe him.

She heard Lucian strip off the tight clothing and drop it to the floor, cursing the entire time. She nearly smiled as her imagination took flight. She saw him vividly in her mind's eye, working off the feel of his nude body next to hers last night.

Everything about Lucian was hard, unyielding, and cold. Now that she'd seen him, she knew no man would ever measure up to his looks. No modern man could possibly have the same...medieval quality Lucian possessed. His rugged looks, the graceful way he moved, even his baritone voice stood out among the men of today's world. What he had couldn't be learned or faked. It was something he'd acquired growing up in the time he had, and surviving the things he had.

Jessica had felt his strength and the tight rein he had on his control each time he kissed her. Just thinking about his mouth on hers caused a wonderful tingle to settle in the pit of her stomach.

Jessica snapped out of her thoughts when Lucian barked her name. She turned and was met by the sight of Lucian standing there in his new clothes looking handsome as all get out.

"What?"

"You were just a million miles away."

Given where her thoughts had taken her, Jessica blushed hotly. "I was just thinking, that's all."

"Obviously." He gave a brief glance down at himself. "Thank you for the clothes."

His voice sent pleasant chills dancing down her spine. "You're welcome."

Jessica loved the way the gray T-shirt molded to Lucian's upper body and arms, hugging every muscle like a second skin. The pants, casual black slacks, cinched tightly around his trim waist and fit to his thick thighs. Her friend Lori would definitely label him boyfriendly, which meant he was boyfriend worthy.

If only he were minus the fangs and plus a soul, Lucian of Penwick would definitely be boyfriend material.

"We'll need to be on the move as soon as the sun sets." She nodded, expecting nothing else. "I need to feed before we leave town."

She eyed him warily. "I figured you might need to."

"You aren't to be more than a few feet from me at all times. You do understand what that means, don't you?"

Jessica most certainly did and she was having none of that. "Lucian, I really don't think..."

He braced his legs apart and crossed his arms. It was an aggressive stance if she ever saw one. She was also unmoved by it—and the frown that went with it. "This isn't up for debate."

"No, it's not." She raised her chin a notch, daring him to argue with her. "I won't be there when you do that. I can't, Lucian. I can't see you do that."

A fleeting look of sympathy flashed across his face. "And I can't leave you alone."

Jessica wasn't going to budge on this. She simply couldn't watch Lucian feed. "Please don't ask me to witness you feeding. Please."

Lucian closed the space between them and ran his knuckles down her cheek. Almost all thought fled Jessica's mind at his gentle touch. "All right, Jessica. I won't ask this of you."

"Thank you." She ducked her head, knowing she was being unreasonable about this, but knowing if she saw Lucian feeding it would be something she'd never *unsee*. Every time she looked at him, that's what she'd see. "I mean...after we kissed and everything..."

The ghost of a smile pulled at his lips as her sentence trailed off. "Jessica, love, if we'd done *everything* you'd still be beneath me doing it."

Chapter Twelve

Though he had to be in agony, Lucian didn't betray a hint of pain as he walked with her down the street. In fact, Jessica had to practically run to keep up with his fast pace as he led her to a pub he'd spied the night before. Nor did he complain about the way she clutched at his hand, squeezing it hard enough to turn her own knuckles white with the force of her hold.

True to his word, as soon as the sun had set, they'd quit the warehouse. In fact, Lucian was the one who woke her just before the warehouse was engulfed in almost complete darkness. Jessica had barely come fully awake before he was dragging her toward the window and hefting her out.

Now that they were out in the open, Jessica felt the same sense of vulnerability take hold of her as this morning. She glanced over her shoulder at their rental car, wishing to God they were already driving away in it. But then she thought about Lucian being in the throes of bloodlust, and knew they needed to delay their escape long enough for him to feed.

Jessica fought her revulsion at the idea of Lucian drinking blood, something she felt every time he'd done so while they were in captivity. She'd seen Lucian drink blood from a cup, had witnessed him taking it from dead rats, she'd even seen him lap it up from the floor after Stephan tossed a cupful at him. Yet she'd never had to watch him drink from a human. Just the idea of him doing that made her skin crawl. It brought her back to the times when Stephan had bitten her.

Her body still hurt from the things he'd done to her. She was still weak from the blood he'd robbed from her, even though Lucian had given her some of his to help heal her. It had only done so much. It couldn't take away all the hurt—or the memories of what had been done to her.

The sting in her side told her the injury that should have killed her wasn't completely mended. Nor were the bite marks that ringed her neck. Most of them were scars now and would act as a constant reminder of her time at Penwick. How she would explain away those marks to people once she returned to her life, she just didn't know. Nor could she think about that now. Not with the possibility of being caught and taken back to Penwick looming over them like a dark cloud.

Jessica must have been squeezing Lucian's hand because he squeezed back and smiled at her—a tense grin, devoid of humor.

"Easy, Jessie. We'll be away from here soon."

"I hope so." She shivered as a gust of cold air blew over them. "I feel as if they're going to jump out at us from every shadow."

Lucian obviously didn't need to know who they were. "From what I can sense, Stephan's men aren't near. I'll take care of my business as quickly as possible and we'll be on our way. I promise."

Jessica glanced at their rental car parked in front of the warehouse. The farther they walked from it, the larger the pit in her stomach grew. She wanted to get in the car and drive away from here, putting as much distance between themselves and Penwick Castle as the night would allow. Every moment spent here heightened their chances of being found by Stephan's men and being taken back to Penwick.

After they came to the pub, Lucian took a moment to peer in through the glass door before pulling it open. As he ushered her inside, Jessica was struck by the overwhelming odor of smoke and stale beer. Never one to frequent the bar scene back home, the strong smells had her gagging and wondering how anyone could enjoy hanging out in a place like this. Especially after she scanned the pub and saw more than a few grizzly old drunks staggering around.

The lively scene of locals already lost in their pints seemed to crash to a momentary halt as Lucian pushed her toward the bar. The men cast suspicious looks his way while the women seemed mesmerized by Lucian's looks. Not that Jessica blamed them. Lucian was too handsome for them not to be struck dumb by the sight of him.

By the time they'd reached the bar, every eye was on them, making Jessica wish the floorboards could swallow her up. Never one who liked being the center of attention, she ducked her head and tried to ignore their stares. Lucian, on the other hand, seemed oblivious to the way everyone watched him. But then, given his looks, size, and the air of authority and arrogance he had, he was probably used to such attention.

Sliding onto a stool, Jessica glanced down the bar at a big bear of a man practically inhaling a thick sandwich. Her stomach growled as she stared at him. He stared back, and she thought he'd call her out for being so rude. Instead, he gave her a wide grin, revealing a mouthful of bad teeth.

The bartender came over to them and Jessica stopped ogling the man at the other end of the bar. "What can I get for you, mate?"

"Nothing for me." Lucian reached into his pocket and slapped a few bills on the bar. "Just give her whatever she wants."

Jessica wasted no time in asking for whatever it was the man was eating. After the bartender went off to prepare her order, Jessica noticed Lucian admiring a group of five women sitting around a table. They were drinking and laughing and, every now and again, sneaking admiring glances at Lucian. One woman, bolder than the others, actually winked at him. Jessica found that incredibly rude given the fact that they were obviously together. At the same time, she knew their appreciation of him would make it easy for him to feed.

Lucian wondered if Jessica realized how easy it was going to be for him to feed. Given the way the women were blatantly staring at him the lot of them would make for easy prey. Returning a smile to the woman who winked at him, he knew it wouldn't take much to persuade her outside where he could feed from her.

Hunger dulled his senses, making it difficult to focus on anything other than the bloodlust. He wouldn't waste any time easing his victim into the feeding. He'd take the attractive blonde outside and feed as quickly as he could without being sloppy and bringing her undo harm.

Though his senses weren't as sharp as they needed to be, Lucian was still able to detect something ancient and mystical. It made the air heavy, drenching it in magic. It was the same sensation he'd experienced the one time he'd been in close proximity to the First.

Remembering this was Druid land, he reasoned that, with Samhain being only days away, it made sense for the First to be here. He'd even thought to go to her to seek aid, but being indebted to the Order of the Rose was a predicament no Templar wanted to find himself in.

The urgency of hunger forced Lucian from Jessica's side. "Stay here. I'll be back shortly."

"Wait." Jessica's hand clamped onto his forearm.

He cocked a brow and looked into her large, frightened eyes. "What is it?"

She swallowed hard. "I'm afraid."

Her whispered confession sliced through him cleaner than a blade. He covered her hand with his, noting how her eyes darted to the brand it bore, and leaned in close to her. "Don't be afraid, Jessica. I'll be right outside."

She slipped her hand out from under his. Sitting there with her head bowed, her hair came forward to shield her face. "Hurry back."

The beseeching tone in her voice twisted at his gut. Right then, he would have done anything—sacrificed anything—just to be able to erase that expression from her face.

The bartender returning with her food was a welcomed distraction. "Go on and eat, Jessie. I'll be right out in the alley if you need me."

The sudden dryness of his mouth and the sharp stab of hunger told Lucian he'd better get this done before the bloodlust overtook him. He turned away from Jessica, leaving her looking lost and lonely at the bar, and stalked over to the group of women. Keenly aware of Jessica's gaze on him, he strode toward the blonde and gave her the same cool, guarded grin he did to all of his victims.

He heard her heartbeat race and felt the breath she released as he held out his hand to her and pulled her up against him. The smell of perfume stung his nose. He heard the giggles of her drunken friends. He paid them, and the woman's offensive scent, no heed.

"Care to elaborate on the looks you keep giving me?"

Lucian concentrated on the sound of her blood rushing through her veins and not on the weight of Jessica's stare boring into his back. He tried to be glad that the woman had eagerly accepted his offer as he pulled her from her chair and led her out of the pub.

Once he had her outside, he pushed the woman against the wall of the pub and pressed his body against hers. Lucian wished she were Jessica and not this strange woman he was about to feed from.

He grabbed a fistful of her hair, yanked her head back, and unceremoniously sank his fangs into her neck. She whimpered and squirmed in his arms but he held her firm. For a moment, Lucian thought he'd hurt her and almost pulled back and let her go. But when she exposed more of her throat to him and moaned, he knew he hadn't inadvertently harmed her in his haste.

He pulled on the woman's neck and drank in her blood with a growing sense of betrayal toward Jessica. No matter how hard he tried to push the feeling aside, there it was. As her blood slipped down his throat and traveled through his body, one word screamed through Lucian's mind.

Jessica.

ഇ⊘ൠ

Though Jessica wasn't new to jealousy, she'd never known it to cut her so cleanly as it did right then. She had no reason or right to feel jealous, and yet the pain bore right through her heart.

Unfortunately, it wasn't only jealousy nagging at Jessica. Disgust that Lucian was feeding on the woman was just as prominent. Neither emotion sat well with Jessica. She tried to excuse away her feelings by telling herself she didn't like that he'd left her after he made damn sure she understood she was not to leave his side. After that failed to work, she tried to tell herself it was because the girl's friends were having a good laugh at her expense. Women could be so mean and catty. It made her appreciate her small circle of friends all the more.

After months of suffering humiliation at Stephan's hands, she *really* wanted to lash out and vent her emotions on those women. Of course, it would bring undo attention to herself and Lucian, so she swallowed her pride as the women made fun loud enough for her to hear and finished her sandwich.

Her next excuse for feeling so emotional was hunger, which she dismissed as soon as she finished eating and found herself still suffering such turbulent emotions. The food hit her stomach like a brick, sitting there as she made a desperate attempt to think about something other than Lucian outside with that woman.

Her one last attempt to explain away her jealousy—and hurt—was stress. That one seemed to work since it made the most sense. Stress. Yes. That was it. Stress was why the thought of Lucian's hands and mouth on that woman had Jessica dangerously close to tears.

She'd tried not to care about Lucian. Jessica tried not to see past the fact that he was a vampire to the man he obviously struggled so hard to remain. She didn't want to see him as anything other than a monster. Yet over the past months his honorable actions made it impossible to see him in the same light as she did Stephan.

Her excuse of stress was proven wrong a moment later when Lucian returned. He came in hand in hand with the woman, who wore a dreamy expression. Jessica hated to admit it, but she looked every bit the well-pleasured woman. Jessica swore she wasn't envious, she was merely stressed and that was why she wanted to slap that look of sexual satisfaction clean off the woman's face. She also noted that the woman bore no mark of what Lucian had done. There were no bite wounds on her neck. No blood anywhere on her. It wasn't like when Stephan had used her.

But then, it had been Stephan's intention to hurt her. Jessica doubted Lucian would do that to the women he fed from. Her assumption was confirmed a moment later. The woman stumbled back to her friends and made the slurred announcement that Lucian's lips were magic.

Disgusted, Jessica rolled her eyes and looked away, but not before she saw the woman collapse on a chair and fan herself. Whatever else she said was, thankfully, spoken in a whisper too low for Jessica to hear. Lucian reached her and went to place his hand on her shoulder but seemed to think better of the idea. Instead, he rested his palms on the bar and stared straight ahead. Something on his jaw caught her attention. Jessica realized it was a smear of blood.

She picked up her used napkin and went to wipe it away. He jumped back a foot. "I don't want you to touch me."

Jessica cocked a brow and tossed the napkin at him. He caught it, obviously puzzled. "You have blood on your jaw. I suggest you wipe it off."

After taking her advice and wiping the blood from his chin, Lucian curled the napkin in his fist. The hard glint in his eyes scared her, as did the rigidity of his stance. He was making every effort not to look at her, which was fine by Jessica. He slammed his fist on the bar and she actually found herself recoiling from him.

"We're leaving."

Jessica didn't need to be told twice. She wanted out of there—and away from the town—in the worst way. She hopped off the high stool and, without thinking, slid her hand into Lucian's. Only after he stiffened and she thought he was going to pull away did it dawn on her what she'd done.

They were almost at the door when Lucian's food—or rather the woman he'd fed from—leapt from her chair and practically bounded into him. She threw her arms around his neck, forcing him to drop Jessica's hand, and tilted her head back so she could stare up into his face.

"You're leaving with her?"

Her accusation was slurred from a mix of ale and whatever it was Lucian had done to her and accented with a stab of a finger at Jessica. Standing so close to the woman, Jessica noticed the glazed look in the woman's eyes, her pasty complexion, and the faint bruises on her neck—too faint to notice if you didn't know to look for them. But she knew. She knew all too well.

The woman was also shivering, something else Jessica knew too much about. It was the cold that came from having blood taken. That cold was unlike anything Jessica had ever known prior to landing in Stephan's dungeon and it was something she knew she'd never forget.

"I'm afraid so. We had fun, did we not?"

The woman smiled dreamily. "Now that's exactly why I thought you'd leave this one here." She tried to cut Jessica down to size with a nasty look. It didn't work. She'd been through too much to be laid low by this woman's glare.

Suddenly everything about Lucian changed. He went stock-still, his muscles straining before going stiff. Jessica went sick with dread when Lucian finally looked at her. "We have to go. Now."

His expression was unreadable, and yet she knew just by the way he stood it was bad. Very bad. "How close?"

"Too close."

"Oh God..."

With a quickness that astounded her, Lucian snatched her hand in his and pulled her toward the door. Jessica glanced over her shoulder to see the woman fall to the floor in a faint. The ruckus of her collapse spared them the attention of the occupants in the pub who crowded around her. It afforded them enough distraction for Lucian to drag her out with a speed that would not only startle most—but also would raise too many questions and bring them undo attention.

Panic lent Jessica the ability to run faster than she ever had, allowing her to have an easier time of it trying to keep pace with Lucian. Still, Jessica stumbled behind him as he moved through the night with an agility that bespoke his inhuman state.

Racing down the street, Jessica could have sworn she felt the devil himself at their heels. Even after they reached the car, she felt the brush of death across the nape of her neck.

Lucian opened the passenger door and shoved her in before hurrying around to the driver's side. He paused for only a moment, staring out into the night. She watched him inhale deeply and look to the left. He got in and started the car. He made sure she had her seatbelt on, told her to hold on, and slammed the car in gear. Jessica did exactly as he said—she held on tight and thanked God they were getting the hell out of there.

℘)(℘

Bloody hell—that had been too close.

Almost too late, Lucian had felt the presence of renegades. The prolonged hunger and the raging emotions emanating from Jessica had clouded his senses, making them dull and unfocused, just as they had been back when he'd first been damned. Those first months had been a hellish experience as he'd tried to control his new abilities. He'd been sloppy and a danger to himself and others. With Jessica depending on him to get her back home, he couldn't allow himself to be that undisciplined again.

Glancing at Jessica, who held fast to the bar on the door with one hand while the other bit into the armrest between them, he knew she had no idea how close they'd come to being found by Stephan's men. Looking back out of the windshield at the road stretching before them, his body hummed with the borrowed life from his victim. He fought against the desire that ripped through him, focusing on the world around him and not on Jessica. He was sure he'd left the renegades behind. Nevertheless, he pushed the car to its maximum speed, putting as much distance between them and Malmesbury as he could before they were forced to stop for the day.

Since this was the first time he'd seen Wiltshire in centuries, Lucian couldn't help but steal quick glances at the countryside as they sped down the darkened road. He remembered traveling down this same spot on horseback as he rode away from Penwick Castle with Guy Sinclair's army. He never expected to return on foot. He'd come back here, bringing death with him.

Back then he'd left with the blood of his father thundering through him, lending him the strength to make it to Seacrest. Lucian had arrived more feral than even Constantine had been. Tristan's family had accepted not only Tristan, but all of the Templars. The Beaumonts gave them more than sanctuary. They'd given the Templars a home.

Even after Tristan had gone off to Damascus in Pennsylvania, the rest of the Templars had remained in Northumberland. God had called them to Seacrest, and it was there they would wait until it was time to join Tristan. They would have all gone together, but the temptation of the relic Tristan guarded was too great for them to have resisted all these centuries. It was a miracle Tristan had resisted it this long with his sanity intact.

Lucian was next in line as Guardian should anything happen to Tristan. It was a burden that sat heavily upon Tristan's shoulders and one Lucian hoped to never have.

"Lucian?"

Jessica's voice jarred Lucian out of his thoughts of the past and what was to come. Brought back to the present, he barely spared a glance at Jessica, instead focusing on the road.

"What is it?" he asked curtly, still angry with himself for nearly getting them caught.

Out of the corner of his eye, Lucian saw Jessica lift herself up and look over the seat to glance out the back window. "Are they following us?"

"No." She sagged back down with a relieved sigh. "But they will be."

Jessica's fear rolled over him, strong enough that he shifted uncomfortably in the seat. Her emotions were raging, bombarding him. Fear and jealousy were the most prominent. Fear, he understood. Her jealousy baffled him.

"Do you think we'll make it to the next town before they catch up to us?"

"We should, but in the event they catch up with us, I'll hold them off long enough for you to..."

"To what?" Jessica interrupted, her tone heavy with panic. "Drive off into the night with no clue where I am or how to get to Seacrest? I don't think so. I won't have you playing hero and leaving me alone. Sorry, pal, but you're stuck with me."

Being stuck with her was the last thing Lucian was worried about. It was renegades overtaking him and getting to her after they took him out that worried him. "Easy, Jessica, I'm not that easy to get past."

Though he offered her a grin, she returned it with a scathing look that told him she didn't appreciate his attempt at humor.

"You'd better not be. I don't want to go back there."

There, he knew, was Penwick. "Once you're back in Damascus, I want you to go to Seacrest castle. Touch base with Tristan. He'll protect you should I fail in stopping Stephan."

Jessica assumed Lucian meant that to reassure her, yet all it did was heighten her doubt and fear. She didn't want Tristan to protect her. She didn't want any Templar besides Lucian to protect her. But more importantly, she didn't want Lucian to fail. She wanted Stephan dead—and to stay dead this time. Though it was bloodthirsty of her, after everything Stephan had put her through, she wanted to see him reduced to dust.

She tried to imagine more vampires like Lucian. "How many Templars are there? Are you guys infinite, like the renegades?"

"No, not infinite. There are only five of us."

She wasn't expecting that. Given what she'd learned of renegades, they were so great in number they were everywhere. Infesting the world, quietly slaughtering innocent humans under the cover of night. It was a chilling concept, knowing no matter where she went, they'd be there.

"If there are only five of you, how do you fight all the renegades?"

"Carefully."

Again, not the answer she was expecting. She didn't want something quite so flippant. "What about the Obyri that Stephan mentioned? Are there as many of them as there are renegades?"

Lucian speared her with a sharp glare before turning his attention back to the road. "Leave it alone, Jessie."

The cold glint in his eyes warned her she shouldn't push him on this. The smart thing to do would be to heed his warning and let the matter drop. Unfortunately, it was something Jessica couldn't do. After all she'd been through, she deserved to know certain things—namely anything that might put her in further jeopardy.

"I can't do that, Lucian. I'm part of this now and I think I deserve to know what's going on."

"The Obyri have nothing to do with this."

Jessica placed a hand on Lucian's arm and felt the strain of his muscles. By the way he gripped the steering wheel until he was white-knuckled told her this was an extremely sensitive subject.

"I'm afraid, Lucian. I'm afraid that even if we make it back to America, I'll always wonder about unknown threats hiding in the shadows. The least you can do is prepare me for what's out there so that this will never happen to me again."

From the change in his expression, Jessica knew she'd gotten through to him. Lucian sighed heavily and relaxed his grip on the wheel. "After being held at Chinon Castle for three years, fifty of us Templars were burned to death. God saved five of us and offered us one chance to earn our way into Heaven. We became Templar Vampires. But there were others who were taken from death as well, only not by God. Lucifer promised them eternal life in exchange for the relic we protect." He looked at her and his sad smile pulled at her heart. "They agreed to steal from God to be spared the torture of Hell."

Jessica shook her head in disbelief. True, she'd always believed in God and the devil, Heaven and Hell—but to be confronted with the reality of Christianity made her mind spin.

"So, these Obyri were Templar Knights too." He nodded, his gaze locked on the road. She saw the sorrow in his expression and it broke her heart. "I'm sorry they betrayed you."

"They didn't betray me." Lucian glanced at her and his pain was there in his eyes. "They betrayed God. All we can do is make sure they never get their hands on the relic."

Jessica smiled and let out a small laugh. "I don't suppose you're going to tell me what the relic is, are you?"

He shook his head and gave her a small smile. "No, I don't suppose I am."

That much she could understand. Some things she knew simply were for him to know. It went beyond Lucian keeping secrets from her. Nevertheless, she certainly had her suspicions as to what the relic the Templars guarded was.

Settling in her seat, Jessica didn't let go of her death-grip on the armrest and the bar on the door. As long as Lucian was driving at over one hundred miles an hour down a dark and winding road with no headlights on—not to mention the fact that at any moment a carload of renegades could come speeding up behind them—she was going to keep holding on and praying they reached their next destination in one piece.

The silence that stretched between them was as thick as it had been in the dungeon. What went unsaid was what had taken place at the pub. Not wanting to dwell on the woman's dreamy expression or the way Lucian didn't want her to touch him, Jessica stared out the window and wished she was home.

Chapter Thirteen

Though Jessica didn't want to think about the night Stephan had kidnapped her, she couldn't control her dreams. In her sleep, she relived the feel of Stephan's hands on her and of his fangs each time he'd bitten her. She could actually feel him drawing on her vein, taking the blood from her as he fed. She felt her strength fading, felt her life leaving...

Her own screams woke her. Jessica bolted upright and rubbed her eyes in an effort to clear away the fog of sleep. She gazed around the hotel room and tried to calm her rapid breathing as the last of the memories of that awful night faded from her mind.

"Easy, Jessie, it was only a dream."

Jessica shook her head before dragging her hands through her tangled hair to move it away from her sweaty face. "No, you're wrong. It was real."

"Come here, Jessica."

Jessica looked to her left. Lucian lay next to her on the bed, which was covered with a stained green spread. He held his arms out to her and, God help her, she fell into them. Fell into them and grabbed onto him, holding him as if letting go would mean her life or death.

And she wept. Her cries came from deep within her, from where she kept her fear of death and desperation to get home.

They were pulled from her in great heaves as tears flowed unchecked. As she cried, Lucian held her, his cheek resting against the top of her head. With one hand he held her to him. The other smoothed through her hair. He whispered words of comfort to her all the while, accepting her tears as he offered her kindness that touched the core of her heart.

With her tears spent, Jessica eased her hold on Lucian. She laid her head on his chest and wished she heard a heartbeat there. He was cold, still, lifeless. Yet he existed. More than that, there was something about Lucian that was gloriously alive. The way he moved, talked, everything about him drew her in and held her captive.

He smelled clean, having headed right for the shower the moment they'd entered this windowless room. His demeanor after he'd fed told her he was as miserable with having to feed as she was. He'd been slightly more at ease after his shower. While he'd been in there, Jessica had practically inhaled the food they'd picked up for her before they'd reached this remote hotel.

With its painted cinder walls, filthy rug, and stained green bedspread, this room was still a world of improvement from the dungeon or the cave. It would provide the perfect place for them to spend the day. Best of all, Lucian assured her he sensed no renegades, which meant they could rest peacefully here for the day.

If only her dreams weren't haunted by the memories Stephan had put in her mind...

"Feel better?"

"No," Jessica admitted. "I hate crying. It solves nothing."

He laughed, causing his chest to rumble. "Most women like to cry."

"True. But I've never been that way. My father taught me better than that."

The thought of her father made her heart hurt. He was a strong man. To her, he seemed invincible. He'd taught her to be strong as well, to stand tall in the face of adversity. The lessons she'd learned from him had her surviving this long.

Her mother, however, was the embodiment of all things feminine. Petite and beautiful, her mother was the exact opposite of her manly father. The two made for an adorable couple. Their type of relationship was one Jessica hoped to have with the man she married.

"Your father did you a great service in that lesson."

Yes, he did. "If he'd been born in your time he'd have been a great warrior."

Lucian's hand was soothing as it passed through her hair. "I'm sure he would have been. Only a great man could have given life to such a daughter."

Jessica swore her heart skipped a beat at the marvelous compliment. "I'm sure the same can be said about your parents."

Was it possible Lucian had gone even more still? "They were...remarkable people."

Her hand went to the scar over his heart. She wondered how he'd gotten it. Given that she knew he'd burned to death, she wondered how he'd survived such an injury. Unless he hadn't survived it. Had he received the wound after he'd been turned?

The questions Jessica had far outweighed what she knew of Lucian and it frustrated her. Here she was, their lives—such as they were—intertwining, and she knew next to nothing about him.

"What's it like to be a vampire?"

Lucian's hand stilled in her hair and there was no mistaking how tense he became. "Imagine your worst nightmare. Now bring it to life. *That's* what it's like."

She knew he was tortured by what he was. The evidence of that was there to see once she knew what to look for. "I'm sorry I treated you badly while we were at Penwick."

And she meant that. She felt horrible for how hostile she'd been in those first weeks toward him. And then after—she'd been cold. Not that anyone could blame her for her behavior. But now, it just seemed wrong since Lucian was...nice. No, he was more than nice, he was...

Exactly what she imagined a man she could fall in love with to be.

Lucian grunted and hugged her tighter. "There's nothing to apologize for."

She unwrapped herself from the cocoon of his arms and came up on her elbow. Staring down at him, Jessica was amazed at how handsome he was. From his Roman nose to the mysterious gleam in his glowing silver eyes, she found every nuance of his face ruggedly beautiful.

But most of all, Jessica liked Lucian's mouth. Full and demanding, his lips woke in her a passion that both thrilled and scared her with its intensity.

Acutely aware of the way he was staring back at her, Jessica leaned toward him. He hissed and placed his hands on her shoulders to hold her at bay. Not to reject her, but to warn her.

"I can't, Jessica." His expression was pained. "If we start this, I don't trust myself to stop."

"So don't stop."

Lucian slid his eyes closed at her invitation. He'd never wanted anything more than he wanted to take what Jessica was offering.

Need thundering through him, he fisted his hands in her hair and dragged her head toward his. He didn't hold back. Instead, what raged in him flowed from him to her as he took her mouth in a kiss that was as raw as it was desperate. He gave her his desire and she accepted it with the same strength she'd shown in captivity.

She moved her hand down his body until it settled on his hip. Her fingers bit into his flesh when their mouths opened and their tongues met. He fought against the insecurities that came with his lack of experience. Instead, he focused on Jessica's taste, scent and touch. She intoxicated him, pushed him toward a place he was afraid once there, he wouldn't want to leave.

He liked the feel of her light panting breaths fanning his cheek. Her thundering heartbeat was musical. Jessica kissed with the skill and confidence Lucian knew he lacked and hoped she didn't realize it. As he fought to keep his raging body in check, he felt the way she pressed herself against him, as if seeking more of him. Lucian was only too happy to comply.

The need to possess her, to take all Jessica had to give, had him repositioning them so that he was over her, grinding into her as he deepened the kiss. Under him, Jessica pressed up into him and Lucian felt his restraint crack, but not shatter. He was still in control of himself, though for how long, he didn't know. With all of her filling his senses, he knew he'd break and centuries of desire would come bursting forth.

Her delicate touch on his bare back had his body jerking and then needing more. Her fingers continued to dance lightly over his back, pulling a groan from somewhere deep within him. She met his groan with a soft sigh that he relished.

Needing to taste her flesh, Lucian pulled away from her mouth and trailed his tongue over the pulse of her throat. He expected her to move away, shove him off her—anything to get him to stop. Instead, her hands tangled in his hair and she pressed his mouth more firmly to her.

Her abandon and acceptance of him was almost more than Lucian could bear.

"Take it away, Lucian. All of it...please."

He knew what she was asking. It was the same thing he'd begged God for countless times over the centuries. She needed him to erase the memories haunting her.

"I'll take the memories away for both of us."

Lucian took a moment to simply look at her and marvel at her fragile beauty. Though shadows darkened her eyes, her cheeks were hollowed, and her complexion wan somehow, Jessica was captivating. He doubted anything could diminish her beauty.

She parted her lips and reached for him. He didn't fall into her arms, as she obviously wanted. Instead, he inched her shirt up. She stiffened and he asked if she wanted him to stop. She shook her head shyly and admitted she was nervous. He nearly laughed at that. *She* was nervous? He hadn't known a woman, not in seven centuries. Though his prowess in battle was without question, his skills with a woman were nonexistent.

For once, he was grateful for all the tales Raphael had carried back to him about his sexual conquests. They just might help him here tonight.

At his hesitation, Jessica sat up and moved his hands aside. She took hold of the bottom of her shirt, and slowly slid it off. Inch by gorgeous inch of her was bared as she removed the offensive piece of clothing and tossed it aside.

She wore nothing else, having come to bed after her shower in only her shirt. Her nudity robbed him of reason as his hands went to her almost with a will of their own. He hissed at how soft her skin was when he ran his palms over her shoulders. She licked her lips, and then parted them, a whisper of breath escaping them when he brushed over her pale pink nipples.

He shook as he knelt before her, his hands trembling as he touched her. "You're so beautiful."

She shook her head and looked away. "No, I'm not."

Lucian trailed his hands down her sides, drinking in the sight of her bare flesh. How could she not see her own beauty? "Never have I known a woman more beautiful than you."

He looked into her eyes and saw they shone with unshed tears. "Oh God, Lucian, make me remember what it is to live."

Back in his day, Lucian doubted the women in his social circle would have been as wonderfully bold as Jessica. Every woman he'd ever known lacked the one thing Jessica seemed to possess in spades. *Life.*

There was nothing still or quiet within her. Her soul sang to him and it was the sweetest music he'd ever heard. Her body resonated with life. No woman he'd encountered in all his centuries affected him as she did. She gave him back life, though he hadn't taken a drop of her blood.

Jessica threw herself into his arms. Her body, warm with life, was a contradiction to his. Yet here she was, begging him to make her remember life. And then her mouth was on him and all Lucian knew was the feel of her beating heart and the warmth of her that flowed into him. At Jessica's surrender, his past faded away. Stephan wasn't a threat shadowing them. Even his damnation and his oath to God failed to matter.

Her life hummed through her and into him as they knelt on the bed in each other's arms. Their mouths came together in a kiss hot enough to spark an inferno. The flame moved through him, and emotions he knew he had no business entertaining followed in its wake.

Her nails, jagged from her time in captivity, scraped his flesh as she clawed his back. He hissed at the mix of pleasure and pain. He dragged his mouth from hers and Jessica whimpered. He released her hair, relishing her gasp as he moved his mouth down her body. He laved her collarbone and she writhed in his arms. His erection strained against his pants at her reaction to him.

"Oh God," she said on a breathy sigh and dropped her head back.

"I want to devour every inch of you."

Her lips curled into a smile that shook him to the core. "And I want you too, but not until you take those off."

She gestured to his pants, the only clothes he'd donned after his shower. How Lucian kept his hands from fumbling in his haste to pull down the zipper, he didn't know. He felt like a clumsy youth, all thumbs and no grace. With Jessica watching him, his awkwardness seemed that much more shameful. Although, to look at her, she didn't seem to notice the way his hands shook or how he struggled not to tear the pants from his body and dive back on top of her. In fact, her eyes, wide and watchful, were filled with appreciation as he pushed down the denim jeans.

Once Lucian had his pants off, the confidence he'd always known on the battlefield was nowhere to be found. How strange that he had faced down entire armies without so much as a moment's hesitation, and yet, standing naked before Jessica, he felt bared clear to his blackened heart.

She watched him with eyes hooded with desire as he climbed back onto the bed. Jessica stretched her arms out to him and Lucian went to her. He pushed her down and spent long moments admiring the sight of her. She did the same with him, her eyes missing nothing, lingering the longest on his scars. He nearly got up and put his clothes back on, thinking how unappealing he must seem to her. His body was terribly flawed, the skin puckered and twisted in certain places. She had to be repulsed, especially since she made no attempt to touch him.

He went to move off her. Her hand clamped around his wrist. Her frown was fierce. "Where are you going?"

"I should have warned you. I don't know what I was thinking."

Now, she simply looked confused. "Warned me about what?" And then she paled to at least a shade whiter than she'd already been. "Oh God, you're not...you don't want to...feed...do you?"

It was his turn to be confused. "No, of course not."

She relaxed visibly. "Then what should you have warned me about?"

He cast a brief glance down at himself. "My body."

One brow cocked as her gaze traveled over him. "What about it?"

"The scars. I should have told you I was scarred."

Her hand fell away and she looked at him as if he'd lost his mind. "You're kidding, right?" He shook his head, baffled that she seemed almost annoyed. She sat up. "Lucian, I've seen your body...well, maybe not *all* of it. But I've seen enough to know you were scarred."

"You don't find me displeasing?"

"Now I *know* you're crazy." Her laughter filled the room, dying off as she turned serious once again. "No, I don't find you displeasing. I don't think any woman would. Lucian, how can you not see how gorgeous you are?"

"I wouldn't know about that." He shrugged with an indifference he didn't feel. Not with her words sending warmth through him.

She ran her hand down his chest, over his scars. Her light touch had him sucking in a sharp breath. "Well I do, and you're magnificent."

Jessica leaned toward him and wrapped her arms around his neck. She touched her lips to his and Lucian was lost. He touched her all over her body, loving the feel of her beneath his palms. Her skin was warm and soft. The calluses he'd earned from centuries of wielding a sword made her flinch, but she didn't pull away. No, not Jessica. She thought him magnificent, even as callused and scarred as he was.

Instead, she pressed closer against him and sighed into his mouth. He pushed her backwards until she was again lying on the bed. He settled over her, the heat and wetness at the juncture of her thighs pulling a groan from him.

The sweet scent of her arousal was an added torment his body reacted almost violently to. She brought her leg up and wrapped it around his waist. His entire being trembled with need at the feel of his cock nestled at the opening of her body. She encouraged him by lifting her other leg to hug him tightly around the waist. He lifted his head and stared intently down at her. Jessica stared back with eyes hooded and unfocused.

"Are you sure, Jessica? I have to know. I have to hear you say you want this."

Her nails grazed his back, causing him to jerk. His back arched, pushing the very tip of him into her. His forehead dropped down to hers as his body ached for more.

"Oh God, yes, Lucian. I want this."

That was all he needed to know. Her acceptance had him pressing into her with a gentle thrust of his hips. He entered her and was immediately hugged by the warmth of her body. As he inched into her, he strained to hold himself back. He fought not to plunge into her as his body screamed for him to do. Her erratic heartbeat and sweet moans had him pressing deeper still, until he reached the depths her body would allow.

Lucian ground his teeth together once seated within her. His fangs cut his lower lip but he barely paid them any attention. He gazed into Jessica's eyes and saw trust in them. With her body squeezing him and her gaze cutting through him, Lucian acted purely on instinct. He began to move, the sensation of sliding into her body was unlike anything he'd ever known, and so much more than he could have ever imagined. He closed his eyes and finally let himself go to enjoy being inside of a woman for the first time.

Thank God it was Jessica he was experiencing this with.

Lucian opened his eyes as he thrust into her. He wanted to take in every nuance of Jessica's expression as he took her. Her hair framed a face flushed with desire. Her lips were parted, an invitation he couldn't resist. He pumped into her as her body contracted around his. She pulled guttural groans from him that blended with her breathless moans. She whispered his name brokenly. He sensed her coming release and knew his own wouldn't be too far behind as he took her with a savagery he wished he'd been able to control.

But Lucian was beyond control. He was beyond anything other than the feel of Jessica's warmth. She gouged deep trails into his back with her nails and released a cry that resonated around them. Her body tightened around him, her muscles flexing—coaxing him toward his own climax.

Lucian's body erupted within her, giving him his first taste of perfect pleasure.

The bloodlust followed in its wake. Somehow he managed to bite it back as his body continued to pump out his release until he was spent.

After smoothing Jessica's hair away from her sweat-dampened face, Lucian kissed her tenderly on the forehead. Her eyes were half-closed and her lips swollen and red from his kisses. Her heart hammered loudly, her breathing erratic. She placed her palm on his cheek and smiled dreamily up at him. It wasn't merely pleasure of the body Lucian experienced, it was a pleasure far beyond anything he could have ever comprehended.

It was the closest he'd come to remembering what it was to have a soul since the day he'd died.

Chapter Fourteen

"This is unacceptable." Stephan leveled a glare at Vincent, a throwback from the Italian Renaissance. "There's no excuse for my brother and that wench getting out of Malmesbury."

Stephan noted, with no small measure of satisfaction, that Vincent had the good sense to be afraid. As well he should be. The Italian was dangerously close to being reduced to ash for his incompetence.

"I don't know how they could have slipped past me, my lord. I picked up their scent at an inn and followed them to a pub." Vincent glanced away, his clasped hands trembling. He was obviously waiting for his death. "Lucian had obviously fed from one of the locals."

Narrowing his eyes on Vincent, Stephan was barely able to hold back his fury at that bit of news. No doubt, with fresh blood in him, Lucian's strength had returned. That would prove to be a problem. "And where is this woman now, Vincent?"

"Upstairs, my lord."

Stephan smiled slowly. By bringing the woman here, Vincent had saved himself. "That's something at least." He'd have the chance to spend his fury without sacrificing any of his men to do so, and he'd rebuild his strength through the woman's blood. "I'll take no more failures. Is that understood?"

He cast a hard stare over his men, relishing the power he had over them. They outnumbered him, were obviously stronger than him, and yet they trembled before him. To have such control over men was the mark of a great leader. His father had been such a leader of men. And though he harbored no false delusions that his band of mangy vampires loved him as Penwick's garrison had their lord, it was enough to have their fear. Through their fear of his savagery, he'd gained the power to control them. And through their strength, he'd captured Lucian.

He'd done so once, he'd do so again.

The four men gathered in the hall bowed their heads in proper submission under his critical scrutiny. "Get you gone. All of you." They scurried out. James, who leaned against the wall, too weak to stand without aid, made no move to go. "I said all of you."

A fleeting look of surprise crossed James's face. He moved away from the wall and, on unsteady legs, made his way out of the keep. Hopefully he'd go to the garrison and take one of the humans they kept there to feed from. He'd need James at full strength once Lucian was brought back.

And Lucian *would* be brought back.

Stephan would not rest until his brother was found. He'd not let Lucian go, not after finally having him and coming so close to extracting revenge for their family.

Putting a hand to his throat, Stephan knew revenge wasn't the only thing he'd come close to. His destruction was another. He'd underestimated Lucian. Stephan had believed his brother didn't have it in him to end him. He'd not make that same mistake twice.

If Lucian had cut a few inches deeper, Stephan knew he'd be in Hell right now, and not trying to figure how to recapture his goddamned brother.

After seven hundred years of savagery, Stephan knew Hell was his only option. He found it odd that having been so devout in life, he'd come to terms with his fate with little regret. He comforted himself with the knowledge that his family was with God. That certainly got him through the nights when their deaths came back to haunt him. Their screams echoed in his ears—or did they still resonate within these ancient walls? He could no longer be sure. All he knew was that there were nights he swore he saw them moving through the castle or heard their whispered voices calling to him.

Lucian was to blame for all of this, and once Stephan had him back here, he'd make sure that his brother knew there were worse places to be than Hell.

Since Heaven was forever denied him, there was no need for Stephan to hold back the cruel urges that came with being a vampire. With wild abandon, he'd cut a terrifying path through history that began the very night he'd been reborn as this...*thing*.

His acute hearing heard the musical sounds of whimpers coming from his chamber. Unable to resist what awaited him upstairs, Stephan climbed the stairs and walked toward his room with a growing sense of anticipation.

He spotted the woman immediately. She was sprawled out on her back across his bed. Her arms and legs were spread wide and thick rope bound her wrists and ankles to the bedposts. She was pretty enough, with her large brown eyes filled with fear and tears. She'd do nicely, even if Lucian had already used her.

His smell on her was nauseating. Stephan smiled coolly, his senses telling him Lucian had only taken her blood and not her body. But then, he knew Lucian remained untouched. His brother had held to the teachings of the church and had not lain with a woman out of wedlock. That his brother continued to abstain in death only proved to Stephan how hard Lucian fought for redemption. It was why it was so important for Stephan to break him.

The woman struggled on the bed, crying behind the gag over her mouth. Her nude body was beautiful to behold as she fought against the ropes that bound her. "Hush now, love."

Stephan closed the distance between them and removed her gag. Much to his surprise—and disappointment—she didn't scream. "What do you want from me?"

Her breath was foul, stinking of ale and fear. Stephan would have gagged at the stench had his body had the ability to do so. He placed a finger over her lips. He didn't think he could take more of the smell.

"I need information."

She nodded frantically. "Anything." His finger slipped from her lips. "I'll tell you whatever you want to know. Just don't hurt me."

Stephan smiled. "I know you will. You'll be a good girl and tell me everything, and then this will be over and you'll go home." He wiped away her tears. "You were with a man tonight, weren't you?"

She nodded again, her simpering grating on his nerves. "He was with a woman, but none of us paid her any mind."

Her Cockney accent was thick and her voice abrasive. He found it highly offensive. Or was it the fact that Lucian's touch was on her that irritated him?

"But he went outside with you."

"Yes."

"And what did the two of you do?"

She appeared baffled. That infuriated Stephan. "We went outside, and then next thing I knew we were back in the pub."

Stephan jumped on the bed and grabbed a fistful of hair on the top of her head. Her scream aroused him. "And then what happened?" She was obviously too afraid to talk and he was having none of that. "Answer me."

"He left." Her voice held a note of hysteria. "He left with the woman."

"Did you hear them say where they were going?"

"No." He tugged on her hair and she gasped. "They just left in a hurry."

Stephan leaned in low and growled. "So then you're no use to me, are you, love?"

She swallowed hard as fresh tears poured from her eyes. "Oh God, please don't hurt me."

His rage exploding, Stephan backhanded her. She gasped at the impact. Her lip split and blood burst from the cut. He dragged his finger over her lower lip before licking the blood from it.

"Say the Lord's name again to me and I'll make your death last for days."

"Yes." Her sobbing nearly made the word unintelligible.

He slapped her to shut her up but that only pulled more cries from her. As Stephan crouched over her, he felt the weight of his parents' stares on him. He swore he could actually feel them in the room with him. The sensation brought back the memory of the night Lucian returned to Penwick. No matter how he tried to shove the memories away, there they were, invading his mind in a barrage of sights and sounds.

Lucian had dragged his battered body through the gates of Penwick, bringing his evil with him. In a fit of mania, he'd attacked their father. Stephan had rushed Lucian, distracting him from their father. He'd taken the brunt of Lucian's violence, his brother coming close to killing him.

The garrison had managed to take him down, though they'd been unable to kill him. Their swords stunned him, but failed to end him. Knowing they had a devil in their midst, the soldiers fought Lucian back. Once they had him out of the gates, Lucian had run. But evil came back.

Other vampires had come to finish what Lucian had started. They killed the servants, and then the garrison. With no one else left, they'd forced Stephan to watch as they'd slaughtered his parents.

Before they left, they'd turned him. He never saw the vampire who'd done it. By the time the vampire exchanged blood with him, he'd been unconscious and on the edge of death. Even after so many centuries, he still didn't know why he'd been turned and who had done it. His guess was the vampires who'd attacked Penwick had wanted to see if it could be done. Once they'd used him to experiment on, they'd left, leaving a bloodbath in their wake.

Stephan had awakened covered in blood, confused, and in agony from hunger that twisted at his gut. His mouth had been so dry he'd thought he'd rip his own tongue out in sheer frustration.

And then he'd smelled it. Blood. Everything he was screamed for it. He'd run from Penwick to Malmesbury. There, he'd fed from the first woman he'd encountered. In a mindless feeding that caused him to tear her apart and drain her dry, he'd felt the power of life—and of his death—surge through him. He'd walked away with a strength he'd never known in life and an awareness of the world around him that took years to learn to focus in on.

He released the woman's hair. She'd made a bloody mess of her wrists and ankles by fighting against the ropes. He continued to feel the disappointed stare of his parents on him. With a grunt, he leapt from the bed. He didn't spare another glance at the woman before he slammed out of the chamber. Her screams followed him down to the hall and filled him with satisfaction.

James was there. He was still nursing his wounds. The Scot perked up when he saw his master.

"My lord?"

Stephan ignored James's questioning stare. He stalked from the hall and out into the courtyard. The frigid night air hit him hard. He remembered the screams of his mother and the empty look in his father's eyes after those monsters tore his throat out.

Lucian was to blame for that, and for the pain Stephan was forced to carry with him all these long centuries. He'd stop at nothing until he made Lucian pay for that night. And then he'd wipe the stain of his brother from this world.

Chapter Fifteen

While Jessica showered, she couldn't stop the dreamy smile that kept creeping across her face. There had been something so—different—about sex with Lucian. Not that Jessica had much experience to compare him to. She'd been with only two men before Lucian, and those had been mediocre experiences, to say the least.

There had been something untamed in the way Lucian made love to her. He held nothing back, while at the same time, it was almost as if he were experiencing a woman's body for the first time. In fact, Jessica sensed something that came remarkably close to awe when he'd climaxed. In that one moment, they'd come together in body and emotion, but the feeling had been fleeting and she was sure, after they were finished, it had been nothing more than her imagination.

But now, thinking clearer since the fog of sexual satisfaction had lifted, she knew it had occurred. She'd sensed, for just a moment, what Lucian had felt. She was sure his pleasure heightened her own. It had been amazing, something she knew she'd never forget and something her body already craved more of.

Yawning, Jessica was bone-weary. No matter that she'd slept a good ten hours—most of which had been spent in Lucian's arms—she was still exhausted. Her mind felt like mush and her body wanted to give out. Or was it give up? She was so exhausted and emotionally spent, she wasn't sure. All she knew was that her legs didn't want to support her and they still had days of running ahead of them.

Washing the shampoo out of her hair, Jessica wondered if it was possible for her to ever feel clean again. Not that the feeling was bound to happen here, in this disgusting hotel room. She missed how immaculate her mother kept their house, especially the bathroom, with its guest towels no one was allowed to touch and the frilly pink accents her father always griped about. Her father's gruff demeanor didn't fool Jessica. He loved how Carmen made their home look like a dollhouse. He might not openly admit it, but Jessica saw the way her father's adoring gaze lingered over her mother as she ran around tending to her family. It was adorable to witness such a big bear of a man get love-struck each time he set his gaze on his tiny wife.

The affection her parents shared was something Jessica wished to have one day. Although, given the direction her life had been forced to take, she wondered if that dream was now lost to her. How could she put aside these last months? She couldn't. No matter how much time passed or where her life's path took her, this would always be with her. Haunting her. If she even made it home. Though she had faith in Lucian, that he'd stop at nothing to deliver her safely home, there was so much standing in the way—namely Stephan, who was equally determined to drag them back to Penwick.

Though Jessica hated to admit it, she understood why Lucian was reluctant to kill Stephan. All she had to do was think of her brother, Anthony, and she knew why Lucian had allowed his brother to do the things he had. The only time Lucian fought back was when Stephan threatened her. She wondered what Lucian had done to earn Stephan's hatred.

Whatever it was, it had to be bad enough to fuel Stephan's fury for centuries. As much as she tried to imagine what it could be, every time she looked at Lucian it was difficult for her to envision him doing something so horrible. Not after he'd shown her only kindness.

Having woken an hour ago, Jessica hadn't even made it off the bed before Lucian snapped awake and asked if she was all right. She'd kissed his lips and assured him she was fine. He'd fallen instantly back to sleep, stretching out beneath the bedspread. His lips parted and, in the light of the small lamp they'd kept on, Jessica saw his fangs. She marveled at how careful he'd been with them while they'd kissed. It would have been all too easy for him to hurt her, not only with those fangs, but with his strength as well. Yet he'd been gentle enough that Jessica hadn't thought about *what* he was, only *who* he was.

Lucian. Not a vampire. Not a damned Templar Knight. But a man who'd shown her what it was to be worshiped.

As she soaped herself, Jessica avoided looking down at her body. She didn't want to see the scars left behind by Stephan. Instead, she thought about Lucian. He'd taken away the pain of the last months and replaced it with pleasure. Her body stirred at the thought of his hands and mouth on her and the way his body had felt beneath her touch.

There was no denying that Lucian had spent his nights keeping his body in battle-ready condition. He was taut, the muscles unyielding. He flexed and moved with every thrust into her, and all Jessica could do was hold on to him as he brought her body to epic heights.

Washing away the soap, Jessica caught sight of her body and cringed. The scars were the least of her problems. She'd always been thin, but now she looked skeletal and she wondered if she'd ever flesh out again. Bones protruded where there had once been curves and contours. Her skin was pasty and ashen. She looked as dead as the vampires whose world she'd been forced into.

Her shower finished, Jessica stepped from the tub and made sure she kept her feet on the towels she'd laid out on the floor. She wrapped a towel around herself and hopped around as she put on her socks and sneakers. What a sight she must make in nothing but a towel and shoes.

Since Lucian was still sleeping, Jessica tiptoed back to the bed. He surprised her by sitting up and giving her a lazy grin. His gaze traveled over her, stopping at her shoed feet. He lifted a brow at her sneakers.

"God only knows what's growing in this rug."

"True," he conceded. He made a face that told Jessica he smelled things she couldn't. He probably saw things her limited human vision couldn't, too. She was sure she should be grateful for that. "You smell nice."

The simple compliment sent chills through her. "The rank stench of dungeon really wasn't my scent."

He smiled wider and his fangs peeked out from behind his lips. "Your sense of humor is astounding."

As she moved to the clothes thrown over the radiator, Jessica tested them to make sure they were dry. She collected everything save their pants, which were still damp. "What other choice do I have but to keep my sense of humor?"

"You have other choices." The intensity of his gaze unnerved her. "You could lose yourself in fear."

She shrugged, catching the towel when it went to slip off. "Because losing my shit would help, right?"

He laughed at that descriptive observation. "No, it wouldn't. But it's how most people would react."

"Like I said, my father taught me better than that." She climbed on the bed and kicked off her shoes. "And speaking of things taught... I'd love to thank whoever taught you to do that thing with your tongue."

"And which thing would that be?"

Jessica crawled up next to him and knelt. "You know what thing. The one that made me scream."

Now Lucian's smile was purely devious. In one swift motion, he ripped the towel from her and tossed it aside. One arm snaked around her waist and he drew her up against him. His tongue cut a chilling path over her neck and Jessica moaned. "That one?"

"No, but it will do, for now."

"I'm pleased you enjoyed my lovemaking. I improvised as best I could."

Jessica pushed away and tucked herself under the sheets, not quite as free with her nudity as Lucian obviously was. "I don't understand."

"I've never known another woman."

Well now, that was a bucket of cold water thrown over her head. "Excuse me?"

"You heard me just fine."

He reached for her breast but she slapped him away. "You don't say something like that and then think it's going to just pass on by. Are you saying you were a virgin?" He nodded curtly. "Are you serious?"

"Decidedly."

She pushed out of his embrace and donned her bra and shirt. "But...what about the women you've fed from?"

His frown marked his confusion. "What about them?"

"I'd assumed that you had sex with the woman from the bar."

"Jessica," he replied patiently, "even if I'd had the desire—which I didn't—I lacked the time."

That much was true, she conceded. Lucian proved he liked to take his time. Or had he taken his time simply due to the fact that it was his first time. Jessica's head spun at that fact. His first time. Impossible. The man had been around since the 1300s.

Not to mention, Lucian had been one hell of a lover. He knew exactly what to do to bring her body to climax. He hadn't been fumbling or hesitant. He'd possessed such confidence that it diminished her own. Given that poise and certainty, it was only natural for Jessica to assume many—many—women had come before her.

"So, you're a seven-hundred-year-old virgin?"

He nodded, and Jessica didn't know what surprised her more, that he was an expert in bed or a virgin.

"What's so hard to believe? My family was devout. The laws of the church were ingrained in me since the day I took my first breath. My faith ran so deep that it was only natural for me to go off on Crusade." Jessica didn't miss the change in Lucian's expression. His pain was raw and it killed her to see. "When I joined the Order of the Templar Knights, my oath involved me becoming a monk. The least I could have done after breaking every promise I made to God was to keep my body pure."

The very least.

Lucian's guilt at having made a mockery of every promise he'd sworn to God festered within him even now.

After witnessing and committing atrocities in the name of the Lord, Lucian had given up his faith. He had no use for it after killing a child in the name of God. He'd filled the emptiness that followed with violence, blood, and bitterness. He hadn't realized how far he'd fallen from grace until the day he'd died and faced an archangel.

For continuing to kill in God's name even after losing faith, he—along with the other Templars—was damned. They were given one chance at redemption, and it was one they held fast to night after night. Should one of their brethren falter, the other four were there as a reminder to stay their course. It wasn't always easy, but somehow, they'd managed to get this far. And since they'd gotten this far, none of them were willing to fail now. Hell wasn't a prospect any of them relished. One innocent kill was all it would take to break a Templar's oath to God.

"How in the world did you—refrain—all this time?"

Jessica's voice brought Lucian back to the here and now. "With great difficulty, I assure you."

He turned so that she was facing him. She tilted her head to regard him oddly. "Why me?"

Lucian smiled at her blush. She looked away, twisting the sheet in her hands. She turned shy at the oddest things, he realized, especially after he'd devoured every inch of her body—just as he'd promised he'd do.

He gripped her chin and licked his lips. He wanted her again. "You are the one temptation I couldn't resist."

Her blush deepened. He thought her adorable in her uncertainty of her own appeal. "You can't be serious."

"I'm very serious."

In the span of one moment to the next, Jessica's expression went from bemused to concerned. "Can I ask you something?"

He smiled and ran his finger over her bottom lip. He ached to kiss her, but would allow her the time to ask him her question before giving in to his desire. "Of course."

"Can I...can we...a condom. Do we need to be using a condom?"

Though he may have been a virgin, Lucian wasn't ignorant to sex. He knew exactly what she was asking. "No, we don't need to be using a condom. My body can't carry disease and I can't make a child."

This being the first time he'd ever said that aloud, that admission brought with it a flood of grief and regret.

"I was just wondering, that's all." She stroked his face, her light touch reaching into him to where his soul once was.

He smiled at her shyness. "I know."

He leaned into her and felt her anticipation as she waited to see if he would kiss her. She was different now that she was out of captivity. There was life to her that had been painfully absent in the dungeon. It went to show just what Stephan had robbed from her by imprisoning her in the dark.

Now that he'd had a taste of her, Lucian was unable to resist the feel of her mouth against his. He brushed his lips over hers, taking the chance of losing himself in her even though they didn't have the luxury of lingering. They needed to leave as soon as the sun set if they planned on taking advantage of every moment of the night to travel.

As soon as their lips met and Jessica sighed, he took her in his arms. Her body melted into his, making him wonder how he'd gone so long without the glory of her life to give him a relief from the dark.

He'd never desired another woman. True, he'd often craved sexual satisfaction, but devotion to God and guilt had given Lucian the strength he'd needed to deprive himself. He'd given up wondering what sex would be like centuries ago. The emptiness that came with not knowing the touch of a woman had eventually faded. He'd believed he'd be able to spend eternity without ever knowing it—and he might have been able to uphold his oath of abstinence. But then Jessica had opened herself to him and he knew he'd never be able to go on without her without feeling the loss of her as keenly as he did his soul.

‸) ℅Ƨ

They left the grubby hotel less than an hour later. Jessica once again sat next to Lucian as he sped down a narrow road traveling north.

Jessica wished she had the chance to see England bathed in sunlight. She wondered what it would be like to see this land without the threat of death shadowing them. She imagined the English countryside must look much as it had in Lucian's day. The roads seemed to be the only visual reminder of the passing of time, adding a touch of modernism to this land steeped in ancient history.

Music played low on the radio as Jessica tried to make sense of the map. Giving up, she folded it neatly and stuffed it back in the glove compartment. How strange it was to be on the opposite side of the car. It threw her off and had made driving the car back to their hideout in Malmesbury a hellish experience. Only the fear of being caught had enabled her to drive down the town's streets alone.

A glance at Lucian told Jessica he seemed to know where he was going. Her trying to read a map and give him directions would probably only steer him wrong. One bad turn could very likely get them killed, so Jessica just gave up trying to follow the map.

"Sorry, but map reading was never one of my skills. I'm an expert at pulling into a gas station to ask for directions, though."

Lucian's laugh was a rich, deep sound that touched every part of her. He swept his hand wide in the direction of the windshield. "That won't help us here."

No, it wouldn't. They were in the middle of nowhere. Only the large pale moon and the low glow of the control panel broke the dark surrounding them. This darkness, unlike the blackness of the dungeon, seemed intimate. Private. As if the rest of the world were far away. It was actually comforting and calming.

She hunkered down in the seat and slid a glance at Lucian. That he had been a virgin still baffled her. She understood his reasoning, and was awed by his resolve. She knew women had to have thrown themselves at him over the centuries. How could they help themselves? He was such a handsome man it was difficult not to be overwhelmed by his looks.

Since feeding seemed such an intimate act—Stephan's treatment of her not withstanding—that Lucian never took it further said much for his self-control. Basically, the man was a rock, and that he'd called her the one temptation he couldn't resist woke emotions in Jessica that confused her as much as they thrilled her.

Remembering the state of the woman Lucian had fed from, Jessica turned to Lucian. "Can I ask you a question?"

"Of course, Jessie."

She loved when he called her that. No one else did, which made it only his name for her. "Why did it feel good for that woman when you fed from her but it hurt me when Stephan..."

She couldn't finish the sentence. Her hand instinctively went to her neck, her fingers moving over the scabbed puncture wounds left behind by Stephan's bite.

Lucian's hand settled over hers. Such simple contact soothed her. "I make sure it doesn't hurt them."

That admission brought a realization to her. "So, Stephan deliberately hurt me."

"He did."

She wasn't at all surprised. Had she expected anything less of the bastard? He'd made it clear he wanted Lucian's soul in Hell and was using her as a means to get it there. Any pain she suffered would only be an added bonus to him.

Well, if Stephan's men *did* catch up with them and they were brought back to Penwick, Jessica wasn't going to give Stephan the satisfaction of breaking her or using her to damn Lucian's soul. Because she'd be as good as dead if that were the case, she'd find a way to provoke Stephan to kill her before Lucian could. At least if she went by Stephan's hand there was a chance Lucian might be spared Hell.

Chapter Sixteen

Jessica rethought her noble stand when she and Lucian arrived at another motel where they'd be able to spend the day. If he just killed her now it would the merciful thing to do. After all, death had to be better than spending the next ten hours holed up in this room.

Although this motel room wasn't as bad as the one from yesterday, it was still grimy and disgusting. The brown rug had seen better days, the wallpaper was peeling, and it was doubtful the television worked, given its cracked screen. But the bed looked relatively clean, which was a bonus since Jessica couldn't wait to get some sleep.

After giving the room a reluctant sniff, she realized it even had the same funky stink. The mix of must and dirt turned her stomach, making the thought of food nauseating.

Behind her, Lucian kicked the door closed and dropped the bags. Jessica peered into the bathroom, relieved to see it was actually clean, a pleasant surprise given the condition of the room.

Glancing at Lucian, Jessica felt her devilish side coming back after months of suppression. She walked up to him, stood on her tiptoes, and grabbed him by the back of his head. She dragged him down for a kiss that had him growling low in his throat.

She pulled away and raked her gaze over him. "When I get out of the shower, you're mine."

Lucian pulled her back when she went to walk away. "I'm already yours."

Oh God...

Jessica's heart skipped a beat as a wonderful thrill shot through her at the implication of his words. She leaned into him and rested her chin on his chest. Looking up at his face, she marveled at the glow of his silver eyes. There was so much emotion shining in them and yet his expression was completely unreadable.

With a tilt of his head he indicated the room. "It should only be for a couple of more nights and then you'll be back home sleeping in your own bed."

That was a good thing, right?

Then why did Lucian's assurance make her heart hurt? Why was the thought of being home with her family and away from him painful?

Jessica caught her bottom lip between her teeth and chewed on it as she stared at him, hoping once they got back to Damascus it wouldn't mean the end of things between them. She didn't want it to end like that. Hell, Jessica didn't want it to end at all.

That made no sense to her. She shouldn't want it to go on. Logic told her it was for the best if they parted ways once they were back in America. She had a life to live and the reality was Lucian wouldn't fit into her world.

She released her lip. "I know."

"You could put more enthusiasm into it." He shook his head, clearly bewildered at her less-than-cheerful response. "Don't you want to go home?"

Jessica pushed away from him but he caught her and pulled her back.

"Of course I do."

Lucian smoothed a hand through her hair. "What aren't you telling me, Jessie?"

"Nothing."

"You're lying. I can sense it." He kissed the top of her head, bringing her dangerously close to tears. "Now tell me what's troubling you."

What good would it do to deny what he probably already knew? "I'm scared."

He looked incredulous. "Of what?"

She shrugged, and this time he let her go when she pushed off him. "Of facing my family after...after everything."

He leaned back against the wall and ran his hands through his hair. Of all the things she could have said, that was the one thing he wasn't prepared for. It hit too close to home.

Lucian had felt the same way after he'd woken in Medina. During the arduous trek to Penwick, he'd often wondered how he'd face his family. He'd found the answer the hard way—by arriving home on the verge of madness.

It had never occurred to Lucian that Jessica might be experiencing the same fear and doubt. "What do you think they'll do, Jessica? Reject you?"

She laughed, though it lacked humor. "My family? Absolutely not. It's me." Her hand moved to her scarred neck. "I'm afraid I'll never fit in again in that world."

"You'll find your place back in that world."

She stopped and faced him, her tears finally released. Lucian moved to grab her but she shook off his hand. "Will I,

Lucian? How? How will I find my place after everything that happened at Penwick?"

Bloody hell, he wished he had answers for her. "I don't know. But you will. You belong with your family and eventually you'll put this all behind you."

Jessica dropped her hand and tilted her head to the side. The scars left behind by Stephan's bites ringed her neck and caused fury to ignite within Lucian. "Until I look in the mirror. I'll never forget what your brother did to me. And I'll never forget you."

Lucian closed his eyes as her words ran though him, chasing away the fury and replacing it with emotions he'd never known he could feel. "You're wrong. You will forget me and you'll find happiness."

A cry escaped her and she sank to the floor. Lucian was at her side in a blur of motion. "I don't want to forget you. I'm afraid of going home and never seeing you again."

Everything within him ached to swear she'd never be without him. Now was the time to tell her how completely he loved her and how they'd find a way to be together.

He wanted it to be him she spent her life with, his children she bore. If he closed his eyes and thought about it, it wouldn't be difficult for him to envision a daughter who bore a striking likeness to her mother and possessed the same strength of spirit.

Such a future wasn't possible and he shoved the idea out of his mind, though the pain of wanting it remained in his heart. He'd never be able to have such a life with Jessica. She'd go off to live her life and he'd go off and exist in his death—but he'd never forget and forever ache for what he could never have with her.

But he said none of that, unwilling to make her promises he couldn't keep.

He was a Templar. Night after night he fought to escape the sins of his past and earn redemption. The time of their greatest battle would soon be upon them. That fight was either going to free them from the threat of Hell or condemn them for eternity. Lucian refused to drag Jessica into his world of damnation and darkness.

He cupped her tear-streaked face, burning to kiss away her sorrow. "There's so much to go back to, Jessie. You have a family and friends who love you and are worried to death about you. All this," he waved a hand through the air, "will fade with time."

If he could, Lucian would take in every drop of her misery. He'd take the memory of the past three months from her, giving her back the innocence she'd had before Stephan forced her into their world.

Only after she'd spent her tears did Lucian help Jessica to her feet. He watched the change take place in her. She squared her shoulders, wiped the tears from her face, and gathered her pride around herself—just as he'd seen her do countless times in the dungeon.

She grabbed their bag and retreated into the bathroom, where she spent the better part of an hour. He'd heard the shower running for most of that time, the spray of water doing nothing to drown out the sounds of her muffled sobs.

By the time she returned to him, Lucian saw Jessica was back in control of her emotions. Wrapped only in a towel, she sank on the bed, crawling toward him. He opened his arms and welcomed her in his embrace. She flipped her damp hair away from her face and settled against him. Her contented sigh moved through him like a warm wave.

"I'm sorry for crying all over you again."

Lucian kissed the top of her head. "There's nothing to apologize for."

Before he'd gotten into bed, he'd removed his clothes. Though he was painfully aware of the fact she wore only a towel, his lack of clothing had been unnoticeable. That is, until Jessica began to stroke his chest. With every pass of her hand over his flesh, Lucian's need for her intensified. It didn't take long before he stripped the towel from her and tucked her beneath him.

Her warmth eased his cold and the life radiating from her countered his lifetimes of dwelling among the dead. He settled his mouth over her neck and lost himself in the taste of her flesh. Her nails scored his back and she let out a whimper but didn't push him away when he scraped his fangs over her. The bloodlust was almost too much to bear and he nearly pushed off her. If she hadn't stopped him with gentle pressure on his back, he'd have fled.

Instead, she moved her hands to his hair and held him to her throat. She whispered she trusted him, her words ripping a groan from him. He didn't trust himself, yet Jessica was putting her faith in him. Didn't she know how close he was to losing control? The taste of her was pushing him toward madness as he dragged his tongue over the gently pulsating vein. Her heartbeat mingled with the roar of blood rushing through her.

He craved to bury himself inside of her, to drive into her until his past was gone—until the guilt he'd carried for the last seven hundred years poured out of him. Lucian needed the relief from his past found only with Jessica.

He wanted to be with her in every way that a man can be with a woman, even though he knew that was impossible. The ache of needing her turned to pain, yet he held back, wanting to savor this time with her while he could. Just the small sensation of her skin brushing against his robbed him of reason.

Excitement rushed through him when he captured her mouth with his. Her taste, the feel of her skin against his, and her breath on his body had Lucian surrendering himself to her. He lifted his head and positioned himself over her. Lucian kept his gaze locked on her face as he entered her in one long, slow thrust. Jessica's lips parted on a sigh as he seated himself in her. The soft and feminine sound mingled with his grunt as pleasure washed through him.

The warmth and moisture that hugged him brought a pressure that threatened to push him beyond control. Every stroke was deeper and warmer than the one before. Lucian needed release. He needed to ease the pressure building within him. Only centuries of training for battle gave him the strength to hold back. A few seconds of ecstasy wouldn't be worth bringing the pleasure of being inside Jessica to an end.

The longer he held back, the greater the pain. He gritted his teeth hard enough that his fangs sank into his bottom lip. The taste of his blood was bitter in his mouth. Growling, he pulled out of her. Panting, sweating, Jessica cried out and tried to drag him back on top of her.

"Don't worry, Jessie, I'm not done with you yet."

Lucian turned Jessica around and, with a hand on the small of her back, gently pushed her down onto her stomach. The glance she gave him over her shoulder was one of the most erotic sights he'd ever seen.

He dragged his gaze down the length of her, taking in every nuance of her. Her beauty was a physical assault on his senses.

Easing himself over her, Lucian slid back in. The altered motions helped him to hold back until he felt her body tense.

Her breathing quickened. She arched her back, allowing him to sink even deeper into her.

Jessica's body tightened around him. She clawed at the sheets and raised herself up to meet his thrusts. She cried out her release and Lucian stopped fighting to hold himself back.

The sensation worked its way through him. It inched down his spine, settling in his cock a moment before he found his own release.

It came hard and fast upon him. Lost to the ecstasy of it, Lucian grabbed Jessica's hair and roughly pulled it aside, baring the column of her neck. If Jessica hadn't screamed and bucked wildly beneath him, Lucian might have done the unthinkable and taken her blood.

Roaring, he leapt off the bed, ashamed at what he'd nearly done. Jessica sat up, dragging the sheet with her. Even though he'd come dangerously close to violating her, she smiled at him. Her lazy smile taught Lucian what true agony was.

How could she smile at him? Didn't she see him for the monster he was?

And then Jessica held her hand out to him and he swore he felt his soul move through him.

"It's okay, Lucian. Come back."

"I can't." His voice was no more than the rumbling growl of an animal.

"Please come back to me."

Unable to deny her—or himself—Lucian walked back to the bed. Jessica opened her arms to him. He gathered her in his embrace and forced her down onto her back. "I'm sorry."

She reached up to stroke his hair. Lucian leaned into her touch and stared down at her. He'd never forget her expression. He'd take the sight of her with him into eternity.

"There's nothing to apologize for." Her small smile caused a new sort of ache within him, one he couldn't explain. "You didn't hurt me. A monster wouldn't have stopped, but you did. That's why I trust you. I know you would never hurt me."

Lucian hadn't hurt her, but he'd come too damned close for his peace of mind. If she hadn't stopped him, how far would he have gone? Would the bloodlust have completely taken him over? Would he have been able to stop once he'd tasted her blood?

Those doubts were a brutal reminder of how far he needed to keep himself from her once he returned to Damascus.

Chapter Seventeen

They were running dangerously low on gas. Too low to continue driving much longer down the endless stretch of road separating them from their next refuge.

The last gas station they'd come across had been hours ago and, from the look of the area, it would be a long time before they reached another.

Lucian banged his palm against the steering wheel and growled with frustration after glancing in the rearview mirror. A car was coming up fast behind them. In it, he sensed two renegades. Normally those were fair odds, but a quick glance at Jessica was a cold reminder that now wasn't one of those times. All it would take was for Lucian to have one moment of distraction for Jessica to end up in harm's way. That chilling fact had his foot slamming down on the gas pedal to push the black Ford as fast as it would go.

Not fast enough, obviously, since the car behind them was steadily gaining on them.

From the corner of his eye, Lucian saw Jessica grip the bar across the door—aptly nicknamed the oh-shit bar—panting with terror. Not good. He couldn't lose her to panic now.

"Breathe, Jessica."

"I'm trying." She turned to him and he stole another look at her. He saw the raw terror in her wide eyes. "But until those bastards are off our tail this is the best you're going to get."

He hadn't lied to her yet and he wouldn't start now. "I doubt we can lose them." He gestured toward the windshield with a nod of his head. To her, he knew, there was nothing to see since her eyes couldn't cut through the dark. But he saw the straight strip of road and the flat, open land on either side of it, leaving them nowhere to run and nowhere to hide.

"Oh God..."

"Easy, Jessica, I'm not giving up yet."

The memory of the three women he'd found back in Pennsylvania propelled him forward. Their dead bodies, used and left to rot like garbage, still haunted him. If he failed and Jessica was taken back to Penwick without him, Stephan would do worse to her than he had to them. He'd smell Lucian's scent all over her and use her to vent his rage. That was something Lucian would willingly sacrifice his existence to prevent.

And, given the degree of Stephan's hatred, he knew that's exactly what it was going to come down to.

Sensing the renegades closing in on them, Lucian swore as he tried to push the car faster. The Ford was simply no match for the sports car. A warning light came on, indicating the low gas tank. He growled again and continued to push the car to go faster.

Lucian knew it was inevitable that Stephan's men were going to catch up to them. He also knew it was going to go down badly. He wasn't about to go quietly this time. Tonight, more than just his existence was at stake.

Jessica peered over her shoulder and choked back a cry. Lucian knew at this point he was merely burning rubber needlessly. They couldn't outrun that car. Lucian might have had a chance alone, but Jessica wouldn't get ten feet before they caught her.

This fight was going to happen. He just wondered how many of those miserable bastards he'd have to fight off at once while trying to keep an eye on Jessica.

Lucian warned Jessica to stay down and to brace herself. A moment later, Stephan's Alfa Romeo Brera rammed into the Ford on the passenger's side. Jessica screamed as she was jolted violently by the impact. Pulling the car to the right, Lucian was able to swerve away, but he didn't get far. They were right there to hit the car again.

This time Lucian was prepared for it. He told Jessica to hold on and met the hit hard. The crunch of metal and the cracking of glass drowned out Jessica's scream. She snapped to the left and would have been thrown around the front seat, but the seatbelt held her. The wind coming in from the broken back window sent a spray of shattered glass around. Jessica covered her head with her arms until it blew past.

The renegade's car moved off to the left, obviously playing with them. A glance to his right showed Lucian that Vincent was driving. Forced to swerve sharply to keep their car from being rammed again, Lucian instructed Jessica to take off her seatbelt. She did and scurried to his side. Holding fast to him, she ducked her head and tried to keep out of the way of his arm and not hinder his ability to steer.

Looking out the side window, Lucian saw a cluster of trees up ahead. Cutting the car to the left, he drove off the road and onto the grass. The Brera continued straight, which was exactly what Lucian had hoped for. It would gain them a few moments—or so he thought. From the rearview mirror he spotted the car skidding into a turn and heading toward them.

Lucian steered over the tall grass and headed for the trees, though at this point it was futile to try to run. The Brera was right behind them.

As Jessica banged around from the bumpy ride, Lucian glanced out the passenger's window to see Vincent was keeping pace with him. Knowing it was futile to continue the chase, Lucian stopped the car.

"What are you doing, Lucian? Are you crazy?"

"There's nowhere left to go." Seeing Vincent pull up next to them, Lucian gave Jessica a hard shake. "Swear no matter what happens you won't give up fighting to get home."

She shook her head. "No, I won't swear it. I won't let them take me back to Penwick."

He brought his face in close to hers and growled low in his throat. "You'll swear it to me. If I fall, don't let me go to my end knowing those bastards broke you."

Lucian didn't need to look behind him to know the two renegades had emerged from the car. He heard them get out and he would have floored it to get Jessica as far from them as he could, but they'd easily catch up with him—if the car didn't run out of gas and stop on its own first. There was simply too much open road ahead of them and not enough gas to get them far enough away. It made trying to outrun them pointless. Lucian's only option was to try to fight their way out of this situation.

Jessica choked back a scream when Vincent tapped on the driver's side window. Brian, one of Stephan's more vicious henchmen, came around to the passenger's side. He leaned down and peered into the car, his scarred mouth twisted in a malevolent grin that pulled another scream from Jessica.

Brian tore off the passenger's door and tossed it away. Jessica threw herself at Lucian, but he pushed her aside so he could reach for his weapon. In one smooth motion, he reached into the backseat to retrieve his sword. He opened the door, sending Vincent back. Lucian saw Brian hauling Jessica from the car. She tried to fight him off, but was no match for his strength.

Forced to forget his worry for Jessica, Lucian turned to Vincent and attacked. Before the renegade had a chance to palm his sword, Lucian struck him across the arm, nearly severing it. Vincent hissed but didn't falter. He pulled his sword from the sheath of his back-hanging baldric and sneered. "You're going to pay for that, Templar."

Baring his fangs, Lucian beckoned him forward arrogantly. "Let's see which of us will face Lucifer first."

Though Lucian knew Vincent was a coward, he didn't dare underestimate his enemy. Jessica's screams tormented him as he faced off with Vincent. It killed him not to run to her and snatch her away from Brian. The bastard was using her as a distraction, purposely making her scream as a means to divert him from the fight.

"I wouldn't be too cocky if I were you," Vincent taunted in his faint Italian accent. "You're not going to win this one."

Not about to exchange verbal taunts with the renegade, Lucian tightened his hold on his sword and attacked. Vincent swung his blade but Lucian was able to deflect it. Vincent went on the defensive as Lucian moved in on him. They danced around as their blades clashed, the sound of steel against steel mixing with Jessica's cries as Brian roughly subdued her.

Though Lucian countered Vincent's onslaught, the renegade managed to get in one good strike. He had a split second to decide which body part he could afford to lose—his left arm or his head. Obviously Lucian chose to take the hit to the arm.

Luckily, Lucian was able to move and fend off the attack without losing either appendage. Vincent, however, sliced him deep. Blood spurted from the gash but didn't hinder him. Surprisingly, Vincent was a good swordsman. He managed to keep pace with Lucian, making it difficult to gain the edge Lucian needed to take the bastard out.

At Brian's howl, Lucian nearly turned to see what was happening. But he refrained, barely managing to keep his gaze on Vincent, who hacked at him with an expertise that rivaled a Templar. Next came a growl from Brian and then the sickening sound of flesh hitting flesh. The dull thud forced Lucian to look away from his fight. He saw Jessica sprawled on the ground with Brian standing over her and feared she was dead.

Lucian's battle cry shook the night when Brian's foot connected with her back. Her limp body jerked from the force of the kick, but she didn't wake.

Fury fueling him, Lucian advanced on Vincent. With a vicious swipe of his blade, he cut the renegade's arm, nearly severing the arm. Vincent stumbled but didn't fall. His sword hit the ground and Lucian kicked it away. As Vincent dove for his weapon, Brian attacked. Lucian knocked him to the side and moved in for the kill but was intercepted by Vincent, who had managed to get to his sword.

The two vampires locked blades in a brutal battle. Lucian quickly gained the advantage. With a brutality that came from years of spilling blood on the battlefield, Lucian growled and fought Vincent with wicked delight. All that hampered him was the need to avoid treading on Jessica, who was lying unconscious on the ground.

Lucian tried not to let himself be distracted by her presence as he battered at the renegade mercilessly. Fury fueling him, his movements were a blur with high and low strikes coming so rapidly it was all Vincent could do to parry each separate move.

Blood seeped from the many slices Lucian inflicted to Vincent's body. Lucian's fighting skills allowed him to get past Vincent's wavering guard to score on his torso, arms and legs. Lucian came in with an overhand slice that would have taken the renegade's head but Vincent dodged and blocked with a weak hanging parry at the last second.

The renegade fell backwards, and collapsed to the grass with a grunt. Lucian tried to run him through the gut but he moved to the side. Instead, Vincent's blade caught him in the right shoulder. Pulling himself free of the blade, Lucian spun on Vincent, who was now back on his feet and crouched in a battle-stance. They were about to clash swords but Brian pulled a gun and released a round into Lucian's left leg. Lucian barely flinched when he took the bullet. Shaking off the hit, he turned to Brian and saw the renegade now had the gun pointed at Jessica's head. In that moment, Lucian knew what true horror was.

Jessica, obviously not realizing the threat, had finally woken and was pushing herself off the ground. She came face to face with a 9 mm and froze. Lucian swore his heart kicked out a beat as he watched her slowly look up and come face to face with the barrel of the gun.

ೞ౧౪

Time came to a crashing halt.

Staring down the barrel of a loaded gun was a chilling way to regain consciousness. Dragging her gaze up, Jessica saw Brian's finger hovering over the trigger. All he had to do was move that finger a hair and she'd be dead. Leveling a look at

Lucian, she was met with an even more harrowing sight—that of him lowering his sword.

To see such a proud man about to give up his weapon shattered her. Directing her gaze back at Brian, she thought frantically of a way out of this, but the intent etched across his face and the cold determination gleaming in his eyes told her that this fight was already over. If Lucian didn't surrender his sword, the renegade would no doubt put a bullet in her head.

Staring into Brian's eyes, she saw determination turn to sinister delight. "I see I finally have your attention, Templar."

"Put the gun down."

Brian barked out a laugh and Jessica flinched, expecting him to squeeze the trigger. "Surrender your sword, Knight."

Jessica didn't take her gaze from Brian. If she was going to die, she wanted to see it coming. She also knew Lucian would give up his sword to save her, and that surrender was something Jessica couldn't witness. Especially not after the last few days with him. He was more than a vampire, more than a damned creature. He was a man. He was—Lucian. And she didn't want him going back to Penwick to face his brother's vengeance any more than she wanted that fate for herself.

"Let her go. This fight doesn't concern her."

Brian dismissed Lucian by casually looking away. His gaze settled on her and Jessica swore she saw her death reflected in his eyes. He tilted his head to the side and regarded her curiously. "I've always been curious to see what a bullet would do to a human head at such close range."

No matter how hard she tried, Jessica couldn't hold back her whimper. Maybe she wasn't as brave as her father had raised her to be. If she were, she wouldn't be so terrified to face death. A bone-chilling sound coming from Lucian took her attention from Brian. The sound was menacing, feral, a mix of a growl and something unholy enough to scare her worse than the threat of a bullet.

"Don't."

Lucian ground that out between clenched teeth and threw down his sword. Jessica sucked in a sharp breath at his surrender. Her heart didn't break. It didn't shatter. It crumbled into dust at the sight of Lucian forced to his knees by Vincent.

Vincent picked up Lucian's sword, laughing as he leveled the blade at the back of Lucian's neck. Jessica fully expected Brian to shoot her anyway, regardless of Lucian's surrender. To her surprise, he didn't, although the gun remained trained on her head. He motioned to Vincent, who looked none too pleased that Brian was the one in control. "Get him in the car."

Vincent prodded Lucian to his feet with a nudge of the blade. Lucian growled, though he did gain his feet. As he moved to the car, Lucian kept his gaze trained on Brian. Just before Vincent shoved him in, Lucian stopped and sized up Brian.

"The night will come when we'll get the chance to finish this fight."

"I look forward to it, Templar."

"Get in the fucking car. One more word from you and I'll start taking body parts from you."

Lucian smiled icily at Vincent. He said nothing, just gave Vincent a long, hard stare that held all he needed to say.

As Lucian was pushed into the car, Jessica was left with Brian. He pressed the gun to her temple and oddly, Jessica's body relaxed, waiting for the pain of death. He took a step back and laughed a second before the deafening crack of gunfire rang out.

In a haze of disbelief, Jessica realized she was still alive. Brian had fired the gun into the ground. Lucian, she saw, was trying to claw his way through Vincent to get to her. His struggles brought the gun back to her temple.

"Cease, Templar, or she dies."

Much to Jessica's relief, Lucian stopped fighting. She wasn't ready to die, even after her noble stand of her life for Lucian's soul.

"Now, get in the car," Brian demanded.

Jessica did as she was told, knowing to resist would get her killed. She moved to get in but Brian stopped her by grabbing her around the waist. He growled into her ear before licking her cheek. Jessica gagged and nearly vomited at his feet.

Brian released her before backhanding her across the mouth, splitting her lip. From the backseat, Lucian went wild again. Jessica grabbed Brian's arm when he aimed the gun at Lucian, who had easily gotten past Vincent. The gunshot deafened her and the horror of seeing Lucian slump forward dropped her to her knees.

She lunged, thinking only to get to Lucian, but Brian stopped her. She fought him with every ounce of energy she had but he was too strong for her. His gaze went to the blood seeping from the cut on her lip a second before he pulled her toward him and licked the blood from her mouth.

Brian shoved her into the front seat. She turned to see Vincent pulling Lucian's limp body into the car. Not even the slam of the car door roused Lucian. Blood oozed from the gunshot wound to his head. The only reason she knew he wasn't dead—permanently dead—was because he hadn't been turned to dust. She repeated that fact over and over to herself in order to keep herself sane.

Brian climbed into the driver's seat and dragged the barrel of the gun across her neck. "I'm going to enjoy you, Jessica. I'm going to use your body and take your blood. See if your noble Templar will want you after you've been soiled by us all."

Brian's threat burned into her mind and stayed with her as she sat beside him in the front seat. They raced back to Penwick, outrunning the coming dawn. The closer they got to the castle the more Jessica wished Brian had shot her.

Brian steered the car with one hand, holding the gun in the other, hammer cocked, keeping Lucian from fighting. The weapon was still aimed at her, keeping her from daring a glance over her shoulder at Lucian. He hadn't woken yet and the bullet wound wasn't healing.

But he wasn't dust and that meant he'd eventually wake. The one thought Jessica held on to was that at least she hadn't died on her birthday.

ꙮ

Since the sun was dangerously close to rising, they stopped at a hotel to hide from the day. Vincent and Brian chained and gagged Lucian before he woke. Eventually his wound healed, though it was obvious he was extremely weak.

Jessica was forced to sit in a corner, secured by rope. The renegades took turns in their vigil. As one slept, the other kept watch, and at one point, obviously bored, Vincent decided to have some fun. He taunted Lucian with words before the game grew tiresome. He then slammed the butt of the gun against Lucian's temple. His sadistic nature unappeased, he fired three shots into Lucian. The wounds weren't drastic, just meant as a taunt.

Lucian kept trying to break the chains. If Jessica weren't gagged as well she would have begged him to stop. His struggles caused the chains to cut into him until he was sitting in a small pool of his own blood. Sometime during the long day he managed to bite through the gag. Another replaced that one, with the warning that if he did it again, Vincent would put a bullet in Jessica's head. The threat was effective, even if Lucian's frustration became a tangible entity within the disgusting hotel room.

The moment the sun went down they were back on the road and speeding toward Penwick. They made it back to the castle that night, cutting it close to sunrise. As they drove through the iron gate, Jessica felt a single tear slip down her cheek. Brought before Stephan, Jessica's last bit of hope that she'd make it home vanished.

Death closed in all around her and she knew they weren't going to make it out of this alive.

Chapter Eighteen

Lucian was stripped of more than just his clothes. He had little pride left, having given it up to save Jessica. He'd done the honorable thing by throwing down his sword. Hadn't Tristan explained enough times to him—to them all—that there was no shame in laying down your weapon to go on to fight another time? If that were true, then why was Lucian's shame eating away at him?

On his knees was not a position he was comfortable in. He'd sunk his fangs into his bottom lip to keep from venting his rage and jeopardizing Jessica. He'd endured the indignities forced upon him by Stephan in silence, knowing one sound from him was all his brother was after. One word and Jessica would suffer worse than she already had since being brought back to Penwick last night.

Keeping his silence while suffering the whip for the past hour took all of the control he'd honed over the centuries. Nevertheless, there were times when James landed a particularly cutting hit that Lucian almost screamed from the pain.

By now, he had to have lost at least a bucket of blood. The loss of it, coupled with the pain, weakened him. The manacles around his wrists and the chains connecting him to the wall were all that kept him from falling forward.

Though he was loath to look at Jessica, Lucian sought her out nonetheless. She was huddled in the corner of the cell, her back against the wall and her knees drawn up. She had her hands over her ears. Lucian couldn't blame her for wanting to block out the sound of the whip taking chunks out of his back. He wished he could, too.

Her eyes were unfocused and tears fell unchecked. He sensed she was teetering on the edge of sanity. A splatter of his blood hit her but she didn't so much as flinch. Lucian wondered if she was even aware of it.

"How much more do you think you can take, Luc?"

Lucian shifted his gaze from Jessica to Stephan. He narrowed his eyes on his brother, who paced leisurely before him. "Fuck you."

"No thank you, brother," Stephan drawled sarcastically. "I plan on fucking her."

Lucian realized Jessica wasn't catatonic when Stephan stabbed a finger at her. As a matter of fact, she seemed all too aware of what was happening around her. She dropped her hands from her ears and hugged her legs, rocking to and fro. Her breathing became erratic and she squeezed her eyes shut. Fear emanated from her in heavy waves, thickening the air and filling his senses.

Lucian strained against the chains and growled. "Touch her and I'll rip you apart."

Heedless of the threat, Stephan strolled toward Jessica. From behind him, Lucian heard James snicker. "How's the neck, James?"

James's snickering ceased and the whip came down hard across Lucian's back. His head slumped forward and he was sure he'd lost a good chunk of flesh with that hit. "I wouldn't be so arrogant if I were you, Templar. You're the one back in chains."

Lucian fought back the pain long enough to lift his head. "Not for long."

"No." Stephan crouched in front of Jessica. "Not for long. Soon you'll be in Hell and I'll still have Jessica to play with. And you do know how thorough I am when I take a fancy to a woman, don't you, Luc?"

He went to touch her but Jessica recoiled. Snarling, he grabbed a fistful of her hair and brought her face close to his. She whimpered but didn't pull away.

"He may have had you first, but I'll have you last." As Stephan brushed his lips over hers she gagged. "You'll carry my touch on your body when you go to God. Tell me, Jessica, do you think your Lord will welcome you after you lay with sin?"

Jessica spat in Stephan's face. "Let go of me."

Stephan released her hair and shoved her back. She hit the wall with a grunt. "That was a stupid thing to do, Jessica."

She matched Stephan's glare as she gained her feet. "I'll make you kill me before I let you touch me."

Stephan rose to his full height and dragged a single finger down the center of Jessica's chest. She hissed and backed up a step until her back was pressed against the wall. "No, love. I'll kill you after I put my touch on you. And then I'll go to America and kill your family."

In a fit of fury, Jessica leapt at Stephan. Her scream mingled with Lucian's roar. Stephan deflected her attack and knocked her to the floor. At the same moment, Lucian lunged for his brother but the chains held him back. James hit him with the whip hard enough to stun him, but he quickly regained his senses. He yanked on the chains again, trying to rip them from the wall, but they wouldn't give. He had to watch helplessly as Stephan hauled Jessica to her feet. She fought wildly until he gave her an ultimatum that stopped her cold.

"Cease or I'll have James finish him."

"No, don't."

Her whisper cut through Lucian. He didn't want her sacrificing herself to spare him. "Let her go, Stephan. She's an innocent. Your fight is with me."

Stephan shook his head. "Innocent, Lucian? I think not. She reeks of you."

Stephan pushed Jessica toward him. Lucian caught her and wrapped his chained arms around her. She buried her face in his chest, shaking violently, her heart hammering in her chest. She smelled of sweat and fear, and yes—him. His scent was all over her and it roused needs in him that were dangerous, given his body's loss of blood.

Unable to stop it, the bloodlust rose in him. He needed to drink her in so badly, his fangs ached. His stomach contracted and his throat ran dry. He needed blood. An unholy growl came from someplace dark within him.

"Ah, there it is." Stephan announced. "There's the monster I remember so well."

Jessica untangled herself from Lucian and dragged her gaze up to his face. He felt dirty, and yet he couldn't stop himself from wanting to take her. Even with Stephan and James watching, Lucian was losing control over himself. He needed her body and her blood and that need transformed him from Templar to monster.

"Get away from me." She didn't move. Instead, she cupped his face. Everything disappeared for a timeless moment as she traced her thumb across his bottom lip. Her acceptance destroyed his shame. If Stephan's growl hadn't shattered the moment, Lucian would have stayed lost in her forever. "Move, Jessica. Now."

Jessica backed away from him until she bumped into Stephan. He put his hands on her shoulders and she sucked in a sharp breath. He thrust her forward. Her feet skidded across the stone floor as Stephan pushed her toward Lucian. Not even the pain on his back or James's laughter could break the spell Jessica's scent wove around him.

"Take her, Luc. You know you need to." Stephan goaded, inching her closer. "Take her blood. End this now."

Lucian fought back every vampire instinct. He struggled to remember his oath to God. The faces of the other Templars flashed in his mind and gave him the added bit of strength he needed to fight down the beast threatening to burst forth.

"You're not going to win this, Stephan," Lucian ground out roughly between gritted teeth.

Stephan's eyes narrowed with menace. "Yes, I will." He drew Jessica up against his chest. Her gasp and her tears hit Lucian like a physical blow. "And I'm going to relish every moment it takes to break her."

"I'm warning you..."

"No!" Stephan roared, passing Jessica to James. Her screams were deafening as the vampire dragged her, struggling, from the dungeon. "You don't warn me of anything, Lucian. Your nights are coming to an end. You *will* go to Hell. I'll make certain of it"

Stephan stalked from the cell, leaving Lucian chained. Lucian's gut twisted as the door closed with a bang. He was instantly engulfed in blackness.

The only reason Lucian could think of as to why Stephan hadn't given up trying to break him yet was blind rage and determination. His brother had always been stubborn, and now as a renegade, that trait had intensified. What had started as an act of vengeance had metastasized into a deranged battle of wills—with Jessica's life as the prize.

He tried to break the chains, but they wouldn't give. Lucian slumped forward, the pain in his body and the torment of his hunger nothing compared to the agony of having to suffer the sound of Jessica's cries echoing throughout the castle.

෨෬ඌ

After she'd been brought up from the dungeon, Jessica expected torture beyond her comprehension. Instead, she was met with a small feast Stephan had laid out for her. She sat at the head of the table with her hands folded in her lap. Her stomach rumbled loudly but she refused to take a single swallow of Stephan's feast.

Stephan sat across from her, calmly watching her. James stood beside him looking bored, though she knew his sharp gaze missed nothing. Brian leaned against the wall behind her. His presence was a reminder of the gun he'd held to her head. She swore she could feel his smirk at the back of her head.

Jessica stole a discreet look around the hall, imaging Lucian and his family here centuries ago. She tried to imagine the days when life thrived within these walls, but she was met with only the stark reality of death all around her.

There were times she swore she saw ghostly images haunting the dungeon. At first she'd believed it was her mind playing tricks on her, but being a world where vampires were real it wasn't a hard stretch for her to realize ghosts were as well.

She often sensed the presence of ghosts all around her. Instead of being scared, knowing they were there comforted her.

Even now she felt them watching her—watching all that went on within the walls of Penwick.

"Eat. I know you're hungry."

Jessica didn't know what this new game of his was, but she was sure she wasn't going to play along. For all she knew the food was poisoned, although she doubted Stephan would give her such a merciful end.

"No." Her stomach growled in rebellion of her denial.

Stephan slammed his fist on the table and Jessica jumped at least a foot. Even James looked startled. "I said eat."

Where Jessica found the courage to defy Stephan, she didn't know. Maybe it was her fear at the prospect of spending another three months as nothing more than a puppet in Stephan's twisted plot for revenge. Or maybe it was foolishness. Jessica pushed away her full plate and jumped to her feet. She slapped her palms on the table and met Stephan's oddly curious gaze steadily.

"And I said no. I won't eat your goddamn food and I won't play your goddamn game. Either you let me go or kill me, because I swear to God, I won't be your pawn anymore."

Stephan leapt from his chair. He swiped his arms across the table, sending dishes and glasses crashing to the floor. Jessica gasped and went to back up but decided against it. She'd gotten this far standing her ground. She wasn't going to allow herself to falter now, even though she was scared out of her mind.

For a moment, she and Stephan stood there facing each other, she heaving with fear and him deceptively calm. Brian made a move toward her but Stephan motioned him away. A slow smile curled his lips. The sight of his fangs repulsed her. If there were any food in her, she would have vomited it up.

Stephan's mock applause at her bravado seemed as loud as a clap of thunder. "There's that fire. I've missed it." Jessica's heart beat erratically with fear as he strolled toward her. "And here I thought you were cowed."

Jessica faced Stephan with defiance, knowing it was both foolish and valiant—though more the latter than the former. Still, she stood her ground, preferring death than being locked back in the cell. "I won't play your game."

Stephan closed the space between them. The scent of his cologne, a spicy aroma, filled her senses. He gripped her chin firmly, forcing her head up. "You'll do whatever I want you to. And if you doubt that, even for a moment, remember that I know where your family lives."

That threat defeated Jessica. "You leave them alone."

He leaned in close enough for her to smell the blood on his breath. He rubbed her cheek with his almost lovingly. She shivered with disgust. "Then behave, pet, or else I'll drag you back to Damascus and make you watch as I kill your family. Then, I'll turn you just so that their screams can haunt you for eternity." He moved back and she saw the conviction in his eyes. "Do we have an understanding?"

She nodded, the nightmare of her life robbing her of the ability to speak. Stephan ran his hands up her arms. His hands were smooth, not at all like Lucian's. He'd obviously lacked the years of holding a sword that Lucian had.

"What was it like, Jessica? Tell me. What did it feel like to have Lucian rutting between your legs?"

She took a step back, surprised when she hit the wall. Glancing over her shoulder, she realized it wasn't a wall, but Brian's chest she'd backed into. James came to stand near his lord, leaving her no way to escape them and nowhere to run.

Brian took hold of her shoulders and held her for Stephan, who trailed his hands over her. She wanted to recoil from his touch, but Brian's hold prevented it. Even if she wanted to run, the threat to her family would have held her in place.

"Did Lucian tell you that you were his first? My brother, so noble even in death, held to his vow of celibacy for over seven hundred years." Stephan stepped back and licked his lips as his hungry silver gaze raked over her. "Makes me wonder what secrets are hidden beneath your clothes to move a man to break such an oath."

"I say we find out," Brian suggested.

Jessica went cold with horror. Thus far, she'd been spared the offense of having these monsters invade her body. Rape would only be the beginning of a new horror, one she knew she wouldn't be able to live with, should she somehow survive.

"Not yet," Stephan replied, which actually pulled a sob of relief from her. "If Lucian doesn't kill her by Halloween, I promise you can have your fun with her before I kill her."

Brian grunted in acceptance and released her. Jessica's legs gave out and she fell to the floor. Waves of cold dread washed through her. Halloween was only two days away.

God help her, she actually wished Lucian would kill her. At least at his hand, death would be quick.

"Now," Stephan said to James. "Gather the men and tell them to be on guard. The First is in Wiltshire and there's no telling if Julian will ultimately lead the Order here."

This was the second time she'd heard Stephan mention Julian of Harwick. The first came shortly after he'd captured her. From what he'd said, Julian was the vampire who was after a Druid relic she'd heard them refer to as the Daystar. From what Jessica had gathered, if a vampire had control of the Daystar he would have the ability to walk in the sun. Lucian had assured her the other Templars would stop that from ever happening. She hoped to God he was right.

Jessica went to push herself to her feet, but Stephan grabbed her and hauled her up. "You," he purred. "Stay with me. I may not use your body to sate my sexual needs, but I fully intend to take your blood and sate my hunger."

Stephan slammed her against his chest. His arm came around her, holding her like a vise. His other hand fisted in her hair and yanked her head to the side. He licked her neck before he sank his fangs deep into her. Her scream rocked the walls of the castle, reaching Lucian, who let out a roar that echoed throughout the dungeon.

Lucian punched the wall hard enough to tear open the flesh and break his knuckles. Rage, helplessness and desperation thundered through him. Lucian ignored the pain of his damaged hand and the blood spilling from the wound as he paced the length of the cell.

The walls closed in on him just as they'd done at Chinon as he suffered the sounds of his fellow Templars' torture. Hearing those screams had been an unbearable torment. Forced to listen to those same wrenching sounds from Jessica and being helpless to do a damn thing about it was so much worse.

Dropping to his knees, Lucian did the only thing he could. He closed his eyes, and prayed for God's forgiveness for what he knew he'd have to do to save Jessica.

He couldn't avoid it any longer. He had to kill to his brother.

ஐௌ

Jessica woke cradled in Lucian's lap. She was shivering uncontrollably and sick to her stomach. Cold from the inside out, she curled into him. He hugged her close, his gentleness shattering her emotions and making her weep until she had no more tears left.

The nasty smell of the pallet was overwhelmed by the wonderful smell of Lucian's flesh. Lying on their sides, Jessica held him, never wanting to let him go. He was her anchor, her strength, and she found she needed him as much as she needed air to breathe.

"I'm glad you're here. Well, not *here*," she indicated the dungeon with a wide sweep of her hand. "I mean...I'm glad we're here together."

"I am too," he agreed gruffly. He kissed her forehead and Jessica felt it clear to her soul.

She shifted, trying to find a more comfortable position but the stone floor was just too unyielding. Her aching body forced her to sit up. Lucian sat up with her and laid gentle fingers to the bite on her neck.

She hissed and pulled away. "No, don't touch it."

He withdrew his hand. "Jessica..."

"Please, Lucian. I don't want you to touch it." A shiver of disgust made its way through her. "I feel so dirty."

His hands curled around her upper arms and he pulled her close enough to him that their lips were almost touching. "Nothing can make you dirty."

"Stephan has."

Lucian shook his head slowly. "No, Jessica, you're wrong. You are all that's clean and good."

Jessica wanted to believe him, but with Stephan's touch lingering on her, she felt filthy. "No, I'm not. I'll never feel clean again."

Jessica's whispered announcement sliced through Lucian. "You will, Jessica. I swear it. You'll wash this all away," he whispered to her before capturing her mouth. She melted into him, giving herself over to him. Lucian deepened the kiss, until Jessica felt the impact of it throughout her entire being. It replaced the cold with wonderful warmth.

Lucian's kiss chased away her pain and fear. It made the world fade away, until all that mattered was him and what he was doing to her. He ground his hips into her, pulling a moan from her as a rush of wetness settled between her legs.

When he lifted his head, she desperately wanted to drag him right back to her mouth. She didn't want to slip away from where she was with him. She didn't want to risk reality pushing its way back into her thoughts.

"You make me feel alive."

Lucian couldn't have said anything that would have touched Jessica's heart more. Though unable to see him, she felt him by brushing her fingers over his face, down the column of his throat, to his collarbone. He sucked in a breath at her touch, which emboldened her to continue her exploration.

She trailed her hands down his bare chest, loving his hardness. She barely gave his scars notice, instead enjoying how his body moved against her palms. She wanted to touch his back, but knew it had to be torn apart and raw from the whipping he'd endured.

If she lived ten more lifetimes, Jessica would never forget the sound of the leather hitting flesh, or the sight of Lucian's skin being torn clean away. And the blood—dear God, there had been so much blood.

She wanted to take that pain from him, rip the memories that haunted him from his mind. Jessica wanted to give him peace. Most of all, she wanted to give him love. Her feelings for him terrified her. If they survived this nightmare, it was doubtful they'd ever find a place where they could fit into each other's worlds.

All they had was this moment, and Jessica wasn't going to waste it.

"I get lost in you, Lucian." She placed a tender kiss on his lips.

At Jessica's whispered words, Lucian growled and pulled her to him. The moment he took her mouth in a kiss that threatened to set them both on fire, the dungeon disappeared around them. His body's pain faded. All that mattered was the two of them and the pleasure shooting through him as Jessica danced her fingers gently up his arms. He loved her hands on him almost as much as he loved touching her.

His body craved her in ways he'd never imagine a body would want another. It transcended the hunger, making the pain of the bloodlust seem like nothing more than a mild inconvenience. His desire for her turned him savage. He pushed her down on the pallet and settled on top of her. Though her arms snaked around his neck, Lucian sensed her pulling away from him. Reality, he knew, was intruding.

"Stay with me, Jessica." He kissed her softly. "Forget everything else. It's just us. Promise me you'll stay with me."

She nodded as her hands traveled absently over his healing back. Though it was torture to have her fingers graze his wounds, the pleasure of her touch overrode the pain. "Take me away from this place."

Though a part of him felt guilty for breaking his last vow to God, it felt right to give himself to Jessica. Inside Jessica, he felt at home for the first time since he'd left Penwick to go off on Crusade. Only with her did he finally have a sense of peace.

He knew a moment of panic at the thought of going on alone after she returned to her world and he crawled back to his.

Lucian awkwardly removed Jessica's clothes. As he bared her body, he relished the sight of her. Only after he'd shed his own pants did he settle back over her. Her warmth flowed into him, chasing away the cold. She buried her hands in his hair and parted her lips in invitation.

Lucian shook with desire as Jessica drew her legs up and wrapped them around his waist. He wanted to take his time with her, but the reality of where they were made that impossible.

Letting go of his restraint, Lucian positioned himself at the opening of her body. She was slick with desire, which only fueled his raging passion. Gritting his teeth, his hips moved forward and the tip of him slipped into her body. Instantly, her heat surrounded him, forcing him to surge forward. Once he was fully inside of her he relaxed and gave over to the pleasure running through him.

He settled his mouth over hers and took in her gasp of pleasure. She squeezed him with her thighs as he pumped into her. The hand she placed on the small of his back seared him as she pressed him into her. The urgency in her kiss grew as his hips rocked forward.

Her erratic heartbeat hammered against his chest as he drew himself out of her, teasing her with the head of his cock before sinking deep into her again. She arched her back, which thrust her breasts toward him. He couldn't ignore the blatant offering of her body. Kissing his way to her breasts, he used his mouth on them until she writhed beneath him and whispered incoherent words.

Nearing his release, Lucian held back. He wouldn't shame himself by finishing before her. He was a warrior and had long ago mastered control over his body. Yet, buried within Jessica, with her body pulsating around him, that control left him. All he knew was her—the feel of her, the scent of her, the sight of her. She consumed him body and mind and pushed him past reason.

Restraint was the furthest thing from Jessica's mind. With every thrust of his body into hers, Lucian stoked a fire within her. Careful not to touch his wounds, she kept her hands at the small of his back, pressing him into her. She matched each thrust of his hips with her own, the length and thickness of him bringing her closer to the edge of release.

Her body convulsed around him. Lucian growled into her mouth as his body erupted into hers. She held back her scream when she joined him, soaring higher than she'd ever dreamed possible.

After he rolled off her, Jessica became all too aware of her surroundings. Though she couldn't see the dungeon, the cold, damp, and stench of the place invaded her momentary contentment. She curled into him, shivering from the chill in the cell and from the spent energy.

It scared her that she wasn't able to see. "Lucian?" Even she heard the note of panic in her voice.

"Easy, Jessica. I'm right here."

He accented his words by tightening his arms around her. The small gesture calmed her. "I wish I could see you."

"I know, Jessica." He kissed the top of her head. "Try to get some rest."

Jessica shivered and tried to get even closer to him, not that it helped much. His body was even colder than hers. "I'm as cold as a grave in winter."

Lucian hissed and went rigid. "Don't ever say that again."

His gruff tone had her frowning even as she curled her freezing and aching body into his. "Say what again?"

"Cold as a grave."

"It's just an expression."

"I don't like it."

Jessica wasn't going to argue with him. The man dwelled in a world of death, with the constant threat of Hell hovering over him like a doom cloud. If he didn't want to associate her with death, she'd honor his request.

Besides, it was nice to know he cared about her enough that the thought of her death bothered him. It told her that he might care for her as much as she did for him.

Not that it mattered. If they ever found their way free of here, they'd go back to their life and death, respectively. But at least in the years to come, when the nightmares haunted her, she'd have the memory of Lucian to help chase them away.

Chapter Nineteen

The stench of his burnt flesh filled Lucian's nose. It transported him back to the day he'd burned to death. Only Jessica's hoarse cries echoing throughout the cell anchored him to the present. Agony robbed him of reason, making pain all he knew. The pain was raw, pure. Somehow, it brought him closer to God than anything else had since the day he'd taken his monk's vows.

He wanted to scream. No—he needed to scream. He had to give voice to the agony. And yet, his mouth worked but no sound came forth. Whatever he might say froze in his throat at the hiss of Stephan's latest torture device. This was the one most likely to break him.

A blowtorch.

Stephan leaned against the doorframe and watched maliciously as James and Vincent took turns using the blowtorch on Lucian. The torture had gone on for over an hour. There wasn't much of Lucian's flesh that wasn't damaged. As per Stephan's command, the maniacal bastards took great pains to avoid his face, lest the overzealous henchmen accidentally burn Lucian's eyes.

The devil forbid Lucian should be spared the sight of his own torture or of Jessica, who was being held by Brian. The fight had long since gone out of her and she now hung limply in his arms. Stephan wanted Lucian to see and hear and smell. Most of all, he wanted his brother to *feel.*

And oh God did he feel. Lucian could withstand most any torture—hell, all the Templars could after the brutal life they'd led—save for burning. This was the one way to bring a Templar low. To take him back to his death was the ultimate torture and the one sure way to break him. Stephan had to know this, which must have been why he'd brought out the blowtorch now, after so many months. He was obviously done playing games.

Memories flooded Lucian's pain-drunk mind. The stench of his burning flesh had him hearing the cheers of the crowd as they'd watched the Templars burn to death. Their cheering mingled with the screams of fifty burning Knights as they were executed in the center of Paris on the order of Philip of France.

One of the unlucky few who hadn't passed out from the agony—as many of the other Knights had—Lucian had been fully aware of the flames eating away at his body. They licked up his legs, first burning away his clothes before working their way up to char the flesh from his bones. After what had seemed forever, he'd died. Only the pain hadn't stopped there. No, it had just begun.

He'd regained consciousness someplace between life and death and was faced with the awesome sight of an archangel in all his golden glory. Lucian learned of his damnation as a vampire only moments before Michael, with profound regret, stabbed him through the heart and took his soul. As the sword was withdrawn, a terrible cold settled deep within Lucian's body.

He'd been thrown back to life, finding himself in Messina. It was the same place he'd set sail from years before, when he'd made the trek to the Holy Land serving in Guy Sinclair's army.

The blowtorch caused his memories to dissolve as fresh pain erupted within him. Chained to the wall, he was unable to fight back. All he could do was stand there, stripped naked, and endure what they were doing to him. Through a haze of agony he focused on Jessica. Tears streamed down her cheeks as she stared back at him. Those tears were the only indication she wasn't as catatonic as she appeared. He wanted to tell her not to care—not to cry for him—but he knew all it would take was one word before his pain burst from him in a torrent of screams.

"Has he rested enough, my lord?" James asked Stephan a little too eagerly for Lucian's comfort.

"Have you, Luc? Are you rested enough to proceed?" Stephan goaded from the doorway.

"Leave him alone," Jessica implored brokenly. "Look at him. You've done enough."

Fearing Stephan would make her suffer for her insolence, Lucian gritted his teeth against the pain and tried to speak. No words left his throat. Stephan smiled at his wasted effort. He was no doubt enjoying this.

Stephan fangs flashed in the meager torchlight as he raked his gaze over Jessica. "I wouldn't worry too much about Lucian. You should be more concerned with yourself. After all, we still have plenty of time to play before dawn arrives." Jessica went even whiter than she already was and Lucian knew if Brian hadn't been holding her, she'd have crumpled to the floor. "You may proceed."

James went to step forward but Vincent stopped him. "No. You've had your fun with the Templar. I want a chance at him now."

James, cradling his arm, looked at Stephan, who shrugged carelessly. "Go ahead. I don't care who does it, as long as you make it hurt."

Lucian's knees nearly gave out at that.

James reluctantly handed the blowtorch to Vincent. The arrogant renegade sauntered over to him, his fangs bared in a sinister grin. "I'm going to hurt you bad, Templar."

Lucian would have shot back some brilliantly sarcastic taunt, but he still had no voice. The pain was too great to speak. All he could do was glare at the renegade while he ignited the blowtorch.

Jessica whimpered and tried again to yank her way free of Brian's hold. "Please don't."

Stephan cut her an icy glare. "You beg for him?"

She didn't hesitate to answer. "Yes."

"How noble of you, Jessica," Stephan purred before he shifted his gaze back to Lucian. "I do believe she cares about you, Lucian. I wonder how deep her affections run. Shall we put it to the test?"

"No." The word came from deep within him.

"Ah, so now my brother speaks." Stephan raised a brow at him as his mouth twisted in a mockery of a grin. "And here I thought we'd lost you."

"I'm here, Stephan." Where Lucian found the strength to speak, he didn't know. "Trust me, I'm here."

"Good, I'd hate to think your mind had broken. After all," he slid a malevolent look at Jessica, "the game is just now getting interesting. Bring her."

Brian pushed her forward but didn't let her go. Her heels skidded across the floor as she fell toward the door. She fought to break Brian's hold on her like a woman gone mad, but it was a fight in vain. She couldn't break his hold, and in fact, only made things worse for herself as she was shoved toward Stephan.

"Get the hell off me."

The blowtorch being passed across his chest took Lucian's attention from Jessica. Unable to hold back, Lucian bared his fangs and vented the pain in a roar that rocked the castle. He panted hard, empty breaths as his flesh melted. The stench had Jessica gagging as Stephan snatched her away from Brian.

"Tell me, Jessica, would you suffer Lucian's pain for him?"

Through a fog of pain, Lucian heard Stephan's question. Vincent moved the blowtorch away from him. In his blessed reprieve, he waited for her answer. She said nothing.

Stephan smiled maliciously. "I don't blame you, love. He's not worth it."

Jessica tried to twist out of Stephan's hold. "Fuck you."

Stephan's laugh bounded off the walls of the cell. He looked to James and then Vincent. "I do believe it's time to teach her a woman's place. What say you?"

James's laugh was more a growl. Vincent brought the blowtorch to Stephan, though he didn't take it. Instead, Stephan pulled Jessica along as he stepped into the cell. "Not only am I going to hurt her, Lucian, I'm going to show her a glimpse of Hell."

The iron manacles bit into Lucian's wrists as he surged forward. Vincent grabbed hold of his charred arm and Lucian roared. James was right there, moving to protect his master as best he could minus a hand. Stephan tossed Jessica to James and grabbed the blowtorch from Vincent. The hiss of the blowtorch drowned out Jessica's screams and Brian's laughter. The sharp, blue flame hovered near his face and Lucian knew it was going to be bad.

"No more empty threats, brother. No more games." Stephan stepped around him and touched the flame to Lucian's back. Lucian arched and bit back a scream as his flesh melted under the heat. "Now I take a pound of flesh for every year that has passed since the night you brought your evil to Penwick."

The pain was unbearable when Stephan dragged the blowtorch over his flesh. Stephan laughed as smoke rose from Lucian's body. He was burnt nearly down to his ribs. His body wracked with agony, he would have fallen to his knees had the chains not been holding him up.

"Does it hurt, Luc?"

"Fuck you," Lucian ground out. His head slumped forward until Stephan demanded Jessica be brought to him. His head snapped back up and he watched sickly as James pushed Jessica toward Stephan. He wished Jessica had taken both of the prick's hands.

"I never did get an answer from you." Jessica's eyes went wide and she kicked out at Stephan. He laughed. "I know you care for my brother. Let's see how deep your affections run."

Stephan widened the flame of the blowtorch and taunted Jessica with it. She hissed and fought to break away from James. "Don't. Please."

Stephan ran his knuckles down her cheek. He let out a *tsk*, pursed his lips, and shook his head. "You see, Luc? Even Jessica doesn't care enough about you to spare you more pain."

"No. That's not..."

The slap to her face opened a deep cut on her bottom lip. "I didn't give you leave to speak." Stephan touched his finger to the blood trickling down her chin and rubbed it on Lucian's lower lip.

Lucian's eyes slid closed at the exquisite taste of Jessica's blood. He wanted—nay, he *needed*—more.

245

"She tastes good, yes?" Stephan brought his face close to Lucian's, filling Lucian's vision with his evil grin. "Imagine her blood filling your mouth. Spilling down your throat. Remember what it felt like to be buried in her heat."

Stephan held her out like a beautiful gift of life. All Lucian had to do was reach out and take her...

"That's it, Luc. Take her. Now. Take her blood and end your pain."

Yes... Her blood would stop the agony. It would heal the burns and take away the pain.

"Drain her, Lucian. Drain her and take her life into yourself."

Life. Her blood would give him back life.

"No."

Jessica sagged with relief.

Stephan raised a brow. "You should have had such restraint when you came home." The look that crossed his face chilled Lucian more than the loss of his soul. "I think it's time Jessica learned the truth about you, don't you think?"

Lucian slowly shook his head. "Don't."

Stephan shoved Jessica away and began to pace the cell. She ran to Lucian. James went to grab for her, but Stephan stopped him with a wave of his hand. Lucian tensed, fearing she'd touch him. He knew if she did, the fragile hold he had on his control would snap. As if able to read his mind, her hands hovered over him. She looked over her shoulder at Stephan. Lucian felt her fury and let out a low moan as it coursed through him.

"You're a goddamn monster."

Stephan cocked a brow at her accusation. "Monster? I'm only what Lucian made me."

"Stop blaming him for what you are."

Stephan stalked back to her and grabbed her arm. Her gave her a hard shake and brought his face a mere inch from hers. Jessica gasped and tried to pull away, but his hold was too firm.

"Oh, I blame him, Jessica. I blame him for the death of our family and for the fate that befell me."

"Enough, Stephan." Lucian demanded. He didn't want Jessica to know what he'd done. He didn't want her to know his shame.

Releasing her, Stephan faced Lucian. "I wish you could have seen Father and Mother's joy when the guards announced your return. Father *wept.*" He spared a quick glance at Jessica. "We knew Lucian was dead. We knew he'd been among the Knights arrested in France. For three years our parents did everything they could to gain his release from Chinon, all to no avail. The day we received word Luc had been executed, I think a piece of our parents died with him."

"Stephan, no."

Lost in his memories of that night, Stephan continued. "He came back to us not long after his execution. He was burnt to the bone, his eyes silver and glowing. We saw his fangs and knew he wasn't something holy. Still our parents wouldn't turn him away. He was their son. They adored him. They threw open the gates and invited in the devil."

"I didn't kill them."

No, Lucian hadn't physically done the foul deed. It was his actions that had lead to the deaths of his family—and to what Stephan had become.

"Yes, you did." Stephan thundered. "Why didn't you stay away? Why did you have to bring your evil here?"

Stephan finally showed the pain buried beneath his anger. It cut Lucian raw, hurting him worse than anything he'd suffered in his life, or his death.

"I needed to come home, Stephan."

"And so you did." He grabbed Jessica, who let out a scream as she slammed against Stephan's chest. "Since I can't break you physically, I believe it's time to do it emotionally."

Chapter Twenty

Stephan bit down on Jessica's neck, ripping a scream from her that infused Lucian with the strength of ages.

Heedless of the pain it caused, he jerked his right arm, dislocating his shoulder and snapping the thick chain. When Vincent swung at him, Lucian caught his fist and crushed the bones of his hand and fingers. Lucian cut off the renegade's howl by wrapping the dangling length of chain around his neck.

Gnashing his teeth against the agony, Lucian jerked his other arm. The second chain broke, freeing him. Growling, he snapped Vincent's neck before James could stop him, and then threw Vincent's twitching body at the wall, hitting the torch that lit the dungeon and knocking it to the floor.

Darkness descended all around them. Stephan and Brian, unused to the blackness that had become natural for Lucian, would need to adjust to the lack of light. That extra moment gave Lucian all the advantage he needed. He moved faster than James, who dove to retrieve the blowtorch, kicking it away before taking James by the neck and shoving him back until he hit the wall.

"You can't win this, Lucian."

Out of the corner of his eye, Lucian saw Stephan back himself away from the fight, dragging Jessica with him. That didn't surprise him. Stephan lacked the strength to fight him and left that to his henchmen. To ensure Lucian couldn't get to him, Stephan ordered Brian to protect him.

Lucian kept his gaze focused on James as he squeezed the renegade's throat with one hand. With the other, he latched onto James's stumped arm and squeezed until the renegade screamed. Though he couldn't choke him, he could hurt him.

James moved his hand toward his waist and Lucian growled out a laugh. The bastard was a fool if he thought Lucian didn't notice him going for the dagger sheathed at his hip.

"Be that stupid, James."

James sneered, palming the dagger in a futile effort to defend himself. Still holding James's throat, Lucian released his wrist and snatched the dagger from him. James proved to be strong despite his handicap. The renegade managed to break free of Lucian's hold.

Now that Lucian had a weapon, the fight for freedom would be that much easier, though his worry for Jessica's life would be a distraction he'd have to fight to ignore.

At Stephan's order, James attacked, tripping over Vincent's twitching body. Lucian sliced James's arm. The gash running down his handless arm was deep enough to expose the bone. James hissed and jumped back. Lucian positioned himself in front of the door. He wouldn't give them the chance to get away. His arm useless, James advanced again, making a sloppy effort to get to him. Lucian grabbed him and slammed his back against the door. The sickening sound of the renegade's spine snapping had Stephan backing away.

Lucian brought his face in close to James. He bared his fangs in a twisted grin, all of the violence that simmered beneath his surface coming to the forefront. "I'm going to bleed you dry."

Though James was obviously severely injured, he managed to choke out a taunt. "Do it."

Lucian pushed past his own pain and pressed his forearm against James's chest. His strength was slowly coming back. Though his body couldn't heal without blood, even in his weakened state he was still stronger than a renegade.

With a viciousness Templars rarely demonstrated, Lucian dragged the blade across James's throat, deep enough to almost sever his head. James's eyes widened and his mouth worked, but he made no sound. Lucian turned the bloody dagger in his hand and, staring James in the eyes, stabbed him through the heart.

Lucian savored James's death when the bastard exploded to dust. He turned intently, moving to crouch over Vincent. Brian attacked before Lucian could end Vincent. With the vision of Brian holding the gun to Jessica's head feeding his fury, Lucian made quick work of the bastard. He slit Brian's throat and threw him backwards. His body exploded into dust even before it had the chance to hit the floor.

With a roar, Lucian pounced on Vincent. His gaze locked on Stephan and, without a trace of remorse, Lucian cut the renegade's throat deep enough to end him. Vincent stopped twitching as Lucian walked away. He evaporated to dust and Lucian faced down his brother.

Stephan growled and thought to use Jessica as a shield. Lucian snatched her out of his brother's grasp and shoved her out of the cell. He kicked the door closed, forcing himself to remain focused on Stephan.

He faced down his brother, wishing to God this moment never had to come. "Only you and I remain, Stephan."

"So it seems."

Lucian's mind rebelled at what he knew needed to be done. "I wish it didn't have to come to this."

Stephan met Lucian's gaze with a hard glare. "You should have never come back here."

"No, I shouldn't have," he agreed with a heavy heart.

"I hope what you've done continues to haunt you for the rest of eternity."

Of that, Lucian had no doubt.

"I'm not going to make this easy for you. I won't give you the opportunity to look back on this night and have you believe yourself righteous in my death."

Profound sadness ripped through him as he gazed at his brother. Their childhood came rushing back. For just a moment, they weren't Templar and renegade, but Lucian and Stephan. He saw his brother as the boy he'd been, smiling up at Lucian as he trailed behind him everywhere he went.

"Your every action took the choice from me. I would have let you go on, Stephan, all you had to do was disappear and all this destruction would have never been."

Hatred in its purest form blazed in Stephan's eyes, robbing Lucian of the vision of his brother as a boy. They were once again two vampires and though that should have cleansed Lucian of his guilt, it didn't.

"Come on, then." Stephan raised his chin and bared his throat. "Slit my throat. Send me to Hell."

Lucian went numb now that the moment was upon him. The dagger suddenly weighed more than ten swords. He didn't know what hurt worse, the pain of the burns or the agony ripping through his heart. Willing his memories to leave him, he stepped closer to his brother and, to his surprise, Stephan allowed him to take hold of his hair and yank his head back.

His hand shook as he lifted the dagger. Bloody tears came to Lucian's eyes and he faltered. He dropped his hand, almost losing the dagger. Stephan's hand tightened around his wrist and brought the dagger back to his throat.

"It's not like being a Templar." Stephan's words were spoken on a broken whisper. "I'm not noble or righteous, nor do I want to be. I relish my victims' pain. I love the power I have over them. What I did to those women back in Damascus was nothing compared to what I've done to so many more."

In that moment Lucian knew he wasn't merely ending his brother, he was wiping the stain of a renegade from the world. He wished to God he'd be setting his brother free, but Lucian knew where Stephan was going. Though his suffering in this world would be over, a new torment awaited him.

A bloody tear ran a path down Lucian's cheek. "Forgive me, Stephan, please."

"Just do it, Luc. End me before you lose the nerve."

"I love you, Stephan."

Stephan met his gaze then, and in his eyes was the regret of ages. "I forgive you, Lucian."

Lucian pressed his lips to Stephan's forehead as he drew the dagger's blade across his throat. In the instant before Stephan burst into dust, Lucian knew he'd glimpsed the man Stephan would have been had he never been turned.

Lucian dropped the dagger, fell to his knees, and wept. He pulled his gaze from the pile of dust that had been his brother and stared down at his bloody hands. He'd never forget the torment etched on Stephan's face.

"It's not like being a Templar."

Lucian slammed his hands over his ears to block out the echo of Stephan's voice. He knew those words would haunt him for eternity. He'd always remember Stephan had forgiven him. In the nights to come, when this moment came back to him, he'd have his brother's forgiveness to ease the pain of what he'd had to do here.

A warm wind blew over him, strong enough to stir his hair and make him look up. He saw no one or nothing that could have caused the breeze, and yet, it took the cold and pain from his body. There was a force here with him, running through him, comforting him. He looked down at himself to see the burns were gone. Whatever it was had healed him and returned his strength.

The scent of roses and leather replaced the stench of the dungeon. Lucian stared into the dark, almost expecting to see his parents standing there. The only sight he was met with was the broken chains and filthy pallets. Yet they were there, he was sure of it. He felt them surrounding him, felt their souls pass through him. He closed his eyes, wishing he could see them once more. Just as he had needed Stephan's forgiveness, he needed theirs as well.

His mind showed him Jessica, glowing with life. She was smiling and positively radiant. All traces of her time here were gone. She was happy, at peace. That place, wherever it was, was where she belonged. She was life and laughter and goodness—she didn't belong in the dark. He'd take her home, and though it would be the hardest thing he'd ever done, Lucian would give her back to the light.

He'd let her go.

ဆာလ

The deafening silence was driving Jessica insane. She sat on the floor with her hand to her bitten neck. A torch set in a rusted sconce gave her enough light to see. Her gaze was fixed on the iron door of the cell.

The loss of blood left her weak, as did the emotional drain of the last months. She didn't know how much time had passed, only that it seemed like forever since the fight had ended. Not knowing if Lucian would be the one to come walking out of the cell was a torture all its own.

She wished she was only worried about her own life, but she wasn't. Lucian was part of her now, in her heart—in her soul. His suffering had become hers, so although she was out here, a piece of her was in the cell with him. How could she hate him? All he'd wanted to do was go home. Wasn't that exactly what she wanted? Home was a powerful force. It called to someone in their darkest hour, offering comfort where there is none. It broke her heart that, in going home, Lucian had destroyed his family. She couldn't imagine carrying around the burden of that for seven hundred years. It would have broken her long ago.

The door of the cell finally pulled open, startling her. Jessica's heart skipped a beat and time came to a crashing halt as she waited to see who would emerge from the dark. Seeing it was Lucian, she hiccupped on a cry and jumped to her feet. She lunged for him and wrapped her arms around him. As soon as their bodies collided, Lucian grunted and hugged her close.

He didn't try to stop her or soothe her. Instead, he simply let her cry. She realized, with some amount of dread, he might be crying as well. Only after her tears had stopped did Jessica step back and meet his poignant stare.

"Is Stephan... Is he dead?"

Oh, God, how she hated to ask him that. She couldn't bear the idea of the pain he must be in. Not of the body, since his burns seemed to have healed, but of the mind and heart. She adored her brother, and could imagine Lucian's pain.

Lucian nodded curtly. "You're safe now."

His voice was thick with emotion and pain. Good God, he'd just killed his brother. Yes, she was safe—but at what cost?

"I'm so sorry, Lucian."

He set her away and cast a sad glance inside the cell. "Don't be. We both know it was unavoidable."

"That doesn't mean it can't hurt."

The tormented look that crossed Lucian's face broke her heart. "I'm fine."

She suspected he was lying, but didn't push him. He'd suffered enough tonight.

He took hold of her hand and pulled her along behind him as he stormed down the long corridor that ran alongside the cells. She nearly tripped up the steep steps as she struggled to keep pace with him. Given how fast he was moving, it was obvious he needed to put as much distance between himself and the dungeon as possible. Not that Jessica blamed him. All she could do was run behind and pray she didn't trip again.

Once in the hall, Lucian stopped so suddenly Jessica skidded into his back. He dropped her hand as he looked out over the medieval hall. It was as if this was the first time he was seeing his home in centuries. When her hand settled on his arm, he glanced down at it before staring back at the hall.

"I can feel my parents here."

"You mean their ghosts?"

Lucian nodded sadly, his grief a tangible thing. "The first time the hunger hit was when I came back here. The pain of it rivaled the flames that killed me. It felt like a thousand blades cutting through my body. And the thirst...oh God, I'd never known anything like it."

He shook her hand from his arm and moved slowly through the hall. "The thirst burned my mouth and throat and the hunger twisted at my insides. I had to stop the pain." He didn't look at her. Instead, he turned his face to the ceiling, as if he could find absolution there. "I fed from Stephan before I ran out of here. I could have killed him."

"But you didn't kill him."

Lucian finally faced her. His eyes blazed with silver fire. His upper lip was drawn back in a terrible snarl. Jessica shrank back, afraid of him for the first time since he'd freed her from the dungeon.

"Yes I did. I might not have done the deed myself, but my actions brought about the death of my entire family."

"Lucian, you can't believe..."

"The Obyri followed me here." He sidestepped her touch when she went to grab his hand. "They have no conscience. They kill with a savagery that puts renegades to shame. They thought I was the Guardian instead of Tristan. I didn't know they had tracked me from Messina to Penwick. They came after I'd left. They slaughtered my parents and turned Stephan." The look in his eyes chilled Jessica down to her bones. "So, yes, Jessica, I am responsible for their deaths."

Hesitantly, believing he'd push her away again, she reached for his hand. To her surprise he didn't. She slipped her hand into his. "You did what anyone else in your position would have done. You went home."

"And now they're all dead. I just sent my brother to Hell." He yanked his hand from hers and moved toward the blackened hearth. He stopped and crossed his arms over his chest, staring at the pile of ash. "I'll take you home and I want you to forget what happened here."

There was an edge in his tone that brought tears to her eyes. "How can you expect me to forget?"

How can you expect me to forget you?

He turned and stalked back to her. Seizing her by the shoulder, Lucian shook her hard. Fire flashed in his eyes and his fangs were bared. "You have to forget it all...even me. You have to *live*, Jessica."

Jessica choked on a sob and tried to put her arms around him but he pushed her away. "How can you ask me to forget us?"

Lucian brought his face close enough for her to see the pain he tried desperately to hide. "There *is* no us."

If Lucian wanted to wound her, he'd succeeded. Those words cut clean through her, made her heart hurt. "No us, Lucian? Then why the hell did you risk your life for me?"

He released her. As he stepped back, he shook his head. His expression was hard, indifferent. "I don't care about you. You were nothing more than a responsibility."

The impact of Lucian's cold statement caused her to stagger backwards. She put a hand to the wound on her neck as her heart hammered painfully, making the wound throb. Her fingers came away bloody. For a moment, she wasn't sure if the blood was from the wound on her neck or the cut to her heart.

"You're lying." She wanted to scream the words at him, but instead they came out in a hoarse whisper. She dropped her hand, letting the blood trickle down the side of her neck.

"No, Jessica, I'm not."

At the cold conviction in his tone, Jessica gathered the tattered remnants of her pride and nodded just as curtly as she'd seen him do. She wanted to believe he was lying, that his pain was talking. She wouldn't risk further humiliation by trying to prove him wrong.

After all, the glaring truth was, of all the women who'd passed through his existence, he'd only given his body to her. Only the strongest of emotions would cause a man such as Lucian to break his last vow to God.

Jessica had only one last thing to say to him. "You, Lucian of Penwick, are a goddamn coward."

For a moment, she thought she'd pushed him too far. He grabbed her by her upper arms and growled. "*Goddamned* is right."

He released her and Jessica stepped back. She watched as he stalked from the hall. He'd left her alone in a place filled with the ghosts of his past. He didn't look back, not once, not even to see if she followed. Jessica knew he couldn't look back, and that a piece of him had died in the cell where he'd killed his brother.

As she walked from the hall, Jessica knew a part of her had died there as well.

Chapter Twenty-One

Lucian hadn't been lying when he'd told her the Seacrest in Damascus was an exact replica of the castle here in Northumberland. Not that Jessica would know if the inside was the same, but the outside was exact. So much so, it was eerie, and she had to keep reminding herself she wasn't back in Pennsylvania.

They were made welcome by Edward Beaumont, a short, thin man with gentle brown eyes. His warm smile and fatherly manner put her at ease. He possessed none of the stereotypical stuffiness of the English aristocracy. Jessica liked him immediately.

The moment she'd passed into his home, Edward had given her a big bear hug, the same as he'd given Lucian. He treated her like long-lost family, making her at home, even though her home might as well be a million miles away.

It took Jessica less than an hour of being around Edward to know he was sick. Fatally sick. Lucian obviously knew it as well, given the way he hovered over Edward, attending to his every need.

Listening to Edward cough made her lungs ache. He repeatedly dabbed at his mouth with a handkerchief. More than once, when he pulled it away, she noticed it was speckled with blood.

They'd been here for two days now. They had to wait for a Templar named Constantine to arrive with Allison Parker's sister, Lexine. From the warning Lucian gave her about Constantine—the only time Lucian had spoken more than two words at a time to her—he had to be an awfully frightening creature. She wasn't eager to meet him, although she was excited at the prospect of traveling back to America with Lexine.

Though they'd never been friends, Jessica was looking forward to seeing a familiar face. She was also dreading it. She didn't know what to say if Lexine asked her about her time at Penwick. She couldn't talk about it, couldn't give voice to the horrors, didn't want anyone to know what had gone on there.

Though the sun had long since set, Jessica hadn't gone down to the hall to join Edward and Lucian. She wasn't up for the contrast of Edward's joviality and Lucian's indifference. It was killing her how he kept on ignoring her. If he was forced to acknowledge her, he did so with a coldness that chilled her to the bone.

His treatment of her forced Jessica to confront the fact that maybe he hadn't been lying. Maybe he really didn't care for her. Shared adversity could draw people close. There was a good chance that's what had happened, and now that the danger had passed, so too had his temporary sense of affection. Such a possibility was a bitter pill to swallow; yet Jessica did just that, knowing she really hadn't any other choice.

Perched on the window seat, Jessica stared out into the night. Earlier today she'd gone out into the courtyard and enjoyed an afternoon spent under the sun. Though it had been cold, she'd stayed outside for hours, enjoying the light after months of suffering in the dark. She wished she'd been able to share an afternoon like that with Lucian, a wish that only acted as a reminder of how different their worlds were.

At the heavy rap on her door, Jessica sighed, dreading having to face anyone. She just wanted to continue hiding in her room. Her heart was safer here, where it couldn't be pierced by Lucian's indifference here.

After calling out for the person to come in, the door opened. The sight of Lucian standing in the doorway felt like a fist crushing her heart. "I just wanted to let you know that all the arrangements have been made. We leave in two days."

This should be good news for her. Great news. She was going home. Yet, she was terrified. How could she face her family? They'd see right through her to the disgusting things that had been done to her. They couldn't know—they couldn't see the ugliness she'd suffered.

Yes, she missed her family, but the main reason she wanted to leave as soon as possible was she couldn't continue to be around Lucian. His indifference was tearing her apart.

"I thought we had to wait to leave until your friends Constantine and Lexine got here."

"They'll be here tomorrow night."

"Oh." She looked back out the window, knowing that after he took her home, she'd never see him again.

"You're doing well?" He looked pointedly at the bandage covering the healing wound on her neck.

Though she returned her attention to him, it pained her to look at him. He was everything she wanted, and yet nothing she could have. It took everything she had to shrug and act as indifferent as he. "As good as can be expected."

Jessica wasn't going to lie and tell him she was fine. She wasn't. She missed the Lucian who'd made her believe he cared about her.

"I'm glad."

He turned to leave. Jessica leapt from the window seat before she could think better of it. "Wait."

He froze and turned back to her. "What?"

She crossed the room and came to stand before him. The sheer size of him made her feel terribly small. "I understand you don't care for me." Her mind screamed for him to tell her she was wrong. He didn't, of course, and her heart died just a little bit more. "But that doesn't mean we're enemies, does it?"

He took a single step back into her room. "No, Jessica, we aren't enemies."

Oh God, she wanted to touch him so badly. She wanted to smooth the frown from his brow and take away his pain. "Good. After everything we've been through together, I had hoped we could at least be friends."

He stared at her in silence for so long that Jessica was about to turn away, unable to bear the weight of his glare. "Once I get you back to your family you won't see me again."

She saw her life playing out like a sad movie. She'd search the shadows for a while, wondering if he was there, watching her. Eventually, she would give up and accept that he meant what he'd said here tonight. She'd never see him again. And so, she'd go about her life, pretending these last months hadn't affected her. Pretend each day she wasn't wondering about him. And when her time came to leave this world, Jessica would look back at her time at Penwick as the worst time in her life—and the greatest.

"I see," she replied with a dignity she didn't feel, fighting the need to look away from his profound stare. "Will you be staying in Damascus or will you come back to England?"

"Does it matter?"

Yes, it matters. It matters so much it's killing me. "No, I suppose not."

He reached out toward her and Jessica's heart began to thunder wildly. He didn't touch her, merely hovered his hand in the space between them. He shook his head and dropped his hand. Her soul shattered.

"I have to go." Lucian turned to leave again and Jessica's heart fell. Without thinking of her actions, she curled her hand around his forearm and whispered his name. He turned back around, glanced down at her hand and then looked back into her eyes. "What is it, Jessica?"

He spat out her name and, in that moment, Jessica was stripped of all pride. "You may not care about me, and that's fine. I have to accept that. But just so you know, I don't give a damn about your past."

Something passed over his face and Jessica thought he'd break. She foolishly imagined he'd take her in his arms and kiss her until her heart stopped hurting. He did no such thing. Instead, Lucian shook off her hold, turned sharply and stormed from the chamber. The silence that followed in the wake of his departure and the agony of her broken heart were too heavy a burden to bear.

She closed the door just before the first tear slipped down her cheek. By the time she made it to the bed, her tears fell in earnest. After she'd finally cried herself to sleep, her dreams were haunted by the vision of Lucian standing in the moonlight, his hand held out for her to take.

ଽଠଔ

As soon as Jessica closed the door, Lucian's legs faltered. He slammed his back against the wall just as Jessica's muffled sobs reached him. They struck him with the force of a hailstorm of bullets. That he was the cause of those tears killed him all over again. He'd sworn never to hurt her, yet he'd done exactly that. He'd caused her pain and there was no way he could take it from her. Not unless he wanted to drag her down to his world—and that was something he wasn't willing to do.

How the hell couldn't she see past his mask of indifference? Edward had, and he'd been torturing Lucian about it whenever the two of them were alone.

Pretending he didn't care for her was the hardest thing he'd ever had to do. All he wanted was to take her in his arms and love her as she deserved. He wanted to kiss away each tear and tell her how much he cared about her, how much he loved her.

Listening to her cries, it took everything he had not to rush back into her chamber. He knew if he did, he'd be lost. His resolve would break and he'd do something that couldn't be undone—such as lay claim to her and pull her down into his darkness.

He touched the spot where her hand had been on his arm. He still felt her warmth, reminding him she didn't belong there.

He couldn't stand listening to her heart-wrenching cries. With a growled curse, he pushed away from the wall. As he passed Edward's chamber the door swung open. There stood Edward, wrapped in a burgundy robe. He looked frail, not at all the robust man he'd once been. The cancer was eating away at him, rotting him from the inside out. Yet Edward refused any treatment. Lucian's senses told him the disease was now in its final stage. They were going to lose Edward within the month. The Templars would mourn the loss of him for eternity.

"You're a bloody fool, son."

"As are you."

Edward waved a hand through the air, obviously knowing exactly what Lucian referred to. "Bah! What good would treatment do me? Leave me hooked up to machines and pumped full of medicines? That's not how I'll leave this world. This cancer will take me on my feet, living the last moments of my life rather than lying on my back, dead before I die."

Lucian admired Edward's strength and fortitude. Edward Beaumont was a man who said to hell with convention and lived his life exactly as he wanted. He was a generous man with all that was his. Not only did he look to all of the Templars as his sons, he also treated his step-niece as if she were blood.

After Edward's sister, Victoria, and her American husband died in a car crash four years ago, he'd invited Frank's daughter to spend the summer at Seacrest. As soon as Brenna Monroe arrived, it was as if she'd always been here, part of the family.

She and Edward were as thick as thieves. She'd even met all the Templars, save Tristan. Of course she had no idea what they were—or at least she pretended not to. Brenna had to have known something was odd about them, yet she said nothing. They'd all simply gone on as if everything was perfectly normal.

"Stay out of what you know nothing about," Lucian warned, not wanting to get lectured about his decision regarding Jessica.

Edward had the nerve to snort at that. He raked his gaze over Lucian, who stood with hands fisted at his sides as the miserable sound of Jessica's tears tore through him.

"I know a fool when I see one. I also know a thing or two about wasted opportunity."

"I'd be a fool if I pretended I belonged in her life."

Edward swayed. Lucian went to grab him but was shooed away. "Leave me be. I can damn well stand on my own two feet." He dragged in a breath as he steadied himself by gripping the doorframe. "Listen to her crying. That girl loves you, Luc, and you well know it. Don't throw that away."

Love. What the hell did he know about love? Jessica deserved more than he had to give her. She deserved sunlight and happiness—and a man who didn't have to hide from the sun. A man who didn't have to feed from other women. A man who wasn't damned. Lucian wasn't that man, nor could he ever be. He had to push her away in order to give her back her life.

Maybe one day Jessica would put her time in the dungeon behind her, and he'd become nothing but a distant memory. It was he who'd suffer throughout time, always remembering her. Forever loving her.

"Leave me be, man," Lucian spat out. "This is hard enough without you adding to my torment."

"Luc..."

"No. I'm taking her home to her family. It's where she belongs."

Chapter Twenty-Two

Constantine came striding into Seacrest Castle a sight for sore eyes. Lucian had never imagined anything would have brought him back to Wiltshire. Yet one look at Lexine Parker told Lucian exactly why Constantine would return to the place where he'd suffered so greatly.

Lucian went to greet Constantine, expecting him to be the same grumpy bastard he'd always been. Instead, Constantine marched right up to him and gave him a crushing hug before landing a punch to his gut.

Grunting, Lucian doubled over. "Good to see you too, Con. Now what in the hell was that for?"

"Don't you ever shield yourself from me again."

"It was necessary," Lucian replied.

"The hell it was."

"I wasn't going to jeopardize any of you." Before Constantine could say more, Lucian held up a hand. "This was my fight, Constantine. It was my brother. You can understand that, can't you?"

It took Constantine a long while, as if contemplating Lucian's words, before he gave him a curt nod. Once he knew that issue was put to rest, Lucian turned his attention to the beautiful woman clinging to Constantine's hand. His first thought was that Lexine looked nothing like Allie. His next thought was that she seemed too fragile to possess a force such as the Daystar within her. And yet, he saw the power reflected in her bright silver eyes.

"You must be Lexine," Lucian said to her. "I've heard so much about you."

She had an enchanting smile, but then, everything about the ethereal little woman was captivating. Taken aback by her unexpected hug, he hissed at the surge of energy that shot through him. The contact lasted only a moment, and yet it shook him to his core.

Lucian stared at her in awe as stepped back to Constantine's side. She smiled as she slipped her hand back into his. Constantine cocked a brow at him, a hint of a smile playing on his lips. "She packs a punch, doesn't she?"

Though Tristan had filled him in on the details, Lucian still couldn't believe that the Daystar was a person. No wonder they'd had a hell of a time finding her. They had expected it to be an it, not a she. It made sense that the Daystar would be found in Damascus, given the town's significance.

Lucian wondered how the good people of Damascus would react if they knew the sort of paranormal power hidden under the surface of the seemingly serene rural towns of Wayne County.

Didn't anyone find it odd half the towns around there were named after biblical places? Galilee, Edessa, Damascus—all of them taken from the Holy Land. And let's not even get into Church Street in Edessa. In the span of only four blocks were ten churches of varying denominations. There was a need for an abundance of God and no one seemed to wonder why.

There had been nights when Lucian walked the land around Seacrest, marveling at how drastically the world had changed over the centuries. Yet many things remained remarkably the same. As much as humanity grew as a people, too many mistakes of the past were repeated.

Though the world had gone on around Damascus, it was slow to catch up. Though it had changed since the time Judas had been there with the relic, it remained sparsely populated and the mountains kept it cut off from the rest of the world.

Judas had chosen wisely.

As the first protector of the relic, Judas had earned his redemption. It gave the Templars, who took his place after over a thousand years as Guardian, hope that they too would one day walk in Heaven.

Over time, the relic's presence drew the unholy to Damascus, making it a hotbed of paranormal activity. It was now not only home to the holiest of relics, it was also populated with all the things that dwell in the shadows. Vampires especially—who could use it to gain unstoppable powers.

Lucian knew there were times when Tristan thought to move the relic, to take it someplace safer. Each time, he'd decided against it. Lucian understood why. Damascus was already overrun with vampires. He didn't want to infect another place with their evil.

So he'd stayed in Damascus despite the constant threat of renegades and the Obryi finding him.

"I heard it went down badly. How fares the First?"

Constantine grunted at that. "Isobel was well on the way to recovery when we left."

"I still can't believe all this time no one realized Isobel of Lowel was the First." Lucian shook his head in amazement. "The Order knows how to keep their secrets."

They would have said more but Jessica descended the stairs into the hall. Lucian had eyes only for her as he watched her approach. She was wearing a snug gray woolen dress with calf-high black boots. Though they were borrowed from one of the servants, they fit her perfectly. She was still painfully thin, but she looked exquisite with her hair unbound and floating around her face, which was still pale from her ordeal.

She froze when she got close enough to Constantine to see the scar cutting down the left side of his face. That and his black T-shirt, which read, *Crazy enough to kill. Smart enough to get away with it.* Though it was just a saying on a shirt, on Constantine, it came off as a threat.

Lucian expected Jessica to turn around and run right back up the stairs. It's what most people would do when confronted with the glare Constantine directed at her. He should have known better. Jessica hadn't backed down from Stephan, and she wasn't going to turn tail and run from Constantine.

"So, this is the female you almost sacrificed your existence to protect?"

Lucian leveled a glare at Constantine. "Yes."

Lucian knew that was all he needed to say. That one word spoke volumes. Lucian made a point to ignore Constantine's knowing—and curious—look that went to Jessica.

Before he could warn her that Constantine was all bark and no bite, Lexine pushed past him.

"Hi Jessica." Lex's tone was light, as if it were the most natural thing in the world for them to be meeting here. "I don't know if you remember me, but we had a common friend. Lori Rutledge?"

Jessica was so captivated by the terrifying sight of Constantine that it took her a moment for Lexine's words to register. Even after she realized Lexine was talking to her,

Jessica found it difficult to drag her eyes from the terrifying—and gorgeous—black-haired man across the great hall.

Dear God, he was huge. Bigger even than Lucian, and that nasty scar down his face did nothing to soften his ferocious appearance. Not that it made him ugly. It simply made him more fearsome.

He was tattooed and encased in a Goth getup that would put anyone who'd ever stepped foot into The Gate to shame. Noticing the brand of the Templar seal on his right hand, Jessica was shocked. She would have never thought such a frightening creature could be a Templar Vampire. He didn't look like he was a path of redemption. Of course, Stephan had seemed the perfect gentleman. Refined, elegant. It just went to show how deceiving looks could be.

Finally able to look somewhere other than at the Templar, she frowned at that ethereal woman gliding toward her. It didn't take her long to snap out of her stupor and realize this was Lexine Parker.

One look in her shimmering silver eyes told Jessica she was far from normal. And yet she bore no fangs, which obviously meant she wasn't a vampire. She was something different.

"I remember you."

Lex's smile was radiant. "Really? I'm surprised. Usually I was the one who always blended into the background. I didn't think anyone noticed me."

Given how gorgeous she was, Lexine could hardly blend in anywhere. "We only met once, but I do remember you."

Even if she hadn't remembered Lexine personally, Allie and Christian's reputations would have preceded her. One was the town nut and the other had been a junkie before he'd been killed. It was pretty difficult not to know who Lexine Parker was.

Jessica barely contained the shiver that passed through her when Lucian introduced her to the black-haired giant. *Constantine Draegon.* Somehow, his name was extremely fitting.

Lucian and Constantine went on about matters that pertained to their world while Lexine tried to engage her in small talk. Jessica couldn't hang on to a single word being said. All she heard in her head was Lucian telling her he didn't care about her. His rejection had left her raw, and she couldn't continue to stand there as if she weren't dying inside.

She'd never been good at pretending, and her heart still hurt too much to begin now. Besides, she was tired. Bone-weary, actually, and she wanted to go to sleep and put another day behind her. She also wanted to go check on Edward. He'd looked terrible before he'd retired to his chamber.

"Would you both excuse me?" She didn't dare look at any of them—least of all Lucian. She was about to hurry up the stairs but Lucian stopped her by grabbing her arm.

"No. You don't have the right to touch me anymore."

"Jessica..."

"Don't, Lucian, please." She shook his hand from her. Instead of going up the stairs, she turned and ran from the hall. Once out in the courtyard, she dragged the crisp night air into her suddenly starving lungs. She leaned over, resting her hands on her thighs as she fought for breath.

Once she finally felt more in control of herself, she straightened and looked to the cloudless night sky. She wondered what it would be like to only see night. She couldn't imagine it. The prospect of never seeing the sun again was something she couldn't even imagine. And yet, that was Lucian's reality.

Maybe it was for the best that she returned to her world and forgot all about Lucian of Penwick. Maybe...

"Eventually it will get easier."

Jessica almost jumped out of her skin when she heard a voice behind her. She spun around to see Lex standing there. "What will get easier?"

Lexine sighed softly and stepped closer. She seemed to understand Jessica wasn't comfortable with the whole vampire thing. And though Lex obviously wasn't a vampire, whatever she was put Jessica on edge.

"I know you think Lucian doesn't want you. I thought the same thing about Constantine. I swear that man made an art form out of being a miserable bastard. But I learned it was because he cared for me that made him that way."

"You and Constantine are a couple?"

"We're mated." Lex let out a musical laugh at Jessica's surprise. "I wouldn't let him get away."

Although Lex's determination was admirable, Jessica wasn't sure what was right—fighting for Lucian or walking away.

"Circumstance threw us together. Whatever might have been between us was only due to the situation we were in. Now that our ordeal is over, so is anything between us."

Lex lifted a single brow. "And maybe if you keep telling yourself that you'll believe it. Eventually. Or maybe not. Maybe you'll carry the burden of your feelings for Lucian to the grave. I'd hate to see that happen."

Jessica crossed her arms over her chest and shook her head. "It won't. Trust me. I don't care about him."

That lie was bitter on her tongue and sounded unconvincing even to her own ears.

Lex placed a hand on her arm. Jessica was startled by the wonderful thrill of energy that passed through her. "I may not know Lucian, but after spending the last months with the Templars, I've learned a thing or two about them." Her hand dropped away and suddenly Jessica felt the cold of the November night. "Don't give up on him, that's all I'm saying."

Jessica's arms unfolded as regret made her throat constrict and her heart feel as if a hand was squeezing it. "I didn't give up on him. Lucian gave up on me."

Jessica returned to the keep, not even bothering to see if Lex followed. She ignored the stares from both Lucian and Constantine and retreated to her chamber. She wanted to check on Edward, who wasn't feeling well and was resting in his room, but knew her present mood wasn't conducive to a pleasant visit. Instead, she closed herself away in her chamber and prayed to God that, once she was home, she'd be able to forget all about Lucian of Penwick.

೮೦೦೪

"Go away, Con."

"I'd rather stay and bother you."

Now why didn't that surprise him? Constantine was getting as bad as Raphael when it came to being an annoying bastard. Doing his best to ignore him, Lucian kept his gaze focused on the flames dancing in the hearth. Given how loud Constantine was when he dropped onto the chair beside him, he wasn't going to be ignored.

"So, you're going to be as stubborn as Sebastian about this?"

"This isn't the same as Sebastian and Allie and you know it."

"No, it's not."

Lucian was shocked to hear Constantine's quick agreement. "Glad you agree. Now, bugger off, Constantine. I want to be alone."

Of course, it wasn't going to be that easy to get rid of Dragon.

"Sebastian wasn't a virgin." Lucian held back the urge to plant his fist in Constantine's face. "Although he did abstain for three hundred years. That would turn any man back into a virgin. So maybe you aren't as different as I first assumed."

"I said leave off."

"I know better than most that we all have our crosses to bear." He gave Lucian a pointed look. "Don't be a fool and push her away."

"You of all people would say this to me?"

"Especially me."

The guilt of his family's fate festering inside him was a wound that would never heal. It would rot in him for all time. It would consume him, until the burden became too heavy to bear. He couldn't condemn Jessica to such a fate.

"I have nothing to offer her but darkness and death."

"And Sebastian and I have more to offer Lex and Allie?"

Allie had stepped willingly into the night. No, she had jumped in eagerly with both feet. Lexine was fated to be here. Jessica was different. She didn't belong here. "I won't trap her in our world."

"She's trapped here whether you want it or not."

"No, she's not." Lucian ran a hand over his eyes and through his hair. "She's going home where she belongs."

Yet, greedy bastard that he was, he needed to touch her one last time before he pushed her from his existence. He couldn't stop himself from getting up, ignoring Constantine's knowing look, and leaving the hall. He walked up the stairs with a heavy heart, knowing what he had to do would only complicate matters more.

He nearly faltered once but his need for her gave him the resolve to knock on her door. After she opened the door, he pushed past her and strode into her bedroom as if he had all the right in the world to be there.

He gave up the last of his heart in the pregnant moment before he claimed her body for the last time.

Chapter Twenty-Three

True to his word, Lucian returned her to her family. Jessica knew she should be relieved to be home. Instead, she was miserable.

They'd arrived back in Pennsylvania in the late afternoon. They'd had to go directly to Seacrest Castle, which was indeed an exact replica of the ancient fortress they'd just left. They stayed there only long enough for Lucian and Constantine to emerge from their crates and be welcomed home by the rest of the Templars. Jessica's head spun from being around such a formidable bunch of men. All five of them were gorgeous, and Allie and Lex, well, two more beautiful women she'd never seen. It was clear how close the sisters were. The way they'd barely left each other's sides from the moment Lex walked into the hall had Jessica missing her brother so badly it caused physical pain.

While they'd waited for the sun to set so that Lucian could take her home, Jessica learned a few things about the Templars. For one, she realized Constantine wasn't half as mean as he looked. Oh, he was ferocious to be sure, but he had a soft side reserved strictly for his fellow Templars. And the way he was with Lex had her longing to be treated with the same tenderness by Lucian.

Of course, it didn't look like that was going to happen. Since the windows had been blocked out, Lucian and Constantine didn't have to spend the flight back to America trapped within their crates. Constantine spent the flight with Lexine. Lucian kept to himself, barely saying more than two words to anyone. Jessica might as well have not even been there for all the attention he'd paid her. She'd kept to herself on the plane, sitting alone and wondering how she'd adjust back to her life now that she was returning home. She'd find a way, though. She had no choice. She'd find the strength to push through the pain and rebuild her life.

Although, on the short drive to her house, Jessica's resolve faltered. She didn't want to have to walk away from Lucian. She didn't want to face a future without him. The prospect actually scared her. So, after they came to her house, she didn't immediately get out of the car. She sat there miserably, wishing he'd say something—anything—that would give her a hint that this was just a cruel joke and that he loved her as much as she did him.

But he sat there in silence, hands gripping the steering wheel as he stared out the windshield. He didn't look at her, not even when she'd said goodbye.

He simply let her go without a word.

Afraid to walk back into the normalcy that was once her life, Jessica's stomach was twisted into a painful knot as she stood before the front door of her house. As much as she'd changed, everything around her seemed to have stayed the same. Seeing how serene everything seemed, Jessica knew she was going to be a stranger in her own life.

Her trembling hand hovered on the doorknob. She was afraid to go inside. What would she say to her parents? How could she explain away the last three months? Sparing a glance down at her body clad in Lexine's clothes, Jessica knew there was no way her family wasn't going to see how her ordeal had ravaged her. They were going to ask a million questions, none of which she could answer.

She listened for voices coming from inside her house. Her heart leapt at the sound of her mother's voice. Her palms went slick when she heard her father. Anthony's Camaro was parked in the driveway. Her entire family was home and yet she stood frozen to the spot, unable to walk in.

Dropping her hand, Jessica spun around and threw a desperate look to Lucian. He was waiting patiently for her to gather the courage to walk into her home. All she wanted to do was run back to him, throw her arms around his neck, and never let him go.

Summoning the strength that had gotten her through the last months, Jessica dared something she never would have if she were standing face to face with him. She took a deep breath and released it on a sad sigh. "I love you, Lucian."

She turned away from the car and faced the door. Curling her hand around the knob, Jessica turned it. She swallowed past the lump in her throat and pushed the door open. Her steps faltered only once as she walked out of Lucian's world and back into her own.

80C3

Though he was certain it was impossible, Lucian's heart hurt as he watched Jessica walk through the door. He should have driven away once she was inside. He didn't—no, he couldn't. As much as he knew he had to, he wasn't ready to let go. So he stayed long after the door closed behind her and the elated shouts of her family broke the quiet of the night. Only after a curtain was pushed aside and he thought he saw Jessica peering out the window did he finally drive away.

His existence played out before him as he sped down the darkened country road. For the first time since the dungeon, the dark seemed to close in on him. As impossible as it was, he felt suffocated from the weight of it. Trapped by it. It was the one prison he'd never escape.

During the short drive back to Seacrest, Lucian dreaded answering the questions about what had happened at Penwick. He wasn't ready to speak of killing Stephan. The moment he'd taken his brother's life was something he couldn't revisit just now—not after he'd just sent away the only woman he'd ever love. One was painful enough to have to deal with. Both together had left him devastated. He wasn't ready to share that pain, though he knew the Templars would sense it. After all, didn't Raphael like to say that when one farts, they all fart? Though a distasteful way of putting it, it was an apt description of the bond they shared.

As Lucian pulled up to the castle's gate, he slowed. The relic housed here called to him, tempted him. Now that he'd have to reside here, he wasn't looking forward to the constant temptation. He honestly didn't know how Tristan did it night after night. Guardian's strength amazed him. Lucian knew if he were in his place he'd not make it seem as effortless to resist as Tristan did.

As he drove under the gate, he immediately saw all the Templars' cars parked near the keep. It was a full house, and as much as it comforted him, it unnerved him as well. After he parked his car behind Sebastian's Charger, he got out and took a moment to get the feel of being back here. Although he hadn't been here long before Stephan had gotten to him, he felt at home here.

He hadn't been standing there long when Tristan came out to meet him. "I can't tell you how good it is to have you back, Luc." Tristan clapped him on the shoulder and looked him over, assessing him. "For a time there, we thought we'd lost you."

Lucian swallowed down a bitter mouthful of emotion. "For a time there, you nearly did."

Tristan stepped back and nodded in silent understanding of the ordeal Lucian had suffered and the things he'd been forced to do to escape his prison. Tension filled the space between them over the things that went unsaid, even as they were understood. After all, it was Tristan who'd first seen him when he'd arrived at Seacrest, burnt raw and near wild from hunger and eaten away with guilt. If anyone knew what it was Lucian suffered now, Guardian would.

"I was...worried. You shouldn't have closed yourself off from us. We could have gotten to you and Jessica sooner."

"This battle was one I had to fight alone."

"You were never alone. We were there with you."

"I know, Tristan. Believe me, I know."

The Templars might have been there in spirit, but Jessica had been there in the flesh, suffering alongside him. His pain had been hers, and now, all he wanted was for her to have peace and to never know another moment of pain. And yet, the agony he'd sensed just before she'd entered her house was epic. He knew, however, that her heartache would fade and she'd forget him as she slipped back into her life.

It was as it should be, no matter the cost to him. Jessica deserved better than him. She deserved life, which was the one thing he could never give her.

"Go easy, Luc. In time, you'll both heal."

"Now that's where you're wrong. I'll never heal from this." Lucian puffed out an empty sigh. "Raphael is going to torment me over Jessica to be sure."

That remark broke the tension of the moment and had Tristan laughing. "He wouldn't be Raphael if he didn't."

How true that was. They fell in step together as they waked to the keep. "I foresee a beating coming his way."

Tristan shook his head in exasperation. "I think even Allie is ready to pummel him for his constant teasing. The only one he seems to play nice with is Lex."

At the mention of her, Lucian frowned in consideration. "When did you realize she was the Daystar?"

"Not long after you were taken. The mark of the Daystar emerged on her stomach just as her power began to grow beyond control. We all feared she'd not make it through the ritual." He shook his head. "If you could have felt the punch her power packed you'd have sworn she'd never be able to survive its strength."

"And yet she did."

Tristan smiled. "She's every bit Allie's sister."

"She's given Constantine peace."

"That she has."

Before they entered the keep, Lucian turned to Tristan and leveled him with a concerned look. "The signs are falling into place, aren't they?"

Tristan raked a hand through his blond hair. "Aye, they are. The Obyri are coming, and they're coming fast. All we can do is be ready."

"I'm not looking forward to it."

"Nor am I."

They entered the keep to find Sebastian and Constantine coming down the stairs looking disgruntled, to say the least. "What's wrong?"

"We were dismissed."

Tristan cocked a brow at Constantine's grumble. "Were you now?"

Sebastian growled at Constantine, who was glaring at him menacingly. "The women wanted to be alone to catch up."

Right then, Raphael came sauntering from the kitchen. "I knew I liked Lex. She's my kind of woman if she gave you the boot already."

"She didn't give me the boot, you bloody bastard." A low growl came from Constantine as he touched down into the hall. "You, out on the lists. You're due a beating."

Lucian pointed at himself at Constantine's announcement. "Me?"

"Yes."

"What the hell for?"

"Let's start with how you closed yourself off from me."

Lucian snorted at Constantine's boast. "I think not, you ornery bastard."

"I think so," he countered.

"I don't care how bloody you two make each other as long as I have at him before the sun comes up," Sebastian demanded.

Lucian glared at Sebastian. "I look forward to the chance, Sage."

"Don't get too cocky, Luc. After he's done with you, I want my chance," Raphael announced.

"Go easy on Rogue, Lucian," Constantine warned. "I've been meaning to have a go at him for months."

Raphael sneered at Constantine. "Pride still stinging that Lex liked me first?"

"Keep running off at the mouth, I dare you."

Raphael looked undaunted by Constantine's snarl. "Oh damn, for a moment there, I forgot to be afraid of you."

As Constantine dragged a laughing Raphael to the lists, Lucian hung back a moment and watched them. As much as he was glad to be back here, and knew this was where he belonged, he couldn't help feeling as if a part of him was missing. He knew he'd never get back what he'd left with Jessica. She'd hold his heart for the rest of eternity.

Chapter Twenty-Four

One month had passed since the night he'd returned Jessica home to her family. Not a moment went by that Lucian wasn't haunted by her. Her face followed him everywhere, flashing through his mind as a constant reminder of what he'd lost by letting her go.

Lucian retreated to his chamber each morning, knowing sleep would offer no reprieve from his torment. He woke each night to an emptiness that was slowly rotting him from the inside out. He couldn't escape it, couldn't outrun it, nor could he take to the lists and use the time there to purge his emotions.

His melancholy had become an almost tangible force around him. For once, even the other Templars gave him a wide berth. He skulked around the castle, much as he had centuries ago in Northumberland, lost in himself, unable—and unwilling—to share what he was feeling with his brothers-in-arms.

Lucian simply couldn't forget Jessica's whispered declaration of love. If he lived a thousand more lifetimes he'd never unhear her say she loved him. It was seared into him, and would stay with him long after he was taken from this world. He'd carry that whisper with him for eternity.

How Lucian had managed to stay away from her, only God knew. As the hours of each night crawled over him, inching toward morning, he fought not to drive to her house and make sure she was home and safe. He knew if he went, even once, he'd be lost. With his body screaming for her warmth and his heart aching for her love, he knew all it would take was one look at her to shatter his resolve and drag her down into his world.

The sharp stab of hunger reminded Lucian of where he was going. He hadn't fed in the last month, too long to go between feedings, even for a Templar. He didn't know how much longer he could fight down the bloodlust, so he drove toward Edessa.

Despite the cold of the early December night and the promise of another snowfall, Lucian raced his Maserati Spyder down Route 371. The dark, broken only by a pale sliver of moon, closed in around him. "Cover Me" by Candle Box played on the radio, the haunting beats adding to his despondency.

He'd almost steered the car toward Jessica's house, rather than making the turn that would take him into Edessa. If the hunger hadn't been riding him, Lucian had to wonder if tonight would have been the night he broke and went to her. As he pulled up to McHenry's Tavern, his hands were shaking as thirst dried out his mouth and hunger ripped through his body. He got out, his boots crunching the snow as he walked through the small lot.

When he entered the smoky tavern, every gaze locked on him. By now, Lucian was used to such a reaction. It was usually worse when he was with the other Templars. They made for an imposing sight, and they never failed to draw unwanted attention.

After ordering a beer, which he had no intention of attempting to drink, Lucian went off to sit at a table in the corner. He immediately noticed a woman sitting alone not far from him. Her melancholy hit him and he knew, of the small crowd gathered here tonight, she was the one who'd be easiest to feed from.

Though he was loath to exploit a human's sorrow, tonight, he had no choice. He wanted to get this feeding over quickly and be on his way. He couldn't linger here, not with his control so close to the breaking point.

Given his mood, even after he sated the bloodlust, he would still be unfit to be around humans. For the first time since he'd learned how to control the raging emotions that cut a brutal path through a vampire, Lucian didn't trust himself to be around humanity.

Sitting at the table, hidden in the shadows, Lucian passed a predatory glance around the tavern. The voices, the song playing on the old jukebox, the stench of smoke, all of it heightened his agitation, which fueled the fire of bloodlust. He gripped the neck of the beer bottle. As his thumb passed over the drops of condensation, his gaze settled on the woman. She looked his way and he was struck by the sadness in her brown eyes—eyes so like Jessica's.

He'd seen that same lost and lonely look on her face as she'd stared into the darkness of the cell. She'd been unable to see him, but Lucian had seen her clearly. Too clearly, since her sorrow was etched onto his very being. So much so, he not only abandoned his plan to feed from the woman, he stalked from the tavern. The woman's emotions had left a bitter taste in his mouth and he knew he'd not be able to take her blood.

Frustrated, Lucian sat in the car for a long while, knowing he should walk right back into the tavern, take the woman outside, and sate the hunger burning inside of him. Instead, he started the car, threw it in drive and sped out of the lot. He knew exactly where he was headed.

Driving down the winding Damascus roads toward Jessica's house, Lucian knew he had to see her one last time. One more time and then he'd let her go from his heart and go on as if he'd never known her.

Of course, he should have known better. If life had proven one thing to him, it was that things rarely worked out as one expected. Such was the case when he pulled up to her house. He heard her crying and it cut through him like a million daggers.

He parked his car across the road and stepped out just as the first flurry of snow started coming down. He peered at Jessica's house, the Victorian home reminding him of a dollhouse. There was a calmness to this home. The very ground was saturated with life. How different from the glorified tomb Seacrest Castle was.

Lucian was about to turn and leave, but a pink curtain was pulled aside, catching his attention. The small figure of a woman blocked the soft light that came spilling out from the window. No, not just a woman. Jessica. In that moment, he knew she sensed him as much as he felt her every emotion. His chest constricted oddly when her gaze settled on him. He actually heard her gasp. Her hand curled around the curtain, as if she needed to hold onto it to keep from falling.

Her other hand flattened against the window, as if to touch him. Her lips worked, but he heard no sound. And then, as if it was pulled from the very depths of her soul, she whispered his name. Lucian knew then that it was long past time to heal them both and find the light in the darkness.

80CB

If Jessica hadn't grabbed hold of the curtain she would have fallen to her knees. *Oh God...* He was here. Lucian was really here. He wasn't a figment of her imagination, but truly here.

Over the course of the last month, her life had slipped into a predictable routine. Jessica hadn't had a single moment of peace. Nor had her heart known a moment without pain. There were times when she woke to the bright morning sun, buried her head under the covers, and cried until she had no tears left. The sun was a harsh reminder that Lucian was locked away in the dark, alone. Then she forced herself to remember that it was his choice to be there alone. She would have gladly given up everything to be with him. Well, maybe not everything. But damn close to it.

She wasn't ready to give up her life.

Since he'd returned her home, not a night went by that Jessica hadn't looked to the shadows and wondered if he was there. Watching her, wanting her, missing her as much as she did him.

Everyone tried to get her to talk about where she'd been and what had happened, but all Jessica would say was that she couldn't talk about it. And that was true. The words had died in her throat the one time she'd tried to talk about it with her brother. All she'd been able to get out was that she'd been held in a castle in England. Beyond that, all that had come were tears.

To say that Anthony had been shocked when she'd told him where she'd been wasn't doing his reaction justice. He'd asked her a million questions, none of which Jessica had been able to answer. She couldn't even explain the wounds on her neck, which had finally healed. The lingering scars would forever remind her of Penwick.

Even if she could talk about what had happened, who would believe her? Who'd believe she'd been abducted by vampires and held in the dungeon of a medieval castle for three months? That was the stuff of make-believe. And yet, memories of the dungeon and of Stephan haunted her. Nightmares woke her in the middle of the night. Her screams would wake her family, and they'd rush in and try to comfort her, but there was nothing to say that would chase Stephan out of her mind.

And when she wasn't remembering Stephan, her thoughts were consumed with Lucian. Instead of thinking about him less as the days went on, he was constantly on her mind. And now he was outside her house, exactly as she'd imagined him every night since she'd come home.

Gathering herself together, Jessica released her hold on the curtain and wiped the tears from her face. She hadn't even realized she'd been crying. She swallowed hard, not knowing if only a second or an hour had passed with her standing there staring down at him, wondering if he was real or not.

Her body numb, Jessica desperately wanted to believe this was real. She shook her head with disbelief. She'd imagined this moment a thousand times—wished for it more times than she could count—never thinking it would actually come true. She couldn't believe he was really here.

She trembled uncomfortably as she stared down at Lucian, too afraid to move lest he dissolve as if in a dream. The sight of him, bathed in moonlight with snow falling all around him, took her breath away. He had the look of a man going into battle.

And then he reached out a hand toward her and Jessica's soul sang. She pushed away from the window and raced from her room. She bounded down the stairs, glad her parents weren't home. She didn't want to have to explain Lucian. She just wanted to get to him, touch him, and make sure he was real.

Her hands fumbled on the knob, but somehow she managed to wrest the door open. He was there, waiting for her. All she had to do was reach out and touch him... "Are you really here?"

"Yes, Jessica, I'm really here."

Tears came to her eyes and she put her shaking hand to her mouth to hold back her cry. "Oh God, Lucian..." Her words were lost, replaced by a wrenching sob.

Lucian took only a single step toward her. "Please don't cry, Jessica." He took another step. "I came to ask for your forgiveness."

Jessica choked back her tears. "There's nothing to forgive. You weren't obligated to love me."

"No, I was never obligated to love you."

Those words made her heart hurt. Didn't he realize he was killing her with his continued rejection of her love? "Don't do this to me again, Lucian, please."

Her plea cut right to Lucian's heart. How could he have ever thought to go on without her? How had he believed they would both be better off apart? Her pain was proof of how wrong he'd been.

"I was never obligated to love you, and yet here I am, Jessica, asking you to forgive me for lying to you."

Her sorrow was killing him all over again. His heart broke more with every tear that fell from her eyes to slide down her ashen cheeks. "When did you lie to me?"

"When I told you I never cared about you." The hope that lit her eyes seared him. "I love you, Jessica, and I pray to God you still love me as well."

She stood frozen for only a moment, and yet to Lucian, it seemed an eternity. He heard the hammering of her heart, the flow of her blood, and every whispered breath. He took in the scent of her, sweeter than anything he'd ever known. As if time had come to a standstill, he drank in the sight of her, from the way her hair hung free to the tips of her bare toes peeking out from beneath dark blue sweatpants.

Then time moved again. Jessica leapt at him, throwing herself in his arms. Lucian caught her and crushed her to him, wondering how he'd gone so long without the feel of her in his arms. "I've missed you, Jessie."

She squeezed him. "Don't ever do that to me again."

Though it took much effort to pry her away from him, he managed to do so. He cupped her face, loving every nuance of it—even the little frown line between her brows. "I swear to God, I'll never hurt you again."

New tears fell from her eyes. They washed over his hands as he leaned in toward her. He touched his lips to hers, relishing her taste. "Tell me, Jessica. I need to hear the words."

"I love you, Lucian. I always will."

He hadn't realized just how much he needed to hear her say the words again. Her love would always be there to guide him away from the temptation of darkness. She was his salvation from his past, the purity of her love cleansing him of the guilt he'd carried inside of himself all these long centuries.

Lucian would give that love back to her tenfold. He'd love her until the stars burned out.

Under the caress of the moon, with the snow lightly falling on them, Lucian could have sworn he felt warmth rush through him. In its wake was the sensation that his parents were there, watching him—no—not merely watching him. Watching *over* him. Waiting for him to reach the end of his road and find redemption.

"Did you feel that?"

Jessica frowned and looked around. "Feel what?"

Lucian shook his head and smiled. "Never mind."

He gathered her back in his arms and kissed her again. The visions and the echoing screams that had haunted him since the night he'd returned to Penwick dissolved on the night. For the first time since he'd dragged himself away from Penwick, his mind was quiet.

After seven centuries of guilt and sin, Lucian was finally at peace.

Epilogue

Tristan stood alone upon the battlements of Seacrest Castle. The clash of swords cut through the otherwise quiet of the winter night. Below, Sebastian and Constantine tried to hack each other to pieces on the lists. Though they both went at it ferociously, both lacked the savage edge they once used to fight with. Oh, Tristan knew that in true battle, they would both be able to call forth the viciousness needed to prevail, but at least the peace they had found eased the need to strive for pain.

Glancing to the right, he spied Lucian and Jessica. The two were inseparable. The love they shared added to the growing sense of calm and happiness that slowly took over the castle. Of course, Jessica was still human, but Tristan had no doubt the time would come when she would let go of her fears and enter into immortality. Not that he was eager to see another human cross over into damnation. However, Jessica was now part of their world. She fit in perfectly with their odd little family and, in truth, he believed they would all mourn her loss should she grow old and leave them.

Moreover, if she chose to never be turned, Lucian would spend eternity mourning her. That was something Tristan didn't want to see happen.

After Jessica told her family the details of her abduction and the risks Lucian had taken to see her to safety, their shock faded and they'd found it within themselves to accept the world where she now dwelled. Her family was now a regular feature at the castle. Her brother was slowly learning the ways of the sword and her parents came here often to visit. The bond Jessica shared with her family helped the Templars all remember—and some of them learn—what being part of a family was.

Female laughter carried on the night. Tristan watched Allie and Lex as they sat huddled together near the lists. They were looking at pictures of their former lives. Though he was some distance away, Tristan was able to discern that the photo they laughed at was of their brother, Christian, who'd died over two years ago.

Raphael was off alone tonight, having gone to the strip club where Cyn Lombardi worked. Rogue did nothing to hide his affection for her, though he refused to speak of it. It simply *was* and they all allowed him his privacy.

All in all, it was a peaceful scene taking place within the castle. As much as it pleased him, he was troubled as well. He knew this peace wasn't going to last. The Obyri were coming and they were bringing a battle with them. Looking to the chapel, Tristan let out an empty sigh. After seven centuries of wondering when, the time was nearly upon them to either earn their way into Heaven or be thrown down into Hell.

Now, all that was left for them to do was wait. Wait for the fight to come to them. And come it would, to this land where the holiest of relics was kept. They would fight for the ultimate prize. The lives—and souls—of humanity.

About the Author

To learn more about Rene Lyons, please visit www.renelyons.net. Send an email to Rene at rene@renelyons.net or visit her at her blog: http://renelyons.blogspot.com

Look for these titles

Now Available

Midnight Sun
The Daystar

Coming Soon:

The Seraphim: Setheus

Realm Immortal: Stone Queen
© *2007 Michelle M. Pillow*

Queen Juliana of the Unblessed married out of love, to share the burden of her husband's throne. Little did she know the true cost of that decision. With war raging between the blessed kingdom of Tegwen and her unblessed kingdom of Valdis, she feels her spirits weakening even as her powers grow. Risking everything for a bit of peace in her newly immortal life, Juliana will do anything to save her family, even if that means casting a spell over herself to end a war. The only thing she didn't count on was the betrayal of the one person she'd asked to help her.

For a brief time, Merrick knew happiness, as much happiness as the king of necessary evil could ever feel. Though he can never tell his wife he loves her—or risk upsetting the balance of both the mortal and immortal realms—the words are understood between them. Or so he thought. Now, with her body trapped in stone, he's left to again face his reign alone with no idea how to free her from her prison.

Available now in ebook and print from Samhain Publishing.

Enjoy the following excerpt Realm Immortal: Stone Queen...

Merrick shot to his feet. A searing pain ripped through him, a cold, barren gash in his power. He felt a burning across his gaze, indicating the whites of his eyes filled with black as he looked up to his bedchamber, every sense on alert. Bitter, icy emptiness greeted him where Juliana's essence should've been.

"What?" Kalen stood, his body tense. "What has happened?"

"Juliana," Merrick whispered, shaken. He'd sensed her great need before all traces of her disappeared completely. Panicked, his body turned to mist, drifting faster than he could run through the great hall to the door behind his throne. Going under it, he arrived in his bedchamber only to solidify. His wife was there, waiting, only she wasn't as she should be. Her body was cast in black stone, frozen in time.

"Juliana, nay. What have you done?" Merrick's heart pounded, a painful slam against the inside of his chest. He swallowed against the agony of it, as he stared at her face, willing her to break free from the stone and come to him.

One of her hands reached out as if to hold something and the other cradled the stomach rounded with their unborn child. He trembled, moving to touch her immobile face. The lingering scent of unblessed power floated in the air around him, as palpable as his own flesh. Though he searched, he could detect no other magic in the chamber. The door flung open behind him, the thick oak hitting the stone wall.

"My king?" Kalen demanded, his tone gruff with tension. "What has happened? Who has been here? Do you sense them?" He reached for his waist, pulling out a wickedly sharp dagger. Merrick smelled old blood on the blade, though it looked clean.

"She did this to herself." Merrick trembled. As he touched Juliana, the warm stone seemed to move beneath his hand with life, her life. And yet, he could see her statuesque beauty with his own eyes. She was gone. She'd left him. His heart squeezed in his chest, nearly choking him with its pain. "She imprisoned herself in stone. Only unblessed magic is... There is no other. She did this to herself."

Merrick felt the nobleman walk around them, saw him from the corner of his eyes as a blur. Kalen searched the chamber, but it was empty. Merrick couldn't take his gaze off Juliana's hard, black face. Every detail was there, the small crease in her full lips, her long eyelashes, the strands of her wavy hair resting over her ears.

Finally, Kalen stopped looking and didn't move as he stared at the queen. Merrick glared at him, demanding, "Did you foresee this? Did you know something was going to happen to her?"

"Nay, my ki—"

"Did you know?" The Unblessed King's voice lifted, rumbling as he surged toward his friend. He grabbed Kalen by the pelt and jerked him violently, dragging him toward Juliana's stone form. "You have read her. You see these things, I know you do. Why has this happened? Why did she do this? How do I free her?"

Kalen looked unconcerned by his king's anger and did not fight back. "If she did this, are you sure she'll want to be free? If only her magic is in the chamber, she must have had reason."

Merrick glanced down at her pregnant stomach, feeling sick. A reason? What other reason could there be? He turned his attention to the nobleman once more, needing to lash out.

"Then you did know!" Merrick lifted Kalen off the ground only to lower him back down and let go as he realized beating his friend would solve nothing.

"Nay. This I did not see. It must have been planned after I met with her last. Or else she didn't know it herself." Kalen touched the queen's outstretched hand. He closed his eyes. "I can't find her in the stone. It's like reading the wall. Are you sure you sense no other magic? To cast such a spell takes great power."

"There is only our magic in this chamber." Merrick pushed Kalen away from his wife, replacing the man's hand with his own. "Her powers were growing daily. I felt it. Mayhap she could not control this."

"You know as well as I that an act like this would take great concentration and skill. If her magic had been uncontrollable, most likely she would have blown up half the castle, not made herself a part of it."

"She's not a part of it. I would feel it if she'd made herself part of the palace. Instead, I feel nothing of her in this statue."

"Kidnapped?"

"Nay, I would have felt her leave. It's just as if she..." The king breathed hard, moving aimlessly as he searched for a sign, anything that would explain why his wife had cast herself into stone.

"She is not dead," Kalen said, though Merrick could tell by the look on his face he had no way of knowing that for sure. "We must have faith that she is safely buried within this statue waiting for the right spell to free her once more."

"I should have called you here sooner. I knew her powers were growing. Mayhap she could not control them. Mayhap we are wrong to think uncontrolled powers merely cause explosions." Merrick tried to will her from the stone, as he willed the castle to move. It didn't work. "If there was a reason, she would have left me a message. She would not leave me, not like this, not alone. She promised…"

Merrick stopped once more before his wife. Kalen touched her again, laying both hands on her. He shook his head in denial, signifying he felt nothing of her.

"No one can know of this. She's too vulnerable. I must hide her. I cannot let the vision I saw in the basin come true. I will not have her blood on my hands." He would never harm Juliana and he refused to let anyone else. "The statue must be protected."

"The Black Garden," Kalen said. "She'll be safe there. No one but you will be able to touch her. Take her to the center of the garden until we can discover a way to free her."

"Leave us, Kalen," Merrick ordered. "Tell no one of my queen. Seek out powerful wizards, whoever you have to. Read them. Find an end to this. I cannot lose her. Not now. I need her."

It was the closest he'd ever come to saying his feelings for her out loud to another person. Kalen obeyed, leaving him alone with his frozen wife in the bedchamber.

"Juliana, fate cannot take you from me now. I only just found you," Merrick whispered, knowing by the magic around him that her state was not easily undone. "You promised to stay with me."

GREAT cheap fUN

Discover eBooks!

Samhain Publishing Ltd

Printed in the United States
115910LV00004B/196-201/A

9 781599 986579